a Dark Earth Rising *novel*

The Root Witch

Debra Castaneda

SHADOW CANYON
press

ISBN: 979-8-9903956-0-2
Edited by: Lyndsey Smith, Horrorsmith Editing
Cover design by: James, GoOnWrite.com

For Micaela

Chapter 1

Utah, October 1970

As darkness filled the campground, the swishing sound of the trees became a dull ache in her ears.

"They're called quaking aspens," her uncle said.

The forest wasn't anything like she'd imagined. It made her feel small, tiny as a mouse or a bug, like she didn't matter at all. The trees seemed to press in on her. They were sad, too, maybe even angry, and she could feel it in her bones.

She had a bad feeling ever since Cousin Rodney shoved her during a walk through the trees and she'd fallen. When she got up, brushing dirt off her hands, she stared in horror at several crushed baby aspen shoots. She looked up, and the trees around her seemed to move closer together, but no one else noticed.

The trunks were white, and the leaves never stopped rustling. A ghost forest.

The campground was next to it, dark and quiet, except for the rustling leaves and the sound of someone snoring, and she had to pee.

That meant going outside, alone. The tent was stuffy and smelled like Rodney's farts and sour apple Blow Pops. She could ignore the smell but not the pressure in her belly.

Squinting in the inky darkness—trees whispering overhead—she unzipped the flap and climbed out. All the tents looked the same. She couldn't be sure which one belonged to her aunt and uncle, and she didn't want to wake a stranger.

In the middle of the campground, she stopped.

The cold, hard ground pressed into her bare feet. Her Snoopy sweatshirt was too thin for the chilly night air. She shivered, wondering if she should go back for her sneakers and jacket, but decided it would take too long to find them in the mess of the tent.

A crackling noise to her left made her heart thump in her chest. She whirled around, half expecting to see the yellow eyes of a wolf. At dinner around the camp stove, Rodney said if she were dumb enough to walk into the woods, a wolf would get her, but her uncle said ranchers had killed all the wolves a long time ago, so she had nothing to worry about. It was just a deer.

She hoped.

Holding her breath, she looked around. She could just see the outline of a squat building. The bathroom.

The moon slid out from behind a cloud. It was almost as good as a flashlight.

She ran.

The cement floor felt cold and damp against her feet, and the room stank so badly she gagged. She pushed down her pajama bottoms with one hand, shoved open the wooden door with the other, and hurled herself at the toilet. Her relief was so great she moaned. Moments later, she was back outside. She hadn't bothered to wash her hands, but she didn't care. No one saw, and she didn't want to spend an extra second in that disgusting, dark place.

The clouds swallowed the moon again. Surrounded by colorless, pointy shapes, she couldn't remember which tent was hers. She clenched her fists and tipped her head toward the sky, willing the moon to come out. When it did, she'd search for the Big Wheel her little cousin left outside. With its bright yellow handles, she'd spot it for sure.

Time seemed to slow as she waited.

A swishing sound overhead made her freeze.

She strained her ears, listening, too afraid to crane her neck and look because whatever it was might look back.

But she had to see what it was. She turned her head upward.

A tree. And not just any tree. A giant one. Enormous. Its white trunk rose into the darkness, much bigger than all the trees she'd seen earlier that day. But what was it doing there? Maybe she'd wandered farther than she thought.

A dusty smell filled her nose. It wasn't horrible, but it wasn't nice either, and the scent reminded her of wet dirt, wriggling worms, and dead leaves.

The sight of the tree erased her mind. She wanted to run, but her legs wouldn't move. She opened her mouth to call out, but a horrible wet sound, like a cough, came out instead. Her tongue felt swollen, dry, and gritty. Leaves rustled high overhead. She thought of her own bed in her own house and wished she was there, instead of the horrible forest with its ghost trees.

The enormous tree bent down, like it wanted to whisper something. Its puffy golden branches lowered, making an awful racket of creaks and groans, and she threw up her arms to protect her face.

One moment, her feet were on the ground, and the next, she was hoisted into the air. Something wound itself around her waist so tight she was sure it would cut her in two, and the white trunk came rushing to meet her.

Chapter 2

Utah, 1986

At first, Knox wasn't sure he'd heard right.

They were less than half an hour into the interview when the regional supervisor said, "Well, that settles it, then. When can you start?"

Knox's knee jerked upward, smacking it under the lip of the desk where he sat facing Bill Skeene, one of Utah's Forest Service supervisors.

When Knox had filled out his application, he understood the Forest Service had several jobs open—one part-time seasonal in Wyoming and another in Idaho. He was holding out for full time. Even if it meant Nevada—which sounded a lot like his home state of Texas, except with gambling. Since he had a wife now, Knox couldn't afford to be choosy.

On the morning of his thirty-third birthday, he woke up to a giant cinnamon bun with candles and the realization he needed to find a new way of life. One that didn't require moving from one seasonal job to another, which Colleen called, "underemployed." Until they'd met, it suited him just fine. The modest inheritance he'd received from his parents after their deaths had filled in the gaps. But in the years since his father's small plane had crashed into a mountain, he'd run through most of the money.

It was time to get serious.

And then, just a few weeks after he'd mailed in his application, Bill Skeene had called and said if he planned to be in Utah anytime soon, he'd sure like to meet. Knox lived more than nine hundred miles away, near Houston, but he and Colleen made it to Ogden in one long, exhausting day in the old Chevy Silverado, his dad's pride and joy.

Knox absently rubbed his knee as he studied the district supervisor. Pushing sixty. Thick around the middle. The man's scalp shone visibly between the gaps of slicked-to-the-side dark hair.

"Just to clarify, which position are we talking about again?" Knox said.

Bill threw back his head and laughed. Then, he snapped his fingers and aimed one in a gun-cocking gesture. "You're quick, Knox. As luck would have it, I've just had a full-time ranger position open in my district, the Fish Lake National Forest down in Central Utah. An absolute gem of a location."

Knox's heart beat a little faster. "I've heard of it. It's huge, isn't it?"

The older man nodded, the smile fading from his face. "It is. Nearly a million and a half acres. It's so big it's divided into four districts. The one I'm talking about is the Fremont River district, which includes Fish Lake itself, the Boulder Mountain area, and an aspen forest."

"Sounds incredible," Knox said. He still hoped, one day, to end up in Northern California, or maybe the Pacific Northwest, but jobs in those coveted locations were harder to get. He hoped getting more full-time experience would help. Anything would beat working at Sam Houston, with its alligators and bugs.

Bill opened a file on the desk and stared at the sheet inside. "It says here your real name is Bobby, but I see you go by your last name. Any reason for that?"

"Bobby is the name on my birth certificate, but it always sounded more like a nickname to me. So, I just use Knox."

Bill nodded. "Well, thanks for clearing that up." He pulled another sheet of paper from the file folder. "Your supervisors down in Texas have nothing but good things to say about you. And the personnel folks have already got your fingerprints and medical info from the seasonal work you've done, so that means you can start anytime. We can do your orientation later this week."

Knox leaned forward, elbows on the table, as Bill began to discuss the details of his employment. The pay was generous enough, and for the first time in his life, he'd have health and dental insurance, and a retirement plan too. It was, after all, a government job.

While his new boss searched a file cabinet for some additional paperwork, Knox studied the large map of Utah's forest districts, trying to figure out the largest town closest to his new job. Colleen had made it clear she wanted to live in a community with a library, a coffee shop, and preferably, a bookstore.

"How far is Richfield from the ranger station in Loa?" he asked.

Bill threw a thick green packet labeled "Welcome to the U.S. Forest Service" on the desk and slid it toward him. "This will answer most of your questions about the benefits and whatnot, but as for Richfield, it's too far, is what it is. My office is in Richfield, when I'm not up here for meetings anyway, and it's an hour's drive from where you need to be every day. But a commute won't be necessary because this position happens to come with a rare perk a lot of rangers would kill for." He wiggled his eyebrows as he tapped his fingers together. "You and the missus get to live in a fully furnished ranger cabin…free. And we're assigning you a Bronco, so the roads won't be a problem." He scooted back in his wheeled desk chair and rooted around in the top drawer, muttering, "Where did I put them?" and then with a triumphant, "Ah hah," pulled out a ring of keys and tossed them to Knox, who caught them in one hand.

Knox's heart soared as his mind raced, calculating how much money they'd save living rent-free. Thousands! And then he thought of Colleen, and his heart plummeted in his chest.

He didn't want to sound ungrateful, but he had to ask. "Is this cabin…remote?"

A shadow crossed Bill's face. "I won't lie. It is. But that's the nature of work like this, and considering the size of your district, it's best you be in it. You'll need to be available for emergencies."

"Of course, of course," Knox said hurriedly, sitting up a little straighter in his chair, as if ready to spring into action. He didn't want any doubts about his abilities. Or his interest. This was just a complication he hadn't anticipated, and when he explained everything to Colleen, he hoped she'd understand. He'd deal with that when the time came. Which would come soon enough because Colleen was waiting for him at a motel in Salt Lake City.

Until then, he had to focus on the matter at hand.

Bill took him for lunch at a diner in Ogden Canyon. Over pastrami burgers, French fries, and oatmeal pie, the district manager explained the biggest challenges Knox would face on the job, which to his surprise involved not the lake, nor the mountain, nor the campers, but the one-hundred-and-six-acre aspen forest.

Bill dragged a fry through a puddle of ketchup. "So, here's what happened. For as long as I can remember—and I've been in this job coming up on twenty years—the big draw has been Fish Lake. And then, ten years ago, two scientists studying aspens in the western U.S. drove along Highway 25, which cuts right through Fish Lake Basin. They stop, take some samples, and lo and behold, discover those aspens are one large clone."

Knox stared down at his half-eaten burger, trying to recall what he knew about aspen clones.

"Is that when the trees are part of a single root system, and the trees are genetically identical?" he said.

Bill squirted more ketchup onto his plate. "That's right. I've got some papers on it back at the office. I'll make sure you get a copy before you head out. Those two fellows wrote it all up for a scientific journal, but eventually, some local reporters got ahold of it, and then it made the Sunday papers, and then the ten o'clock news, and then the national news shows started sending crews and doing stories. Suddenly, our little forest is famous, and everybody wants to see it. And it's not just families from Salt Lake City. It's folks from Colorado and Wyoming, down for the weekend. In the summer, when kids are out of school, we've got folks coming from all over the place. Even California and New York, if you can believe it. And don't get me started about the tourists from Germany. The lodge down there can hardly keep up, and the campground closest to the forest is full to the brim. So now, we've got all these people trampling around, especially during the fall, when the leaves change color, and that's a bad thing for the tender, new shoots. And believe me, the new growth has enough trouble because of all the browsers. And if you want to know who to blame for all the deer, well then, we've got to go way back to the ranchers who killed all the predators and threw the whole ecosystem out of whack, but that's not exactly a popular opinion, as I've learned the hard way."

Bill fell back in his vinyl upholstered booth and crossed his arms in front of his chest with a scowl. "You say a word against the ranchers, it's like thumbing your nose at the mob in Chicago. They'll come after you."

It was a lot to take in. Knox's district covered a vast territory—the entire southeast portion of the Fish Lake National Forest. A whopping five hundred thousand acres spanning four counties that included lakes, streams, reservoirs, and hiking trails. And yet, Bill Skeene seemed focused on an aspen forest of less than a square mile. Knox was excited about the new job, but alarm bells began to ring.

"Are you saying the ranchers are dangerous?" Knox finally asked.

"No," Bill said. "Most are decent folk. But a few are a pain in the behind and don't like being told what to do. And if you even insinuate their cows might be damaging the forest, they don't like that one little bit." He hesitated. "But there is something you ought to know."

Knox crumpled his napkin and waited expectantly.

"You're not from around here, so chances are, you've never heard of it," Bill said. "But that aspen forest is famous for other reasons. There's an old story about something scary living there. The Root Witch. It's a local legend, and every once in a while, you'll get people hollering and screaming they saw a monster or a creature, or they got chased by something, or something took their dog. Which, by the way, shouldn't be off leash anyway."

Knox nodded. "Sam Houston has ghost stories too."

"Then you know what I'm talking about," Bill said. "Dang annoying, is what it is. And boy, do the crazies come out on Halloween."

They polished off their pie and slid out of the booth. Bill caught him off guard by clapping him on the back and welcoming him to the team. When they got back to the office, it was nearly two o'clock. Colleen was probably wondering what was taking him so long. Knox had expected it to be a couple of hours for the interview, at the most, including the drive to and from Ogden. But when Bill asked if he could stay so they could finish up, instead of returning the next day, he readily agreed. That would mean only staying one night at the motel.

Knox called the motel room from an empty office next to Bill's. Colleen squealed when she heard about the job and offered to take him for a celebratory drink at a private club she'd heard about.

"They don't have regular bars here," she said with a laugh.

The plan was, she'd fly back to Houston the next day to close up their one-bedroom apartment, then drive to Utah in her Honda, accompanied by her brother.

Knox spent the next four hours holed up with Bill in his office, staring at maps and pouring over lists of campgrounds and other facilities. They reviewed a checklist of his daily responsibilities. By the time they were finished, his head was swimming with details he couldn't possibly remember, and he was glad he'd taken so many notes. Bill promised to drive over from Richfield early the following week to see how he was getting on. They said goodbye, and when Knox left, he could hear the district manager pick up the phone and punch in a long set of numbers.

Long distance, he guessed.

Chapter 3

The tall, white trees lined both sides of Highway 25 like sentinels—emerging from the earth just feet from the blacktop. To his left, the ground rose steeply to a ridge so high he couldn't see the top from his truck. At least, not without stopping and sticking his neck out the window. The aspens grew so close together they formed a nearly impenetrable wall of white bark and green leaves. To his right, the ground sloped down. More generous spacing between the trees allowed glimpses of open meadows and ponds. It was a beautiful view, but he found his gaze drawn to the darker, denser part of the forest and the shadows beneath the canopy.

He'd got an early start. It was just before ten o'clock, and the sky overhead was a vivid, crisp blue with a scattering of thin clouds in the distance. The way the shadows lingered beneath the trees didn't seem natural, not with it so bright outside. He didn't like to imagine what it was like when darkness fell. Or in the dead of winter.

Just after he'd passed a "Shooting Prohibited" sign riddled with bullet holes, the forest seemed to take a giant step back from the road, keeping to the foothills. Then, Fish Lake came into view. Enormous. A blue so brilliant he knew it was icy cold, just by looking at it. To his right, he spotted the turnoff to a campground, one of many in his jurisdiction. He'd check it out later. For now, it served as notice he'd gone too far— overshot his turn. He made a U-turn, the ridge ahead visible now. Except for a few bald patches of dirt, the aspens covered the undulating hills. He hung a right onto a service road marked with a large boulder, just as Bill Skeene had described. The road was rough but paved and without potholes. He came to a rustic fence that stretched in both directions, presumably to keep out the browsers. Knox hopped out, opened the fence, drove in, then closed the fence behind him.

He sat in the truck, gripping the steering wheel. There it was. His place. A cabin at the far end of a small meadow—a wooden building painted gray, with white trim and a green roof. Two Adirondack chairs squatted on the wide porch. The setting was beautiful.

Colleen would hate it.

It was, literally, in the middle of nowhere—exactly the kind of place she'd made clear she did not want to live. Ever. While they were in Salt Lake City, Knox hadn't been able to bring himself to tell her about the rent-free cabin that came with the job. He hadn't wanted to ruin their night. Besides, by that time, they'd both had too much to drink at the private club, shouting over some raucous covers of early punk classics. After that, they'd gone back to the room, and things between them had got so hot he had to take extra care pulling on his boxers in the morning. When he dropped Colleen off at the airport, her pressing against him as they kissed, that hadn't seemed the right time either.

Once, Colleen had accompanied him to his previous job at Sam Houston National Forest, then refused to stay in the small cabin he rented for fifty dollars a week. He'd had to drive her all the way back to Houston and wake at dawn to make his shift. That was before they got married, but it didn't make any difference. The gold band on her finger hadn't changed her sentiments about remote living.

"It gives me the creeps," she said, not long after they'd started dating.

If his outspoken mother had survived the fiery plane crash, she would have pointed out the obvious problem. His chosen career was in direct conflict with Colleen's preferences, but Colleen had assured him she was fine with living in a small town, just not in the middle of a swamp, or on top of a mountain, or in the middle of a forest.

Like the cabin standing in front of him.

It was well-built, and the porch was solid. He stopped to read a plaque to the right of the door. "Deer Run Cabin 1911." That explained the fence. To keep out the deer. Not that a fence would do much good—deer could probably hop right over it—but he didn't object. At least it would alert tourists this was private property.

Inside, the cabin had four rooms. The largest was the main room with a wood stove, a long wooden table, a plaid couch in maroon and green with yellow stripes, and two matching easy chairs. They looked clean and relatively new, he was relieved to see. Colleen hated old, stained furniture. The bedroom at the back of the cabin had a sturdy, knotty-pine bedroom set, but no mattress or bedding. Bill had warned him about that. He'd drive into Richfield later and get the bedding, along with whatever else he might need to get him through the next few days.

The kitchen and bathroom were basic but bigger than they had in their Houston apartment, with plenty of natural light and wooden walls and ceilings to add some charm. The best feature was off the kitchen—an enclosed sunroom with large windows overlooking a field and a dramatic upslope carpeted in aspen.

They were at the edge of the forest.

When he'd daydreamed about his future as a ranger, this was what he'd imagined. Better even. His territory included a stunning, varied landscape. On his days off, he could fish. The lake was full of mackinaw, rainbow trout, and yellow perch. Bill said he could take out one of the rental boats when he was off. There were plenty of hiking trails to explore. Colleen loved a good walk. They had that in common.

Circling the cabin, he spotted a shed at the back of the property. Inside were two kayaks, paddles, the usual assortment of tools, and a snow shovel. Bill said the temperature varied greatly, which should keep things interesting. At least he didn't have to worry about plowing the road to the cabin. Bill assured him the maintenance crews would take care of that. He didn't want his rangers getting stuck.

Knox drove an hour to Richfield. There, he was able to get everything on his list. At the department store, where the floorboards creaked under his feet, he bought a mattress, sheets, blankets, and towels. They'd need a bedspread, too, but he thought it best to leave that to Colleen. The cabin came with a set of battered pots and pans, but he splurged on an eleven-piece set on sale, along with dinnerware in bright colors and the least expensive silverware he could find. That only left the food shopping. He stocked up on the staples, and when the cashier rung him up, he was surprised at how much he'd spent.

When he got back to Loa, the tiny town closest to his new home, his stomach rumbled, and he realized how hungry he was. He was driving slowly down the main street, looking for a restaurant, when he spotted the ranger station. It was a tidy, nondescript brick building, a white Bronco with green stripes parked outside. His, probably. He'd never had his own service vehicle before. But it could stay parked there until tomorrow—his first official day on the job.

Bill Skeene had warned him Loa didn't have much in the way of amenities, but it was even smaller than Knox had expected. Population: 400. There was an inn, a gas station, a feed store, a machine shop constructed of corrugated metal, a yard full of ancient, rusted trucks, a long low building that rented heavy equipment, a handful of government buildings, and eventually, a cafe with a wagon wheel outside.

Several men sat in a booth against the front window. Judging by the hats, mustaches, and beards, Knox assumed they were local ranchers. If they stood up, he was positive he'd see shirts tucked into high-waisted jeans. He gave them a friendly nod, made his way to the counter, and ordered the special written on a chalkboard—club sandwich and fries.

Knox was about to ask the waitress what kind of beer they had when he remembered he was in Utah. It had funny liquor laws, laws that mostly meant you couldn't buy any unless you were at a private club or a state liquor store. Loa was probably too small to have either. He should have stocked up in Richfield earlier. Knox was halfway through his sandwich when he felt someone standing behind him.

"Excuse me. I couldn't help but notice that Texas license plate."

Knox looked up to find one of the men from the booth leaning on the counter next to him. He was a big man. Around the same height, six feet, but heavier around the chest and shoulders. Pushing forty, maybe, with brown hair and a coarse red beard.

Given what Bill Skeene had said about ranchers, he gave what he hoped was his best disarming smile. "Yes, I just drove in from Houston. I'm Knox. And you are?"

"Lee Bradley," he said, sliding onto the stool next to him. He propped an elbow on the counter, as if settling in for a long chat. "That Silverado is a nice ride. Is that a seventy-eight? Nine?" The man had an eye for trucks.

"Seventy-nine," Knox said. "You live around here?"

"Oh, a way out. But let me ask you something. We hear there's a new forest ranger up at Fish Lake who just arrived from Texas. That wouldn't happen to be you, would it?"

Bradley gazed at him with such a mixture of incredulity and amusement that Knox bristled. How the hell would the man know something like that? He had connections, obviously.

"I am." Knox dug into his pocket to retrieve his wallet.

Bradley snatched the check off the counter and waved it over his head. "I've got this, Becky. Don't you dare take this man's money."

Knox forced a smile to his face. He wasn't about to get into a wrestling match with the burly stranger. If the man wanted to buy him a sandwich, he'd let him. "My thanks," he said. "What do you do around here?"

Bradley's head pivoted slowly until their eyes met. "I own Circle B Ranch."

The two men at the booth chuckled. The skinny one said, "Come on, Lee. Tell him the rest of it. Get it over with so the games can begin."

Knox kept his expression blank and waited. Bradley's eyes were the color of granite. They watched him, hard and glinting.

Finally, Bradley cleared his throat and said, "My dad passed about five years ago, so now I'm running things." He jerked his head in the direction of the booth. "Those are my cousins over there. It's a bit of a family affair." He grinned.

"Tell him the best part," the skinny cousin called from the booth.

Bradley's red-bearded chin jutted out. "We've got public grazing leases all over your neck of the woods. If you see any cattle, you can be sure they belong to us. We've got the preeminent grazing operation in Central Utah." He paused long enough to hand the waitress a twenty-dollar bill. "And we've got another eight years before our lease expires. I hope you don't get any ideas."

Knox had the feeling he'd walked into a long-standing argument and was expected to take a position, right then and there. His predecessor, or predecessors, must have run afoul of Lee Bradley and his ranching enterprise. Maybe even threatened his lease. He'd have to ask Bill. But in the meantime, he needed to get onto neutral ground and friendlier terms. After all, their jobs intersected.

"Thanks for the sandwich," he said, getting to his feet. "I've never been on a ranch of that size. What do you say about giving me a tour one of these days? Once I get settled in?"

Bradley's head jerked back. His jaw worked. Clearly, he hadn't expected that. When Knox glanced at the booth, the cousins were staring at him with open mouths, and he allowed himself a moment of satisfaction.

"We can do that," Bradley said stiffly.

As the three men strode out, boots clacking against the linoleum, Knox called after them. "See you around."

When he got to his feet, Becky, the waitress, came over, flashing him a sympathetic look. "Good for you. You put him in his place. Lee's all right. He just got a real big head since he inherited that ranch."

Not knowing what else to say, Knox nodded. For all he knew, she could be another of Bradley's cousins, so best to keep quiet.

There was no reason to hang around. The rancher had paid the bill, and he didn't want Becky to get the idea he was interested in chatting. She had teased brown hair and a sweet face, but he was a happily married man. Colleen said he didn't understand the effect he had on women, and he didn't. He was just an average-looking guy. Medium build. Straight black hair he preferred wearing on the long side, a nose a bit too wide.

"My friends think you look like Robert Redford," Colleen had said with a laugh. "But I think you're cuter."

Knox thought it had more to do with the aviator glasses he wore than any true resemblance.

He dug out a couple of dollars for a tip and left them on the counter.

Knox was nearly at the door when Becky said, "I heard you say you're the new ranger. Have you seen it yet?"

Knox frowned. "Seen what?"

Becky spread her hands wide, rolling her eyes. "What else? That thing in the forest."

He stared at her. "Are you talking about the ghost stories? Or whatever they are?"

"They're not stories. And it's not a ghost."

He swallowed. "What is it, then?"

She grimaced. "That thing is too real to be a ghost. And way too big. Or, at least, that's what I've heard."

Chapter 4

Salt Lake City, 1986

Sandy scooted out of the news director's office before he could drop any more bombshells. She raced past the assignment desk, muttering, "I'll be right back. Forgot something in my car." Sandy, ignoring inquiring stares, cut across the newsroom toward the door.

Dry hot air met her in the parking lot, along with two reporters heading in for the late shift. She was furious, but not so upset she didn't note the significance of Jennifer's long legs emerging from the passenger seat of Karl's RX-7. Sandy had heard the rumors. Everyone had. The two were practically living together. Good for them. As long as they didn't gang up on her when she was producing, or give her a hard time when she cut their live shots, she couldn't care less.

She gave a little wave as she raced to her red Escort parked at the far end of the parking lot, away from the fleet of news vehicles lined up near the back door and a safe distance from the employee spots. Usually, when a panic attack came on, she bolted into one of the editing booths, but at that hour— two hours before the five o'clock newscast—they were all full, and she'd learned the hard way the bathroom was a terrible place to fall apart.

Pushing the seat back as far as it would go, she stared up at the fabric roof and replayed the meeting that had just ended. As her psychologist advised, she respected her feelings and acknowledged the source of her agitation. Sandy squeezed her eyes shut, covered her mouth with her hands, and screamed.

When that didn't bring the relief she was hoping for, she pounded her feet on the floor of the car, accidentally slamming her knee into the bottom of the steering wheel. It felt good. Sandy did it again. She'd have bruises tomorrow, but she didn't care. As long as it kept her from hyperventilating, she was okay. Better than okay. Good enough to continue working.

No matter what, she had to stay on her shift. It was death to her career if she bailed early, barring a serious medical emergency. The one time a full-blown panic attack forced her to leave, she told her boss she had an unexpected recurrence of asthma and had to go to the doctor. But that was the kind of excuse she could only use once, especially since she wanted her own show. She'd spent the last year filling in and was getting desperate to have a show she could call her own.

And now, some new guy—from a fancy school and with practically no experience—was poised to jump ahead of her. The news director hadn't come out and said it, not directly. But she wasn't an idiot. And the insulting part was, her boss expected her to train him.

Fuck. Fuck. Fuck.

Jack Danielson, during the day, was bad enough, but getting stuck with him on the overnight shift had quickly become unbearable. The regular morning show producer was on a two-week vacation, so Sandy was filling in, with Jack acting as associate producer. When she complained to Brody, the managing editor who did the schedules, he'd shrugged.

Brody had premature wrinkles around his eyes and mouth from too much skiing and golfing. "He's got a master's from Columbia, Sandy, and he interned at one of the TV stations there. He'll be fine."

"That doesn't mean he knows jack shit," she'd said, then laughed at her own joke. Even Brody thought it was funny. Later, when Brody—who was a good manager, she had to admit—asked how Jack was doing, she was forced to admit the truth.

"Fine," she muttered through gritted teeth.

As much as she'd come to detest the new guy, he wrote solid news copy and had even progressed to writing teases for the first half of the two-hour show. The rest she insisted on doing herself because she was, after all, the producer in charge.

At least he'd stopped flirting. He'd given up after she'd made it clear there was no way she'd go out with him. As one of the few young, single women in the newsroom, she had some experience in rejecting unwanted advances. In Jack's case, she'd had to spell it out for him. With almond-shaped eyes and a profusion of dark hair, some admirers had called her "exotic," to which she replied, "You mean, not blond." Utah was a very blond place. She was one of a handful of Mexican Americans at the station, and the only one in the newsroom. The others worked in production and programming.

The trouble was, Jack didn't know when to keep his mouth shut, and she needed quiet to work. The newsroom was noisy enough as it was, with the police and fire scanners blaring, the row of TV monitors at full volume, and the constant racket of the teletype printing out wire stories from around the world. The guy just yacked away.

She was double-checking the length of a story when Jack said, "Have you guys ever done anything on the Root Witch?"

Jack was sitting on the edge of his seat, as if he'd asked an urgent question that required an immediate response. She ignored him.

He kicked her chair. "Have you?" he said. When she said nothing, he continued. "Because that story is insane. My neighbor told me about it. He's a real granola-eater and a big hiker. He swears he saw it. Scared the shit out of him. And he's not some nut or anything. He's a high school teacher."

Her heart skipped. "Would he be willing to talk about it in on camera?"

"No," Jack said, sighing. "I asked him. He said the principal would think he was out of his gourd and fire him."

"That's the problem with stories like that," she said. "No one ever wants to go on the record, and it's not like Big Foot—no one's ever caught it on camera. Which makes doing a TV story kind of hard, don't you think?" Her voice dripped with condescension.

That got the desired reaction. Jack scowled and went back to work.

Later, in a rare lull, she asked, "How did you end up here?" Because the station hadn't had any openings when Jack had arrived and, as far as she knew, hadn't advertised any positions.

Jack swiveled in his chair and studied her over the coffee mug that always seemed to be in his hand. Every night, he'd shown up in a polo shirt of a different color, and that night, it was yellow, the same shade as French vanilla ice cream. He had a mop of dark hair and a ridiculous mustache too big for his thin face.

Propping his gangly legs on the desk, he said, "My dad is a GM in San Francisco, and he's friends with the GM here. The plan is for me to get some experience here, then give me my own show in SF." When she didn't say anything, he added, "GM. You know. General manager."

Sandy sat there, fuming. Of course, she knew. The GM ran the station from a huge corner office upstairs, with a view of the Wasatch Mountains. Jack had confirmed her worst fears. The little plan he so nonchalantly explained was *not* how it worked in TV news for most people. They worked crappy shifts for years—years!—in smaller markets, putting in their time before making it to a top market like San Francisco. *Maybe* making it. The competition was fierce.

She knew better but couldn't resist. "Spoiled much?"

Jack snorted. "Spoiled? Working here? In this town? I don't think so."

Sandy stood and marched to the teletype, where drifts of yellow paper covered the gray industrial carpet. She felt a flash of irritation. That was the associate producer's job—to rip and scan the stories, see if there was anything worth including in the newscast. But Jack thought he was above it. Too important to do the stuff she'd done for years without complaint.

"Salt Lake City is a mid-sized market," she said hotly, ripping the paper free and clutching it to her chest. "You're lucky to start here. Most people in this newsroom came from tiny markets, like Yakima-Pasco and Idaho Falls. I mean, I was lucky because I'd interned here all through college, and then a desk assistant job opened up, and I fought for it. I worked the desk for a whole year and then was an AP for two years before they let me produce." She dumped the pile of paper in front of him.

"Boo hoo," Jack said lightly. "Come on. Put yourself in my place. I can't help it. My dad has connections. I'm going to use them. Simple as that. You would. Wouldn't you?"

It was a ridiculous question, and she wasn't about to answer it. But she didn't have to because the scanners came to life, and at one o'clock in the morning, that meant something was up. She leaned over Jack and turned up the volume.

"Report of a dead body in a dumpster," a flat voice said over the air.

She groaned. Dead anything on the overnight shift represented complications. Not much breaking news happened between midnight and dawn in Salt Lake. Not enough to warrant staffing a photographer to sit around and do nothing. So, if news broke, she had to wake up the photographer on call, and if it was something big, she'd also call in a reporter. It was impossible to tell from sitting in a newsroom what exactly was happening out on the streets. For that, you needed boots on the ground. Most of the time, it turned out to be nothing.

Jack eyed her eagerly. "Are you calling somebody?"

She bit her lip. "Call dispatch first. See how big this is."

"Are you kidding? Let's roll!"

She grabbed the call sheet off the desk and studied it for a moment. "Shit. Chuck's on call."

Of all the photographers, Chuck was the surliest and crankiest. The last time she worked overnight, she'd called him out on a report of a dead body in an alley behind a bar, but it turned out to be an intoxicated tourist unused to drinking at high altitude, and she'd heard about it for weeks.

Jack gave a nonchalant shrug. "So?"

"Just call dispatch, Jack," she said.

She could do it herself, but she was supposed to be training him, and she wanted to see how he did. Fine, as it turned out. Jack was as smooth as could be, sweet-talking the dispatcher. And it seemed to be working because Jack was nodding and saying, "Uh huh, uh huh." Then he hung up, looking smug.

"Well?" she snapped.

"The dispatcher was playing coy, but she did confirm they found a body in a dumpster. Kinda sounded like it was…something."

Sandy stared at the ceiling, blinking, fists clenched. "Yes, Jack, we just heard that. Body in a dumpster. Yay, you confirmed something we already knew. But who is it? Because it's probably a drunk. We've got a lot of those around Main Street, and we've had dead drunks in dumpsters before."

She'd made that mistake too. With Chuck, of course.

Jack squirmed in his chair but shook his head stubbornly. "She wouldn't tell me. The only way we're going to find out is if we send someone."

Sandy pressed a hand against the side of her head. She hated overnights. No staff to send, and if she blasted someone out of bed and it turned out to be nothing, it was overtime. And Brody, the managing editor, hated overtime. But he also hated missing breaking news. Either way, she was screwed. Sandy tried explaining that to Jack as patiently as she could, but he sat there, listening with a smug expression that made her want to throw a stapler at his head.

He picked up the on-call sheet and shook it in the air. "I do not see what the problem is. This exists for a reason. We're supposed to use it. Who cares if Chuck Nobody doesn't like getting called out. It's his *job*, San-dee. If he doesn't like it, he can find another one."

Jack made it sound so simple. But it wasn't. Because he wasn't one of the few women in the newsroom, surrounded by men waiting to bust her chops. He was the son of a GM who was friends with her boss's boss's boss.

"Fine," she said. "You call him, then."

Jack leaned back in his chair. "Oh, no. I'm just the AP. You're the big shot producer. That's a *you*. Not a *me*." Then, he spun around and began tapping away at his computer.

She stared at the back of his head. Never, ever, had an AP refused a direct order. But he wasn't just any associate producer. He was Jack Danielson, the Ivy League prick with a closet full of polo shirts, here for a short time to get some experience before leapfrogging to the big time.

Asshole.

The scanners had gone quiet. If it was, say, a murder, surely, there would be more chatter, not less. She snatched up the phone and punched in the police department's number. The dispatcher was annoyed to receive a second phone call so soon after the first one.

"It's a body in a dumpster," the woman said. "How many more times do I need to tell you?"

The woman sounded more frustrated than anything, and a bit bored, which was enough information for Sandy. Just the idea of Chuck's reaction to hearing from her in the middle of the night made her hands go clammy. With her luck, the body in the dumpster was another dead drunk. But the decision didn't sit comfortably. Several times, she almost reached for the phone to call Chuck, but as the hours passed and she got busier with the approach of the newscast, her jitters abated and the more confident she felt she'd done the right thing.

They were printing out the rundown when Jack stopped in front of one of the TV monitors tuned to the competition. It was five-fifty a.m., and the anchor was teasing the top story. Sandy's heart fell when she saw a reporter standing in the street in the glow of camera lights, yellow tape and police cars in the background.

"Oh, oh," Jack said, crossing his arms in front of his chest.

Over the rushing sound in her ears, she heard the reporter say, "Police say they are investigating the murder of a still-unidentified woman this morning. We'll tell you where she was found, coming up at six o'clock."

Her mouth went sour with bile. She'd been wrong, wrong, wrong.

Chapter 5

Colleen hadn't spoken to him in forty-eight hours. No goodnight. No good morning either. She was still furious about the cabin. Correction—she liked it well enough. It was the location she objected to, just as he knew she would.

"Jesus, Knox. Are you trying to drive me crazy? What's next? Are you going to put up ugly yellow wallpaper?"

He didn't get the reference but decided not to ask. Colleen was an author, and she frequently spouted book references he didn't get. He stood, helpless, staring out the kitchen window, watching a deer tiptoeing through the aspens.

As she banged pots and pans into place, she said, "No, Knox. This place is not free. It's a giant golden handcuff. Don't you see that? They've got you living at work. You're at their beck and call. Is that what you want? Because that's what's going to happen. It's not like you're a doctor, trading your personal time for big bucks."

He let that go. The drive to the isolated cabin had set her on fire, and she hadn't burned out yet. Knox thought if he just let her get it out of her system, without interruption, maybe she'd calm down. But her anger had continued, unabated.

"But Colleen," he said, steering her by the shoulders into the sunroom. "Look. This is the perfect place for you to write. Better than a library or coffee shop, even."

She'd always complained about the small size of their apartment in Houston, with just enough room for a desk in the corner of the living room, overlooking the parking lot.

"I mean, it's got a nice view and everything. We can get a desk when we go into town. A bookcase, even." He kicked himself for not thinking of that when he'd done the shopping in Richfield. The sight of her own work area might have softened the blow.

She pointed at the aspen grove. "That is not a view, Knox. The ocean is a view. The lake is a view. That is a wall of trees."

Knox thought that was a bit unfair because the aspen grove was beautiful, but he was in no position to argue. Instead, he tried a different tactic. "Colleen. Remember when you wanted to go to that author's retreat in Colorado Springs to finish your book, but we couldn't afford it? You showed me the brochure. It was up in the mountains in the middle of nowhere, with goats and chickens." He gestured at the meadow. "Well, call me crazy, but I'm not seeing the difference. You've got the same set-up right here, don't you?"

Colleen's long brown hair was done up in a braid hanging down her back, and when she whirled around, it nearly cracked him in the face. She reminded him of the feisty main character from her science fiction series. Her books were good, but they were short on science. He once made the mistake of referring to them as "fantasy" when they first started dating. She'd gone on a passionate tirade against the "utter uselessness of realism," and from then on, he'd obliged by calling them "science fiction." When she'd introduced dragons in book two, he wisely kept his mouth shut. He'd already overheard her on the phone, arguing with her editor.

"They're genetically engineered dragons! That's science!" Colleen had insisted.

Now, she turned and looked out the window once again. "I might as well be on Mars," she whispered, then shut herself in the bedroom.

Knox was forced to sleep on the couch.

It was seven o'clock, and Colleen was still asleep—at least Knox couldn't hear any noises when he pressed his ear against the bedroom door. He'd just started the coffee when he heard knocking at the front door. He'd planned to inspect the campgrounds with one of the part-time rangers, but that wasn't for another hour and a half. Knox pulled open the curtain and saw a man in uniform standing outside, twirling his hat in his hand. Whatever brought the man to his door wasn't good, by the grim expression on his face.

Knox slipped outside and joined him on the porch. No use waking Colleen.

The deputy was a few years younger than him, with brown skin and brown hair with sun-bleached streaks. Like the other Utahns he'd met so far, the man probably spent a lot of time outdoors.

"I hate to bother you so early, but I need your help. I'm from the Sheriff's Office. My name's Pete Sandoval. You're the new ranger?"

Knox glanced over his shoulder. The bedroom door remained firmly shut. He nodded. "I sure am. I'm Knox. What's the problem?"

"Not sure yet. Hopefully nothing. One of our officers is missing. He didn't show up for his shift last night. Which isn't like him. So, I went to his house to check on him. He lives over in Koosharem, off sixty-two, but his car wasn't there. His wife said he'd spent the day fishing with his brother up at the lake. His name's Lane Carroll. We're always joking how he's got himself two first names." Sandoval paused and gave a strained smile. "Two girl's names, at that.

"Anyway, they'd rented one of the cabins off Fremont River Road and planned to fish in the morning, then nap until Lane had to leave for work at nine. I just talked to the brother. Said he last saw Lane when he left for work just before nine, and everything was fine as far as he knew. So, I headed up Highway 25, thinking he might have had car trouble, or an accident." He paused. "I found his car, all right, but no sign of him."

Knox ran a hand through his hair. It felt greasy, and he needed a shower. But there was no time.

"Any signs of…violence?" he asked.

Deputy Sandoval shook his head. "I know what you're thinking. Maybe he pulled someone over and found himself in trouble. No. Nothing like that."

"Okay, let's go look for him, then," Knox said. "Just give me a second to get dressed."

He pulled on his clothes in the gloom of the bedroom as Colleen sat cross-legged, staring at him.

"And so it begins," she muttered as he kissed her on the head.

Knox was pulling away when she reached around behind his head and pushed her mouth against his, her other hand squeezing his crotch. That got the reaction it usually did, and he smiled at her, melting with relief and desire. She stuck her tongue out at him, flashed her breasts, then pointed at the door.

He took a moment to compose himself, then trotted to the deputy's steel-gray truck. It smelled of stale cigarette smoke, and the white plastic trash bag hanging from a radio knob was filled with empty Coke cans.

Once they reached the highway, Deputy Sandoval drove away from Fish Lake and headed south where the aspen grove thickened. Knox scanned the forest for the missing deputy. He hadn't bothered asking for a description of the man. He'd be the one in a uniform, looking a little worse for wear.

Sandoval drove fast, leaning forward slightly, anxious to get to their destination. A car on the side of the road loomed into view, and they pulled up behind it. Pete rummaged around in the back seat, retrieved a pair of hiking boots, and changed into them. When he was done, they got out and stood, hands in pockets, surveying the white Ford for a moment.

"The door was open when I found it," the deputy said. "I locked it before I left."

It was only June, but the morning chill was already gone, and it was heating up fast. Knox wouldn't be surprised if the temperature hit ninety. The day before, it had reached eighty-five.

"Do you know your way around yet?" the deputy asked hopefully.

"No," Knox said. "I just started the other day. Maybe we should have gone into town to round up some of the others."

Sandoval shook his head. "I thought of that, but it would take too much time. The station doesn't open until 8:30. We can get a start at least. He's gotta be close by."

"Sure." Knox spoke with a confidence he didn't feel.

They decided to split up to cover more ground. If it had been dark, they would have stuck together, or waited until more help had arrived.

They made their way up the slope, following a trail meandering between the trees, looking all around as they climbed. Eventually, the trail faded, and it was there they went their separate ways—Sandoval to the left, eyebrows scrunched together, Knox to the right.

It was quiet among the aspens, but it would have been wrong to call it silent. The leaves fluttered in the still air, a constant noise he found disconcerting. Shafts of sunlight struck the fallen trees, branches bleached as white as bones. Dark blotches marred the white trunks. Knox wondered what they were. Bugs or disease, probably. He hadn't gone far, but he was so surrounded by trees he'd lost all sense of direction. A truck rumbled past, which meant the road was still close.

He understood, then, how stories about ghosts and witches started in such a place. There was something unusual about the forest. More of a feeling. That you were being watched, or something lurked just out of sight.

A shadow darted among the trees, and his heart nearly stopped. But it was only a bird. An enormous raven.

"Get a grip," he muttered to himself.

He'd gone another hundred yards or so, his boots crunching through the dry grass, when he heard a yelp, and then, a scream. It was short, terrified, and belonged to Sandoval. Knox had flashes of a mountain lion leaping from a tree, biting into the deputy's neck, or a bear charging, striking with its claws and teeth.

With a jolt, he realized he'd brought no weapon. Bill Skeene said he was free to arm himself, and should, but Knox hadn't felt comfortable checking out the firearms at the station in Loa. Not until he could get the proper training.

Knox blundered across the slope, the sun in his eyes, until he found the deputy hunkered next to a boulder, eyes squeezed shut, breathing heavily, one hand resting on the pistol in its holster. His fingers, Knox noticed, were trembling.

Knox crouched next to him. "What happened?" he asked, glancing around uneasily.

"I thought I saw something," Sandoval panted. "But it was nothing. I was just…imagining things."

Knox looked at him sharply. "Bullshit."

Deputy Sandoval slowly got to his feet and sucked in his breath. "No. Really." He hesitated, pointing at a long dirt embankment.

Much of it had eroded away, exposing a network of heavy roots. From where they stood, it looked like the front flank of trees were creeping forward. A strange illusion. Knox tried to say something reassuring, like it could have happened to anybody because all those roots were creepy, but his tongue stuck to the roof of his mouth.

The two men stared at each other. Sandoval willing him to understand, to be cool about it. Knox trying to convey he didn't think the man was chicken, without coming out and saying so.

"Should we keep looking?" he asked.

Sandoval nodded eagerly. They continued their search, this time together. At nine o-clock, after finding nothing, Sandoval got on his radio and called for a multi-agency search and rescue.

Chapter 6

Sandy couldn't seem to escape Jack. They'd worked every shift together since he'd started, and she couldn't believe how quickly he'd taken to producing a TV newscast. Some people never got it. Couldn't handle the unforgiving deadlines. Couldn't figure out what made a good lead story or how to organize the show. Dozens of editorial decisions. The technical stuff. Video feeds. Coordinating live shots. Sitting in the booth during the live show, making split-second decisions.

Some new producers cracked under the strain and quit of their own accord. Sandy felt like she'd been born to the job. For her, producing was like sitting in front of a wall of levers and knobs, and she knew exactly which to pull and turn at just the right moment. With one eye on the clock for the entirety of her shift, she started from nothing—zero—built a show from bits and pieces she'd assembled, and then, usually just seconds before airtime, she'd haul ass down the long hallway to the control room, throw herself into the seat next to the director, and the newscast would begin.

Most of the other producers had a single job—they produced a newscast. But not Sandy. With experience on the assignment desk, she could also act as assignment editor, deciding which local stories to cover, assigning the reporters, and coordinating with them to get their pieces on the air. Much to the delight of management, she could do all of that *and* produce a newscast, which was how she ended up floating from show to show.

She'd become the station's Swiss army knife. A producer called in sick that day? Sandy could fill in. An assignment editor out on vacation? Schedule Sandy. Both at the same time? Come save us, Sandy.

Even Jack couldn't handle assignments, but that brought Sandy no satisfaction. She worked twice as hard, splitting her focus between two separate jobs, but at the end of the day, she was judged on the quality of her newscast. Management seemed to forget she'd spent half her time yelling at reporters to get their packages in, or listening to their sob stories about how their stories fell through, then racking her brain to find them a new one. Sandy spent most of her free time scouring the local papers, squirreling away story ideas she kept in a notebook for occasions like those, or chatting up aides to state lawmakers for an inside scoop. It's what made her so good.

One Friday, the phone rang in Sandy's Second Avenue apartment at six o'clock in the morning.

It was Brody, the managing editor, his voice groggy with sleep. "Can you save the day and do the five and the desk?"

She could guess what that meant. The five o'clock producer and the assignment editor called in sick. Unbelievable. The two were buddies, and the weather forecast was clear and warm. They were probably on their way up to Jeremy Ranch for a day of golf.

Sandy swung her feet to the floor, the phone cradled under her chin. Friday sick calls were highly suspicious in her book. Brody, perhaps to keep his sanity, seemed to take them in stride.

"Can't you do the desk?" she asked.

"I would," he said, sounding sympathetic for once. "But I'm having a root canal at one."

"Sorry to hear that," she said. Sandy had made it halfway to the bathroom when she stopped. "Brody, I was supposed to co-produce the six with Jack. There's no way I can do that too. And the desk. And I'm not sure Jack is ready to produce alone."

The six was one of the day's most important newscasts.

Brody didn't hesitate. "He'll be fine. Can you sit with him in the booth, though? Just to make sure everything times out okay?"

As she snatched a towel from a hook, she caught a glimpse of herself in the mirror. It looked like something had nested on top of her head. Her bangs badly needed trimming, and so did her long dark hair. She should never have let the new hairdresser talk her into so many layers. And all because he said she looked like the singer, Susanna Hoffs. It wasn't the first time she'd heard that. Many people remarked on the resemblance. Even Jack. Which jerked her back to the present moment.

"And Sandy," Brody said, "do me a favor. If a dead body turns up in a dumpster, can you please send out a crew?" He gave a throaty chuckle and hung-up.

That mistake had cost her, but not as much as she expected. At least not with Brody. He'd been surprisingly supportive. She'd been such a mess, Brody had whisked her into his office.

"It's done, Sandy," he said, closing the door. "We've all made a bad call. Or two. Or three. You sent a crew at six that morning, and we had the story by the noon show."

It had been an entirely different story with her co-workers, especially Jack. There was a hard edge to their teasing, a not-so-subtle signal there was something off about her news judgment. That making tough decisions didn't come naturally or easily to her. That she didn't have the balls to work in TV news.

She hung up the phone and quickly showered, dressing in black jeans and a purple top, then applied more black eyeliner than usual because that's the kind of mood she was in.

Another day. Another newscast. Another chance to prove them wrong.

When Sandy walked into the newsroom, Jack was already there, sitting at his computer and eating a donut, wearing a pink and green polo shirt. She threw her purse on the assignment desk so hard it skidded across the counter. The Desk, as it was called, was built on a raised platform with a view of the entire newsroom.

Jack glanced up when he heard the noise and frowned.

She pointed at the empty chair next to her. He raised his eyebrows in silent inquiry.

"We've been reshuffled," she said. "You're doing the six, solo. Mostly. I'm on the desk and the five. But I'm not making all the beat calls alone. We're splitting them up."

"But…," he sputtered.

"No buts," she said.

Jack scowled over the top of his mug. "Don't we have an assistant to do that?"

Sandy shook her head. "Bonnie quit, remember?" She eyed the clock. It was eight-thirty, and she still had the assignment calendar to go through before the ten o'clock editorial meeting.

"Don't we have another assistant?" Jack said, shoulders slumping as he trudged toward the desk.

"Like a spare tire?" she said. "No, we don't. Brody's hired someone else, but she doesn't start until next week, and it'll take at least a week to train her." She shoved a Rolodex toward him, several cards spilling from the rotating spindle. The little notches holding them in place had worn away, and the desk assistant had never gotten around to fixing them with tape.

Jack held up a card and squinted at the contact information scribbled there. "How am I supposed to read these? It's like a monkey wrote them."

Sandy's fingers froze over the phone. "This isn't the first time you've used the Rolodex. Please, Jack, today is not the day to play helpless. We have to work together." Then, she swiveled in her chair so her back was to him, and only when she'd heard him sigh heavily and begin punching numbers did she began making her own calls.

With Brody out and the news director attending a conference, she led the morning editorial meeting. The two veteran reporters didn't bother sitting down. Leaning against a wall, they pitched their stories—both good ones—and left as soon as Sandy had given the thumbs-up. She wondered what she, or the station, would do without them. Both men had reliable sources at all levels of government, and even in the LDS Church. They'd never let her down, not once.

Unlike Karl, who'd joined the station last year from a smaller market in Arizona. He excelled at live breaking news—it was the reason he was hired—but struggled to come up with ideas of his own. That morning, he threw himself in the chair opposite Sandy with such a pleased expression that she pointed at him first.

"Morning. Got something good for us?"

"Oh yeah," he answered, grinning.

Karl had upped his game for once and had come prepared. "I can get a sneak peek at the construction on those pumps they're putting in at the Great Salt Lake so it doesn't flood again."

They wouldn't be breaking any news with that story, but they'd be pushing it along, and the visuals ought to be good. Anything involving water and machinery usually was.

"Nice." Sandy eyed him, impressed.

Like most reporters, he was good-looking in person but even-better looking on camera. It was only after she started working in TV that she truly understood what photogenic really meant. Karl was tall, with a square face, wide jaw, and a head of thick, wavy hair that was the envy of the newsroom. But when he stepped in front of the camera, he looked like a movie star.

She glanced out the window. Chuck, the surly photographer, was sitting around, drinking coffee and wearing his sunglasses. Nursing a hangover, probably.

"Why don't you take, Chuck?" she said to Karl.

Jack snorted and drummed the conference table. "Harsh, Sandy. Harsh."

Her eyes went wide with feigned confusion. "I have no idea what you're talking about." It was the one time since he'd started that she felt even the faintest flicker of camaraderie with Jack.

Karl saluted and hurried toward the door with a backwards glance at his girlfriend, Jennifer, who winked and gave him a thumbs-up. He returned it with a sappy grin.

Sandy envied their confidence. Both had high opinions of themselves, opinions that exceeded their actual talent. It was as if they expected the world to shower them with congratulations just for showing up, while she, somehow, had become trapped in an endless cycle, proving herself over and over with little to show for it.

She turned her attention to Jennifer, who was studying her nails. Jennifer had honey-blond hair, so perfectly feathered it could have been a wig, and a slight gap in her front teeth that gave her an approachable, distinctive look.

"And what do *you* have for us today, Jennifer?" she asked, in the sort of exaggerated speech one used on preschool children.

Jennifer looked up, seeming to notice Sandy for the first time. "Wow, look who's got big ol' raccoon eyes today. Did you even go home last night?" Then, she laughed because everyone in the newsroom under thirty-five knew Sandy didn't get out much.

"Do you have a story today?" Sandy said—without smiling.

Jennifer shrugged. "I thought that's what the assignment desk was for."

Sandy felt her toes curl. Jennifer didn't dare pull that crap when Brody was around, and it was unlikely anyone in the meeting would snitch. Jack sat back in his chair, smirking. Most days, she and Jennifer got along just fine. When she was in a producing role, Jennifer had no problem taking direction. It was only when Sandy stepped into an editorial role that Jennifer pushed back. Like now.

If she'd learned anything on the job, she couldn't afford to let Jennifer appear to win, because then other reporters would think they could get away with it, too, and the next thing she knew, she'd have a mutiny on her hands. It was bad enough the other producers questioned her judgment, thanks to the body-in-a-dumpster debacle. Sometimes, you had to play hardball.

Sandy pushed back in her chair and got to her feet so abruptly, Jennifer looked startled.

"Jennifer," she said. "I'm doing two jobs today. I don't have time for this. I really, really don't. So, if you can please do your *one* job, that would be great. Can you do that for me? Your *one* job, which is to show up with *one* story. Just *one*. And then we can all start…our…fucking…day."

Jack drummed the table again.

Jennifer pursed her mouth angrily. At last, she said, "Can I have ten minutes to make a few calls?"

Sandy felt the tension drain from her neck and shoulders. She'd won that round. Ten minutes later, Jennifer confirmed it by slinking up to her desk with a story about a new baby gorilla at the zoo, and Sandy showed her thanks by assigning Mitch as her photographer.

Everybody loved Mitch. He could do most technical jobs in the newsroom, from editing, to camera work, to operating the satellite truck, and even directing a live newscast. The operations manager was thrilled to have someone so flexible capable of doing it all. It was rumored the ops manager would soon retire, and Mitch would step into the job. Which made sense to Sandy. Nothing rattled easy-going Mitch.

He sat next to her now, as he usually did when he had a few minutes. Several days into his job, Jack had asked if they were going out, and when she'd shouted an indignant "No!" Jack had snorted and said, "Yeah, right."

The truth was, Mitch had asked her out. Several times. And while she was tempted, she'd always resisted. First, he wasn't her type. Too tall, for one thing. Big boned. Dirty blond hair. And he wore work boots—all the time. Mitch was raised on a cattle ranch in Wyoming and still dressed like it. The few guys she had dated were dark-haired and compact. When Mitch was around, she found his physical presence overwhelming. Like now. He sat with his legs far apart, one knee practically touching hers. He'd brought her a coffee, just how she liked it. No sugar. Lots of cream.

"Can you keep an eye on Jennifer? Make sure she doesn't screw me by flaking on her story?" she asked him in a low voice. A story about a baby gorilla was a no brainer, but sometimes, if a reporter was feeling disrespected, they retaliated, like turning in a story that was too long just before air, with no time to shorten it.

Mitch smiled. His teeth were white against his skin. She wondered how he'd gotten so tan, when she remembered he'd gone camping in Moab with friends. He'd invited her, like he always did, but she'd refused. She hated camping. And sleeping in tents. And the places Mitch liked to go didn't have bathrooms. With her luck, she'd start her period.

"I'll watch her like a hawk," he said, smiling. Mitch understood Sandy's challenges.

He had the most amazing eyes. Hazel.

She tore her gaze away.

"I heard what happened in the meeting with Jennifer," he said.

She gave a terse nod but avoided looking at him again.

"Don't let the bastards get you down," he said, squeezing her shoulder as he got up.

A lump formed in Sandy's throat. She had to take a swig of lukewarm coffee to swallow it.

In the commercial break after weather, Sandy was in the darkened control room, calculating whether she needed to cut a story in the last segment to make the five o'clock show end on time, when the technical director said, "Hey, Sandy. Looks like they have a breaker."

Sandy's heart fell. She knew exactly what he meant by "they." The competition, the station with the huge ratings. Her head snapped up to look at the small monitor on the counter.

Sure enough, a reporter, dressed in jeans and a pink Oxford shirt with the sleeves rolled up, was standing with feet wide apart in the middle of an empty road. A bright blue banner appeared at the bottom of the screen reading, "Breaking News: Fish Lake National Forest."

"Some tourist probably drowned," the technical director said.

Sandy turned up the volume.

"Officials say the missing sheriff's vehicle was found, abandoned, where I'm standing now, on an isolated stretch of Highway 25. Coming up at six, we'll tell you about the search that's underway for the forty-two-year-old deputy."

"Oh heck," the technical director said.

Sandy collapsed into her chair, stunned. How the hell had they missed something like that? She'd heard nothing on the scanners, and she'd put together the newscast while sitting at the assignment desk in front of the damn things. Sometimes, the agencies in rural areas didn't blast all their business on the radio—everyone knew that—which was why they made beat calls. The dispatchers were obliged to tell them if something was going on. The public had a right to know.

A commercial ended, and the anchor began reading the lead-in to Jennifer's story about the new gorilla at Hogle Zoo.

Looking at the monitor next to Sandy, the director said, "They must have sent their satellite truck for that deputy story. There's no way they'd get a signal out of there otherwise."

Sandy forced herself to study her rundown, one eye on the red numbers of the digital clock. All good. On time. No need to cut any stories. The director, a grandfatherly type who'd been at the station forever, could handle the last few minutes of the newscast without her.

"Can you see us out?" she asked.

He waved her off. "No problem."

At the door, she stopped. Her knowledge of the geography of the middle of the state was somewhat fuzzy. There were several big parks down there, and she had a hard time keeping them straight.

"Is there anything special about Fish Lake?" she asked, aiming her question at the assistant director, who was as outdoorsy as Mitch.

"Well, it's massive," he said. "But where that reporter was standing tells us something. That was the aspen forest behind him." He paused. "You know. *That* one."

Her throat went dry.

The AD raised his hands into the air and wriggled his fingers. "The one with the ghost."

A harsh laugh erupted in the far corner of the room. Everyone glanced over at Jessie Yang, the graphics operator, a recent college grad with short spiky hair. She said, "It's not a ghost, dummy. It's a monster. Everyone knows that."

Sandy's fingers tightened on the doorknob. "I don't," she said.

As she made her way on unsteady legs down the long hall toward the newsroom, the floor and walls seemed off-kilter.

When she reached the newsroom, Jack's hands came up off the keyboard. Sandy noticed the flicker of unease in his eyes

She slapped her stack of scripts on his desk. Thin sheets of gold, pink and green paper fluttered to the carpeted floor. One landed on his lap.

He grimaced. "Looks like you missed another story, San-dee."

She kicked the leg of his rolling chair. Hard. Sandy made no attempt to lower her voice. In fact, she spoke at full volume. "Before I call dispatch in Richfield County, is there something you want to tell me, Jack? Because if I remember right, that was your job this morning."

He shifted in his chair. The skin on his narrow throat was so thin she could see him swallow. Instead of answering, he gave a little shrug. She rubbed her temple as she glared down at him. An editor stepped out from the feed room and stared. Good. Let there be a witness to the confession she was about to extract from Jack's annoying puckered mouth that looked like an asshole. Because there was no way in hell she was taking the blame. Not for this screw up.

"Did you, or did you not, call dispatch in Richfield County?" she said through gritted teeth.

Jack threw up his hands. "No, I did not because I didn't have time. How am I supposed to make all those stupid calls when I have a show to produce? And I wasn't asked to cover the desk." He jabbed a finger at her. "You were. You were trying to get me to do your work. So, you can't blame me, San-dee."

"That's not how it works, Jack," she said through gritted teeth. "When Brody's gone and he's left me in charge, I get to tell you what to do. If you couldn't do it, because you can't do two things at once, then you need to tell me so I can pick up the slack or get somebody else to do it because we don't skip beat calls. That's how we miss stories."

"Like you did," he muttered, avoiding her wrathful gaze.

"Well, you get to join the club now, buddy," she snarled. "Haven't you got a show to produce?"

Jack slunk down the hall toward the control room. Sandy remained in the newsroom, watching the competition to see what they had on the missing deputy from Central Utah. She was listening so intently she was barely aware of Mitch standing next to her. Jennifer's story was running as a taped package for the six o'clock show, so he must have high-tailed it back to the station. He pressed a mug of hot tea into her trembling hands. She sipped it gratefully, shivering, hoping it would calm the mad fluttering in her stomach.

The camera cut to the reporter. "We have new information at this hour. Search and rescue teams are combing the woods of this aspen forest behind me, looking for forty-two-year-old Sheriff's Deputy Lane Carroll. His vehicle was found this morning near where I'm standing now. Officials say there were no signs of foul play. This aspen forest is well known to many Utahns for the legend of a mysterious creature that is said to haunt these woods. Visitors to the forest tell stories of an enormous black shadow…"

Sandy lurched forward, spilling her tea. Mitch grabbed her elbow to keep her from falling. He was so tall he had to bend his head to search her face, trying to see what was wrong.

"Sandra? he asked.

She continued to stare at the TV screen. As the camera pushed into a close-up of the quivering leaves of an aspen, her heart stuttered. She fought to keep her voice even as she turned to Mitch, gripping his sleeve.

"Should I send a crew down there tonight?" Sandy croaked.

He shook his shaggy blond head. "You'd need to send the satellite truck to get a live shot for the ten, and the truck's in the shop."

Sandy sagged from relief. That gave her a solid excuse not to scramble a crew to play catch-up. If the deputy was still missing tomorrow, she could always send a crew in the morning. She steeled herself, picked up the phone, and called Brody at home. It was time he learned the truth about Jack.

Chapter 7

For once, Sandy looked forward to her therapy session. Of all the psychologists she'd seen, she liked Celeste Munson best. Celeste, with her long straight hair and round glasses, wore tie-dye tops and hippie-style jeans. It was as if the 1980s had never arrived.

Celeste worked out of her house in the upper avenues. They sat facing each other in easy chairs. It was a beautiful room, with blond wood floors and moldings, the walls painted a soothing cream. Celeste didn't believe in knick-knacks. A single print—a mountain scene—hung above the fireplace. Sandy found the room as restful and soothing as Celeste. The windows were open, letting the fresh morning air stream in.

She sipped her mint tea, wondering where to start.

"Any panic attacks?" Celeste asked after a moment.

Sandy closed her eyes, thinking of the crew she'd sent to Fish Lake National Forest to catch up on the story they'd missed. Todd was a senior reporter who'd been at the station for ten years. Usually, he covered politics and stories that required more finesse, but he'd been happy to go. She knew she'd made the right choice when he and the photographer had returned in the afternoon, interviews and B-roll in hand. When Todd was sent to get a story, he delivered. They crammed into an edit booth to preview the video.

She hadn't been prepared for the sound bite that began one minute, thirty seconds into the tape. It was the second sound bite with a forest ranger named B. Knox, who looked a bit like actor Robert Redford, except with black hair.

The editor, the only woman in the production department, named Nadine murmured, "Oooo. He can search and rescue me any time."

When Todd asked him to confirm if any visitors had reported seeing an unidentified creature in the aspen forest the day before the deputy had gone missing, Ranger Knox looked distinctly uncomfortable.

"Not to my knowledge, no," he'd replied.

And then, the follow-up question. "And what are your thoughts? About the legend of the Root Witch?"

The ranger looked past the camera, as if searching the trees. "That's a little outside my area of expertise," he finally said. On camera, it translated into a dramatic pause. It made it seem like the ranger knew something but wasn't telling.

During the five o'clock newscast, while the story ran and the camera followed Todd as he did his stand-up through the aspens, Sandy avoided watching the video, instead shuffling through her scripts. When the show was over, she saw Jack sitting in Brody's office. The door was closed, but she could hear Brody's raised voice.

Her shift had ended, but she waited around at her desk, wishing for once that Brody was the kind of manager to issue a scolding in front of the entire team. But when the two men finally emerged, Brody clapped Jack on the shoulder, and the younger man had sauntered past, wearing his usual smug expression. Avoiding her questioning gaze, Brody slipped back inside his office and closed the door.

It was all too much.

She'd snatched her purse, storming from the newsroom and into the parking lot, past the satellite truck, back from maintenance and in its usual spot.

Mitch hopped out the back and shouted after her, "Hey, come with us for a drink after the six."

With her luck, that drink would include Jack, so she'd said, "Got other stuff to do, thanks."

Which was a lie. Instead, she drove straight to her apartment, stared at her empty refrigerator, and burst into tears. She treated herself to take-out Chinese, drank too much white wine, watched a British costume drama on VHS, then went to bed just before nine o'clock.

The panic attack had come as a sneak assault in the middle of the night. She awakened from a nightmare, being chased through a forest by something. Something huge and terrible, she knew, but she couldn't see it. Sandy bolted up in bed, panting. She felt like an iron band was squeezing her chest, making it hard to breathe. Maybe she had a problem with her heart and didn't know it. That's what happened to her dad. A massive heart attack at the age of forty-eight.

But finally, the episode subsided, and she was left weak and exhausted.

When she'd explained all that to her psychologist, Celeste said, "That's very sad to have lost your father at such a young age. But that's a legitimate concern. Have you ever spoken with your doctor about it?"

Sandy gave a bitter smile. "That's how I ended up seeing a shrink."

"Of course," Celeste said apologetically. "What do you think set off last night's episode?"

Sandy squeezed her eyes shut, trying to rid her head of the horrible images that haunted her through the night. In the morning, she realized her dreams must be connected to the man who vanished from his car in the aspen forest, the deputy who'd gone missing without a trace. She hoped they found him soon.

"I'm not sure," she said, shifting in her chair. "Have I told you about Jack?"

"Yes. The young man you're working with who went to Harvard?"

"Columbia," she said bitterly. "He has a master's in journalism."

Celeste folded her hands on her lap and crossed her ankles. "And you're training him?"

"Yes." Sandy gripped the sides of the chair. "It feels so unfair. I got into the University of Missouri. On a scholarship. But then I couldn't go. Because of my dad, and I didn't want to leave my mother alone. Not after what happened to my brother."

"Yes, your brother. Let's get back to him in a moment. First, I'd like you to tell me about Jack. How he's making you feel now. I know your job is very important to you, and if something is upsetting you there—"

"Jack," Sandy said, blinking back tears of frustration. "Jack is making me crazy. He's such a know-it-all jerk. And he's got connections I've never had. His dad is a general manager, and he knows the GM at my station, which is how he got the job. And Jack just waltzes in, and within a couple of months, he's producing! It took me years to work my way up. Most of the other producers went to big schools, too, and they're always rubbing my nose in it. I went to the University of Utah. My parents didn't go to college at all." Sandy was breathless, and she sounded like a petulant child, even to her own ears, but it felt good to admit her stupid, petty feelings that felt like ground glass churning in her stomach.

"It's a good, solid school," Celeste said, a faint smile playing around her lips. "I went there. There's another way to think about it, Sandy. You've complained about the hours you have to work. And the relatively low pay. You've said you would be making much more if you'd taken a job in public relations. But you followed your passion. And it sounds like you are very good at what you do. Have you considered that the others, who went to what you consider more prestigious schools, may have overpaid for their education in relation to their career choice?"

Sandy bit her lip, thinking that over. "No, I haven't," she finally said.

Celeste nodded. "In the end, Sandra, it doesn't matter where the others went to school, or what advantages they may have. You'll contend with that no matter what field you're in. The workplace is filled with inequities. Especially for young women coming up in traditionally male-dominated fields. Should we discuss some coping strategies with the time we have left? To help you focus on you? On what you want to achieve?

"Yes," Sandy said.

"I do have some questions about your brother's accident, and how that might be contributing to your agoraphobia, but we can leave that for our next session."

By the time she'd reached her red Escort parked at the curb, she'd already come to dread her next appointment.

Chapter 8

Officer Lane Carroll was not found in the first twenty-four hours, the window when most people lost in the back country are discovered.

Nobody could understand how such an avid outdoorsman so familiar with the land could get lost. The aspen forest presented some challenges for out-of-shape tourists, but it was by no means considered extreme terrain. The search expanded to a broader area of Fish Lake Basin. A helicopter searched from the air.

Six days later, the search was suspended.

And then there was the matter of his abandoned vehicle.

"No signs of foul play," the sheriff insisted.

Staged. That was the latest theory to make the rounds. Sheriff's Deputy Lane Carroll had staged his exit from a miserable marriage. The relationship had gone bad, according to Lane's brother and fishing companion. The rest was conjecture, with not a whole lot to back it up, from what Knox could gather. But it made more sense than an able-bodied man vanishing, and it sure beat that ridiculous story of the monster, or ghost, or whatever the Root Witch was supposed to be.

With his growing to-do list, Knox decided it was time to look at the papers his boss had given him on the aspen forest. Those aspens were truly a stunning sight, but they loomed larger than they should have. The aspen forest represented a tiny fraction of the hundreds of thousands of acres that fell under his jurisdiction. Knox couldn't account for the uneasy feeling he got whenever he was in the forest, and he couldn't banish the memory of Deputy Sandoval hunkering in the wood, spooked by God only knew what, because he never would say.

He arranged his day so he'd be alone at the ranger station in Loa, which would leave him free to read without interruption.

That was the beauty of his position in a remote location. No manager to look over his shoulder. Free to direct his own work, set his own agenda. If only Colleen would settle in, get back to her writing now that she had a desk. Instead, she stared out the window, scowling, as if blaming the forest for her writer's block.

"It's so oppressive," she said. "I feel like I'm boxed in here. Surrounded by all these damn trees."

He'd suggested moving to the living room and setting up at the big table in there, where she'd have a view of the meadow, but she'd refused. "I like my desk, thank you."

One day, he'd come home to discover she'd hung curtains across the windows in the sunroom. She'd driven into Richfield to get them. He stared at the fussy pattern, scratching his head.

When she'd noted his expression, she said, "I know, but that's all they had, and I was desperate. I felt like the trees were watching me or something."

The curtains were a busy pattern of pink and yellow roses. Not her style, not even remotely. But he kept his mouth shut. As long as she was busy working, her mind occupied, they'd both be better off. Her manuscript was due to the editor soon.

After instructing the part-timers to put up the new "No ATV Riding" signs, he met the maintenance crew in the parking lot and sent them out to inspect the campgrounds. He'd stopped by the site closest to his cabin on his way home the day before and hadn't liked what he'd seen. It was the middle of summer vacation, and the visitors had left a mess behind. Trash on the ground. Piles of dog waste. Graffiti in the men's bathroom. Disgusting.

When they'd gone, he sat at his desk and opened the file.

The papers were in no particular order. He skimmed a faded photocopy of an academic journal published in 1976. Finding it a bit too dense, he picked up a department memo that summed it up well enough for his purposes.

The forest was a single organism, a clone forest, made of genetically identical trees that sprouted from a massive root system. New trees sprouted from the ground in a form of asexual reproduction.

The description made it sound like something from one of Colleen's science fiction novels. He'd seen the roots, exposed by erosion, while searching the forest for the missing deputy. Rubbing the nape of his neck, he pictured them as part of a larger network of roots buried under the ground.

Since the identification of the aspen clone, the memo read, rangers had been concerned about the lack of natural predators in the area to check the growing population of mule deer and, to a lesser degree, elk. Ranchers, to protect their herds, had killed off wolves, bears, and cougars, and now the number of browsers had exploded.

The problem, the memo continued, was simple. Voracious mule deer were eating the saplings before they had a chance to grow to full size, and if that kept up unabated, the forest wouldn't be able to regenerate.

One ranger named Spence expressed his concern with refreshingly plain language. "Something must be done *now* or the deer will kill the forest!"

The memo had three large exclamations in the right margin, along with a note that read, "Deal with Spence asap."

The next document made him sit up straighter. Written by a ranger named Orson in 1984, it detailed disturbing discoveries he and his staff had made over a period of six months. Each incident, Orson noted, had been reported shortly after they occurred, but he wanted to provide a summary as he would soon be leaving his position. Twelve mule deer and one elk had been found dead in the forest, the major bones in their bodies broken. One was found in a tree, positioned as if the branches had caught it mid-leap. Others were found hanging upside down in trees, hooves caught between the V of branches, the remaining located on the forest floor. All were in different parts of the clone forest. No cause of death was established, because by the time the maintenance crew returned to retrieve the carcasses, the animals were gone. Photos taken before the animals vanished revealed no sign of chronic wasting disease.

"Local prank???" was written in the margin.

Another ranger had submitted a year's worth of reports of "incidents" in the forest, mostly involving visitors staying at the campgrounds—everything from claims of an enormous black shadow following them through the forest to dogs disappearing while on walks through the aspens. Some campers heard disturbing, loud noises but had trouble describing them in any detail.

Then, there was the odd report made by a German man who had sprained his ankle running from an attacker. At first, he said an unknown assailant had beaten him around the head with a tree branch. After returning from the hospital, he amended his report, claiming he'd been attacked by a tree. The German lost credibility when he admitted to the occasional use of psychotropic drugs, although he insisted he'd been sober at the time.

Some reports involving incidents in the forest were made to outside law enforcement agencies. That made it difficult to track how many separate complaints there were, and a district manager proposed the creation of a system that would integrate the reports. Nothing seemed to come of it, as far as Knox could tell.

A single document remained in the file folder—a photocopy of a newspaper story dated October 17, 1970.

It was just a few lines, but it made his skin crawl.

> *SEVIER COUNTY, UT. A 10-year-old child underwent emergency surgery Saturday after an attack in an aspen grove in Central Utah, hospital officials say.*
>
> *The child sustained severe injuries while on a family visit to Fish Lake National Forest. The family, who wishes to remain unnamed citing privacy concerns, said the child had gone missing from the Doctor Creek Campground Friday afternoon and was found unresponsive shortly after dawn, a quarter of a mile away in the quaking aspen forest.*
>
> *The Sheriff's Office says it is investigating. The Ranger District in Loa, which oversees the forest, was unavailable for comment at press time.*
>
> *The child is not expected to survive, hospital officials say.*

Sixteen years ago. That was a long time. But it was significant enough Bill Skeene should have mentioned it. If only to add a few more details, which were lacking in the article. Like, what kind of attack? Were any suspects ever named? Which agencies conducted the search and rescue?

The ranger station must have been involved. How could it not? Why wasn't the official report included in the file?

Knox couldn't help but feel his boss was holding something back. Too many things were off.

But that's why they'd invented telephones. To track down negligent bosses.

Knox dialed the number of the district office in Ogden. Bill Skeene picked up on the first ring. When he heard who it was, he no longer sounded distracted.

"Did you find that deputy?" he boomed.

"Nothing like that," Knox said hurriedly. "I just happened to go through that file you gave me. On the forest. And I have a question about that newspaper article—"

"Which one was that?" Bill interrupted.

Knox cleared his throat. "The one about the kid."

A long silence followed. Knox waited, knee bouncing up and down.

Finally, Bill sighed. "Well, I'm afraid there's not much I can tell you. I was on vacation when it happened, and I only heard about it when I got back two weeks after the fact. And we were in between rangers at the time, if my memory serves me right, so we weren't present when the kid went missing. But as I understand it, the family went to Lakeside Lodge, and somebody called the sheriff's office, and they conducted the search. The sheriff back then was stingy with information, but I got the impression they were looking into it as a kidnapping sort of situation. They seemed to think some pervert who liked little kids got into the campground and, well, you can imagine the rest."

Knox had a perfectly good imagination, but where they found the victim didn't add up. If someone was intent on kidnapping or assaulting a child, wouldn't they have forced them into a car and driven off? Why would someone drag a child all that way, zigzagging through trees, where anyone could have seen or heard them?

As he listened to Bill breathing on the other end of the line, he realized the file did not include a single mention of the aspen forest's urban legend. Since he started, he hadn't gone a single day without hearing someone mention it. The waitress at the cafe in Loa, the locals he ran into, the news coverage about the deputy who'd vanished off the highway that ran past his cabin.

"What about the Root Witch stories?" he blurted out.

His boss dropped the phone. Knox heard the receiver bounce on the desk, followed by a curse and the sound of fumbling. Finally, Bill said, "Oh, for crying out loud, kid. Listen, it's a big forest you're working in, and guess what? People aren't used to being out in nature like that, and the next thing you know, you've got the forest coming alive, chasing after them. It's like our very own Sasquatch, but thank goodness, not anywhere near as famous. So, was there a real question you had, or were you just trying to rile me up?"

Without waiting for an answer, Bill said he was late for a meeting, then gave a good-natured laugh before hanging up.

That night, Knox did not sleep. Colleen had insisted on leaving the windows open to cool the stuffy cabin. From bed—his wife's skin hot against his—he could hear the ceaseless fluttering of the aspen leaves. His thoughts kept drifting to the forest and all the trees that lived as one.

Chapter 9

In the brightness of the summer morning, Knox spotted something moving behind the trees off to the left of the highway. He slammed on the brakes of the Bronco, heart thudding, as he hung out the window, squinting. After the night he had—nightmares of a child left bruised and bloodied among the aspens, of roots twisting beneath the earth, snaking toward his cabin—his tired mind was apt to interpret the most mundane sights into threats.

It was just an animal. A cow. And then, as if in confirmation, a deep lowing reached his ears.

He hadn't seen a cow this close to the aspen forest before and wondered where it had come from. It was on the side of the road where the aspens were thinner. He looked around and saw more cows, grazing in a distant meadow dotted with small ponds. And then, he remembered Lee Bradley, the rancher, and his grazing leases. These must belong to him. He wondered how those arrangements had come to be— ranchers striking deals with the government to let their animals graze on public lands.

It was his day off, so he was in no hurry as he drove into Richfield to shop for groceries. Colleen had awakened at five to work on her book. He'd carried her desk and typewriter to the front porch, where she could work in the cool morning air, and left her drinking coffee, facing the meadow, back turned firmly against the wall of trees.

Knox had just rounded a gentle curve in the road when he hit his brakes again. Three cows were crossing the road from a sun-drenched field of dry grass. In search of shade, no doubt, and better eats. They sauntered past, oblivious to his vehicle, and once across the highway began nibbling around the base of the aspen trees.

He recalled the memo his predecessor sent to the district office—the warning that over-grazing was killing the forest. The scientific paper he'd skimmed explained the aspen reproduced asexually, sending up shoots from the roots. Or "suckers," as the scientists called them. Even from where he sat, he could see that's what the cows found so tasty, and he gripped the steering wheel, fighting a wave of irritation, fast turning to anger.

Like many people he'd met in college, Knox had strong views about conserving the environment. Which, in his mind, usually meant saving ecologically sensitive areas from the powerful chemical and petroleum industries. Never, in all the rallies he'd attended in his university years, did he imagine a forest might be destroyed by a hungry ungulate and a rancher legally grazing his cows on sensitive land.

Another movement across the road caught his attention. A half dozen or so cows were making their way to the road, stopping at a cluster of aspens on the other side of the gravel buffer, near the blacktop. The green shoots, measuring a foot high, disappeared into those wet, chewing mouths. He realized then, with startling clarity, the trees on both sides of the road were the same being. Not a distant cousin, a brother or sister, but an extension of the strange clone network his brain had trouble comprehending.

Workers had built the highway through the forest, bisecting it, but the roots extended underneath, connecting the two sides together. Damage done to one side was damage done to the other.

He'd reviewed the lease shortly after he'd met Lee Bradley and found it was just as the rancher described. There wasn't much he could do. The cows were allowed to graze in the area for one week in July while workers completed irrigation work in his meadows, and another two weeks in October.

The sight of cows eating away at the new growth irked Knox on the long drive to Richfield, and by the time he'd finished his shopping, he was incensed. Voicing his concerns to his boss would get him nowhere. Bill would dig out a copy of the lease, wave it around, and order him to simmer down.

On the drive home, he slowed down where he'd last seen the cows. They were still there, except there were more of them now, closer to the roadway, munching away.

A black cow lifted its head and stared at him with far-apart eyes. After a moment, it went back to eating the sprouts as Knox watched, a terrible feeling of helplessness blooming inside him.

Chapter 10

Sandy had just finished producing the noon newscast when the phone rang at her desk. She ignored it. Her shift had ended, and she was drooping with exhaustion, eager to get home. The regular noon producer had called in sick, so Brody blasted her out of bed at four a.m. to fill-in. She'd stayed up too late the night before, watching movies and drinking wine, and she'd slept through Brody's first attempts to wake her.

Sandy was halfway to the door when she heard her name shouted from the opposite end of the newsroom. It was Harbin, the assignment editor, waving the phone over his head.

"You probably want to take this, Sandy. Says she'll only talk to you."

Despite her fatigue, her pulse quickened, and she raced back to her desk.

It was Janelle, the sheriff's office dispatcher in Richfield.

"Is it about your missing deputy?" Sandy asked breathlessly, reaching for a pen and legal pad.

"I wish, one way or another," Janelle said. "But no. It's something different, and I thought I'd give you the jump on it. The gal who calls me from the other station is a real you-know-what, and you've always been so nice. So, here it is. One of our officers responded to an incident at a campground near Fish Lake. A group of men caught a fellow sneaking around in the wee hours of the morning. Apparently, this guy had been seen the day before, watching teenagers swimming at the lake, and early this morning, he tried to grab one of the girls on her way back from the bathroom. But she had a good set of lungs, and she put up a real fight, and so a bunch of people came running, and, well, let's just say they weren't tolerating it. They sent him to the hospital."

An electric prickle raced up Sandy's spine. "You're kidding,"

"I am not. And here's the doozy. The part you'll be interested in. They ran a background check on that fellow, and turns out, he's a real bad man. Served time for rape and attempted rape and was recently released. It looks like his first stop was that campground."

Sandy readjusted the phone receiver under her chin, which had begun to cramp with the awkward position. "Will the sheriff give us an interview?" she asked, looking over at Harbin, who was staring at her with hopeful eyes. It was a slow news day.

She gave him a thumbs-up, and he punched a fist in the air.

"He sure will," Janelle said. "But you better send your people quick. The sheriff has a buddy at your competition, so he could be calling over there right now, for all I know."

They hung up, and Sandy explained what she'd learned to Harbin. "I don't know why Janelle would only talk to you," he sniffed. "I've only talked to the woman every day for the last I don't know how many years." When she rolled her eyes in response, he added, "Well, it just seems like you gals stick together."

"Oh, and you guys never do that," she said.

When she finally got to her car, she sat staring out the window for a long time, feeling the summer sun warm her bones. The air conditioner was always running full blast in the newsroom. It was so cold in there she kept a thick sweater to keep from freezing.

Sandy sat, immobile, clutching the steering wheel. Her head swam with thoughts of the teenage girl fighting back against her assailant. A flesh and blood bad guy.

Chapter 11

Knox wasn't even at his desk for ten minutes when the phone rang. It was the district manager, Bill Skeene, who didn't bother with a good morning.

"Just thought you ought to know," Bill said. "I just got a call from the sheriff in Richfield, and there was a whole lot of excitement at Doctor Creek Campground this morning. They arrested a guy for attacking a teenage girl near the bathroom. Apparently, tried to drag her into the forest. Sounds familiar, doesn't it?"

"Sure does," Knox said, thinking back to the newspaper article from 1970 about the attack on the unidentified child. "But that was a kid. Not a teenager."

Bill snorted on the other end of the line. "The girl was just fifteen, and a pervert is a pervert. The guy was a convicted rapist who just finished doing his time. He was originally arrested in January of 1971, so the timing is right, and for all we know, he returned to the campground because he was already familiar with it. Mystery solved."

Knox rubbed his hand over his face. He felt like he'd somehow failed at his job—to live within a fifteen-minute drive from the campground and not to have known about the attack and arrest practically in his backyard. "I wish I'd have known about this earlier," he said. Even to his own ears, he sounded dejected.

"Well, even if you had, you're not a cop," Bill said in a gruff voice. "We leave law enforcement to the sheriff. Your job is big enough as it is without having to worry about catching bad guys. Besides, it's pretty tame here. Not like Yosemite, which seems to attract all kinds of weirdos."

When they hung up, Knox drove to the campground. Only a few people were still around, packing up to leave. They seemed glad to see him, if only for the opportunity to share their story to a fresh face in a uniform. The girl, they said, had her arm broken in the scuffle and had been taken to the hospital.

Knox spent the rest of the morning stewing over the assault, and when the time came to tour Lee Bradley's ranch, he was grateful for the distraction.

He spent two hours with Bradley, getting the grand tour of Circle B Ranch, which turned out to be larger and grander than he'd imagined. Six hundred acres. Hundreds of beef cattle, although Lee wouldn't say exactly how many. A main house situated next to a creek with four bedrooms and a living room with a soaring, open-beamed ceiling.

Bradley's well-worn jeans and cowboy boots had been misleading. The Bradley's had money, which accounted for his swagger. From what Knox had heard, farms and ranches around the country were mired in financial trouble, but Circle B Ranch seemed to be thriving. It only added to his dislike of the man.

After touring the "pre-eminent cattle operation," Lee invited him for a drink back at the house, and he'd reluctantly agreed. It seemed rude not to accept. They settled next to the creek in old rattan chairs—scratched, faded, and comfortable. A large umbrella shielded them from the hot sun. Bradley drank a beer, while Knox sipped an iced tea.

The rancher regarded him with cool gray eyes. "How's the new job treating you?" he began. Before Knox could reply, he added. "Started off with a bit of a bang, didn't it?"

Knox dipped his head in acknowledgment. "It did."

Bradley chuckled. "And practically under your nose. It's what? Ten minutes from where you live?"

It had taken some effort, keeping the irritation he felt off his face. He was a ranger, not a security guard. And, as he reminded himself several times during his visit, he was there in his official capacity. He had to stay professional.

"You want to know what I think happened?" Bradley asked, staring at Knox as he sipped his beer.

Knox was curious about what a local might have to say. Go on. I'd like to hear it."

Bradley set down his Budweiser. "My cousin's wife is friends with Eileen Carroll. They've known each other forever, apparently. But Eileen isn't the easiest woman to get along with. She's bossy as all get out, but they're strict LDS, and as such, they are sealed together forever. The church doesn't believe in divorce, so what's a man going to do? He's going to disappear himself. Move to Mexico and find himself a nice little *señorita* who's not going to backtalk him to death. Live out his days nice and peaceful."

"You've got it all worked out," Knox said mildly.

Bradley threw up his hands. "It's the only thing that makes sense, right?"

Eventually, the conversation returned to the ranch, and Bradley started talking about his modern approach to running it. "You see, it's all about business. Balance sheets, cash flow, deciding how much risk to take. Now, my father, he hated debt. More than anything. But I have a higher tolerance, and so far, it's paid off. It allowed me to grow this operation quite a bit since I took over. And I'll let you in on another secret. If you're in agriculture, you have to get involved—and stay involved—in local politics. Otherwise, those environmentalists will do all the talking, and the next thing you know, they're telling us what we can and can't do with our land and taking away our water."

That reminded Knox. There might not be much he could do about the grazing lease, but there was no harm in raising the issue of the aspen forest with the man. After all, he had a stake in the land too. The men had that in common. They were both stakeholders.

"I saw some of your cattle while I was driving around today," he began.

Bradley cocked an eyebrow. "That's right. They'll be back out again in October."

Knox chose his next words carefully. "It's the first time I ever had anything to do with quaking aspen, so I did a little reading up on them, and it turns out, this one is special. It's what they call a clone forest."

Lee was staring at him, mouth slightly open, eyes narrowing. He cleared his throat and hurried on.

"Meaning all those trees are like carbon copies of each other. Which is crazy, if you think about it. And the way it grows is different too. It doesn't make new trees by dropping seeds. It sends up shoots from the roots."

Bradley was shaking his head slightly, clearly baffled. "And you are telling me this because..." He let his voice drift off.

Knox took a deep breath and pressed on. "Because each shoot represents a new tree, and if the cattle are allowed to continue eating without some sort of control, you can imagine what that might do to the forest." Just so there was no ambiguity, he added, "The cows will destroy the shoots, and the forest won't be able to regenerate."

Bradley rose slowly to his feet. His red beard twitched. "I have a lease," he said, sticking out his chin.

"I know. There's no question. I just thought we might be able to work together. You know. Find a solution to the problem."

"I was given a lease, and my cows are allowed to graze on that land. And now you're telling me you want to change things up." His eyebrows lowered. "What is it you're proposing, exactly?"

The truth was, Knox hadn't thought that far. He'd been hoping to open a conversation, not settle an argument. "I'm not sure. Maybe consider not putting out the cows in the more…sensitive areas."

Bradley exploded. "And how would we do something like that? I'll tell you how. There's only one way to do it, and that's with fences. And the land I'm leasing doesn't have any, and if you're thinking about installing them, I'll fight you. That document I signed gives me the right to let my cows go where they may and eat what's there. And if it means they're eating tree roots or whatever you called them, well, that's not my problem."

The part of the rancher's face not covered by mustache and beard had turned a mottled red, the veins of his neck corded. Knox rose to his feet and did his best to smooth things over. But the damage was done. Lee Bradley had pegged him as an adversary. Raising such a touchy issue on their first meeting—when his boss had given him clear warning—had been a terrible misjudgment. A stupid, rookie mistake.

At the truck, Knox held out his hand. Bradley considered it for a long moment before giving it a brief automatic shake, then dropped it and stalked toward the house. The last thing he noticed was the angry set of the rancher's shoulders.

Knox threw open the door of the cabin so hard it bounced against the wall, startling Colleen, who appeared wide-eyed in the doorway, hair pulled back in a ponytail, one hand to her chest. She was wearing a short white slip dress. He felt a flicker of desire, and then it was gone, consumed by frustration with himself and dislike of that pompous jerk of a rancher.

He pushed past Colleen without a word and reached into the refrigerator for a beer.

"Hello to you too," she said, standing behind him so close he could feel her breath on his sweaty neck.

Knox took a swig of his beer and said, "Yeah. It's been a day." There was still plenty of daylight left. The tops of the aspens moved. A shaking canopy of green.

She sniffed. "That makes two of us."

The words came out hard. Sharp. Like a trail of ground glass. He had a choice—step warily around it or walk right into it.

"Have you finished your story yet?" he asked. The question came out sounding more accusing than he intended. He might as well have lobbed a grenade over a wall.

She nudged him aside and grabbed a beer out of the fridge. "Have you forgot your manners? You could have got me one." She yanked the tab from the can and dropped it into the trash. "And no, I haven't finished my book, Knox. Jaysus. And it's not a story. It's a full-length novel."

He held up a placating hand. "Okay, okay. I get it. Just calm down."

Colleen dipped her head and glared at him over the top of her Moosehead. "Don't tell me to calm down. You know I hate it when you say that. Whatever bad thing happened to you in ranger world, don't come home and take it out on me."

Her hair had slipped from its band and fell around her shoulders. The skinny straps of her little white dress contrasted with the tan of her skin. For a moment, he considered pushing one down, just to see what happened, break the tension between them. But the way "ranger world" had tripped off her tongue…Another jab. Another poke at his career. Colleen had never showed much respect for the work he did, the work he loved. Sometimes, he thought she'd be much happier if he'd just get an office job somewhere in a city. But he couldn't stand that, trapped in a room all day. He needed to be outside. In the fresh air. Free from walls.

Knox shrugged. "Well, God forbid you'd ever ask me about my day. Because that would be a miracle."

She flinched as if he'd struck her. "Screw you, Knox. You know what? I'm sick of this."

The hot emotions that had him on boil drained from his body. Exhaustion remained. He watched her dispassionately as she paced the kitchen in bare feet, arms crossed tightly in front of her chest, fists shoved under her armpits.

"Sick of what?" he said, voice flat.

She stopped, lip lifting in a sneer. Even with that expression, she looked beautiful, like she was posing. Colleen had very pretty lips.

"You're kidding me, right? Sick of this place, Knox. *Little House on the Prairie,* except worse. Way worse. How could you have brought me out here? You tricked me. And I can't work here. Can't write surrounded by all these fucking trees. They're making me crazy!" She was shouting now. Full volume.

"Well, it's where we live for now," he said, walking out of the room.

Colleen followed on his heels. "No. It's where *you* live. I'm moving."

That stopped him cold. "What do you mean?" he demanded. "Where?"

"Salt Lake. I can rent a studio apartment or something. Cheap. You can visit me on your days off. It's only a few hours."

"We can't afford that," he said, shaking his head.

"You told me we're not paying anything for this place, so yes we can. I can find a part-time job."

She was serious. Knox could see that now. A promise is all she wanted. He knew that. A promise he'd find another job in a location more to her liking. But he didn't want that. He'd just started and hadn't even had a chance to see all the land in his jurisdiction.

He grabbed both of her hands in his. "Colleen, please. I'm sorry. You're right. I've not been very…" He searched for the right words.

"Supportive," she supplied, a smile dawning around the edges of her lips, her eyes.

"Supportive," Knox said firmly. "I'm sorry I was a jerk." He lifted her hands and kissed her knuckles. "I'm sorry I brought you out here, but I swear, the next job, we're making the decisions together. All the decisions. But please. Stay. Please, please, please, stay."

"It would help if you came home just a little earlier," she said.

Knox kissed her forehead. "Yeah. I can do that." After a moment, he added. "I guess we're both in a bad mood, huh?"

"I admit, I've got PMS pretty bad. And it gets lonely out here, all by myself." She wrapped her warm arms around his neck. "You know, husband, maybe all you need to do is pay a little more attention to your wife."

Chapter 12

Autumn, 1986

When October arrived and he'd passed his three-month probationary period, Knox marked the occasion by stopping at the state liquor store in Richfield after a regional meeting and buying two bottles of champagne—one for him, one for Colleen for starting a new book.

"A dark fantasy," she'd explained. "Time travel with dragons."

After a candlelit dinner of spaghetti and too much champagne, Colleen yawned, kissed his forehead, and headed off to bed. Knox laid on the couch and stared up at the wooden roof beams as logs crackled in the fireplace. They'd left the windows open to let in the cool fall air, but the whole place smelled of wood smoke. A pleasant smell.

Somehow, they'd managed to survive the last few months without any major blowups, mostly because he'd arranged getaways to Salt Lake City as often as his time off allowed. As a show of support for her work, he surprised Colleen with a used IBM Selectric typewriter he'd found at a garage sale. She'd shrieked with delight when she'd seen it.

Deputy Lane Carroll was never found, alive or dead, lending credence to the rumors he'd faked his disappearance to escape a bad marriage.

As summer turned to fall and the leaves of the aspens turned from deep-green to golden-yellow, the number of weekday visitors to Fish Lake Basin dropped. Kids were back in school. But oddly, the number of complaints to the ranger station rose—the same sort of reports about the aspen forest that had been documented in the Forest Service memos. Strange shadows, unusual sounds, lost dogs never found, and a few mutilated hares, which were attributed to a coyote that had wandered down from the mountains.

Then came the calls about "satanic markings" on the trees.

When Knox went to investigate, he knew exactly what they were and heaved a sigh of relief. Insects had bored into the bark, creating strange designs. And then there was the time a family had driven straight into town, demanding to talk to whoever was in charge, insisting Knox follow them to the aspen grove to see what had so shocked them.

He'd made the trip warily, not sure of what he might find. The Arkansas couple, stout and middle-aged, pointed triumphantly at the white trunk of an aspen, then another, and another.

"Those are eyes if ever I saw them," said the woman.

And that's exactly what they appeared to be—eyes carved into the white bark, staring back at them.

Knox had laughed, mostly out of relief. "Aspens don't like shade, so they keep growing toward the sun. But their lower branches end up in the shade, so they do something a bit tricky. They cut off the sap supply, and that causes the branches to fall off. That "eye" you're looking at is just the spot where a branch used to be." He picked up a fallen branch from the ground and held it up. It didn't quite match, but it made his point well enough.

That was met with widened eyes and sheepish laughter. The teenage children teased their parents, and the oldest, a girl, apologized for dragging him out there.

On a particularly raucous weekend at Doctor Creek Campground, one of the part-time staff had spotted several young men carving their names in the bark in the light of day, right off the highway, and had issued citations. When Knox arrived the next day at the station in Loa, the front window was broken, and inside, he found an empty bottle of cheap whiskey.

He'd run into Lee Bradley a few times, and the rancher had acknowledged him but barely. Which was fine by Knox. The less he had to do with that man, the better.

All in all, he mused, the job had gone well. He'd spent most of his time with routine work and overseeing long-overdue campground improvements.

On one of his visits to the Loa ranger station, Bill Skeene gave him a warning delivered with a wink and a mischievous smile. "Halloween's just around the corner, Knox. And you know what that means."

For a moment, Knox thought Bill was about to tell him he was expected to show up for work in costume.

Instead, Bill said, "Don't plan on going anywhere that weekend. It's an all-hands-on-deck situation. Halloween is one of our most popular days. Fall colors. Spooky stories around the campfire. Smores." He clapped Knox on the back. "And usually, a little too much to drink, and the next thing you know, someone's calling the sheriff's office, saying they've seen a monster."

As Knox glanced, bleary-eyed, at the calendar tacked to the wall on his way to bed, he counted sixteen days to October 31st.

Knox sat on the bed, watching Colleen pack for their weekend getaway to Salt Lake. She'd had her heart set on going to a Halloween dance party at a club she'd heard about, but when Knox explained he was expected to work that weekend, she'd sulked for days. Colleen was twenty-eight, five years his junior. She liked going out more than he did.

Before she started complaining again about living in the isolated cabin, he suggested heading north and checking out the club. It wouldn't be Halloween, but she'd still get to go there. He hated seeing her so unhappy.

Colleen had agreed but hadn't completely gotten over her disappointment about the Halloween party she was going to miss. She reached into the knotty pine wardrobe and held out a black lacy top and shiny black pants. "I had my costume picked out and everything," she said.

Knox frowned. "I don't get it. What were you going as?"

Colleen rolled her eyes, tossed her clothes on the bed, and snatched a black scarf from the top of the dresser. Knox watched, mystified, as she tied it over her hair until there was a giant, droopy bow sitting on top of her head.

"Now do you get it?" she asked, hands on her hips.

He grimaced. "No, I'm sorry. Just tell me."

Colleen stamped a foot. "Oh my god, Knox. Madonna in *Desperately Seeking Susan.*"

Knox plucked up the top with two fingers. "You can see right through this." He flicked it at her, and she caught it with one hand. "You can still wear it to the club. Why not? Except maybe don't wear that thing on your head. It's a little weird."

"I guess," Colleen said, shoulders slumping.

Through the walls of the cabin, he heard wheels on gravel. Colleen lifted her eyebrows, and he shrugged. He wasn't expecting anyone. A moment later, a door slammed.

Knox went to investigate, Colleen on his heels.

Lee Bradley stood, one booted foot on the bottom step, breathing as noisily as if he'd just finished a run, chest thrust out. His truck was parked in front of the porch, tailgate open.

"What's going on…" The words drifted from Knox's mouth when he noticed what was in the truck. A badly mangled calf, just a few weeks old and dead, by the looks of it.

Colleen gasped. "Oh no. That's so sad. What happened to it?"

"Why don't you ask your husband?" the rancher said, nostrils flaring.

Knox felt Colleen's hand grip his arm as he continued staring at the calf, then glanced at the ranger in surprise. He couldn't imagine what had caused its wounds.

"You're going to have to fill me in, Lee, because I don't know what this is about."

Bradley scowled. "I found this calf about a quarter mile up from here. It was on the side of the road. But if you look carefully, and I advise that you do, it's obvious it got tangled up in a barbed wire fence. And you're the one who did it. The last we talked, you were going on about my cattle grazing where they have a perfect right to be—"

Knox held up a hand and interrupted. "Back up a little. You found a fence?"

Bradley shook his head. "No. But I don't need to waste time looking for one. It's out there. Somewhere. You tell me where it is." He jabbed a finger at the dead animal. "I know what caused that horrible mess because I've seen it plenty first-hand. People take the lazy way out and string up barbed wire instead of the right kind of fence that doesn't hurt the animals. And I can't abide that."

"My husband would never do something like that," Colleen said hotly.

Bradley gave a dismissive snort, his gaze dropping to her bare legs in her jean cutoffs. "Then you don't know your husband, ma'am."

Knox registered the look. He turned to Colleen and in a quiet voice said, "Why don't you go inside?"

Colleen looked like she was about to argue.

Bradley shifted, planting his feet wide, and stared at Colleen's breasts. Since they hadn't expected company, she was braless, wearing her favorite old sweater with holes at the elbows.

Colleen's mouth dropped open. "Fuck you. Get off our property."

"Colleen," Knox said in a warning tone. That's the last thing he needed—his hot-headed wife mixing it up with the volatile rancher.

Colleen turned on her heel and stormed back into the cabin.

"Your wife has a mouth on her," Bradley said. "And a nice ass."

Knox felt all the muscles in his face tighten. When he spoke, his voice was low and icy. "You can shut up about my wife."

Lee raised his hands in a placatory manner. "I guess I'm a little rough around the edges sometimes, but it's just my way of paying a compliment."

"You can keep your compliments to yourself," Knox said roughly.

He approached the bed of the truck. Bile rose in his throat. He swallowed hard and began his inspection. Lacerations covered its entire body, but the worst gashes were concentrated between its knees and dewclaws. Its muzzle was also torn up, as if it had tried to chew the barbed wire. That didn't make sense. The extent of its injuries was surprising, but the calf had probably struggled to free itself and cut itself up even more in the process. While the wounds were many, it seemed unlikely they were enough to kill a healthy young animal. It had probably died of shock. Knox thought back to the memos he'd read about the dead mule deer discovered in the forest, bones broken. No cows. No terrible gashes. His gut told him the incidents had to be connected. But how?

Knox said, "Whether you believe me or not is up to you. But I'm telling you, I didn't put up a fence in the woods. Why would I? It wouldn't do any good. It would have to be one helluva long fence to be effective. But I am concerned if there is a fence, it's going to catch other animals. So why don't you show me exactly where you found the calf so I can start looking."

Bradley glanced around and for the first time seemed to notice the wall of trees edging the meadow. "I guess I can do that."

The anger and outrage had left his voice. Now, the rancher sounded uncertain. Eyebrows squeezing together, he raised the tailgate, gingerly, as if the calf were alive and he didn't want to disturb it.

After a quick word to Colleen, who'd heard the entire exchange from an open window in the living room, Knox got in the Bronco and followed Bradley up Highway 25. The rancher pulled over at the same spot in the road Knox had seen the cows crossing back in July. Bradley rolled down the window but remained behind the wheel.

Knox immediately spotted blood on the gravel, his eyes following a spattering of red through the trees. The calf couldn't have wandered far after it extracted itself from the barbed wire. The fence had to be reasonably close, somewhere on the upward slope. When he returned his attention to Bradley, the man was staring straight ahead.

"Aren't you going to help me look for that fence?" he asked.

Bradley shook his head. When he turned, his eyes slid to the trees and, after a moment, back to Knox's face. "I'll leave that to you. My brother and his family are visiting from Wyoming. We've got a ranch up there too. Smaller. I promised my nephews I'd take them hunting, and they're probably wondering where the hell I've gone to."

The rancher's explanation, and the tone in which it was delivered, confused Knox. "Okay. Well, you don't want to keep the nephews waiting."

Bradley hesitated. "If you find something, can you call the house? Leave a message on the answering machine?"

Knox nodded. "I can do that. If you don't hear from me, we didn't find anything."

"Thanks," Bradley said, voice gruff. He cleared his throat and coughed. "Sorry about all that. About your wife and all." Without waiting for a response, he drove off, leaving Knox to stare after the truck.

A chill morning breeze ruffled the ranger's hair as he picked his way through the juniper and sage brush, weaving his way through the rows of white trunks. He followed the blood drops about a dozen yards. They led to the base of an aspen. The blood seemed heavier there, confined to a small area. No sign of a fence, though.

As his boots crunched over the dried leaves, a spicy, bitter smell filled his nose, a scent he'd come to associate with the forest. The golden leaves sparkled in the sunlight, twisting in the air. It was a spectacular fall morning, and despite his grim task, he found his mind drifting and his body relaxing as he wandered through the aspen grove—any unease he felt there forgotten.

There was no sign of a fence, but he did spot a cluster of healthy shoots in a small clearing filled with autumn sun. They were several feet high. The sight of the new growth, undisturbed, brought a smile to his face. They'd survived. Survived the cows, the deer, the pests, the tourists trampling through the forest.

He knelt and touched one lightly. "Good for you. One of these days, we're going to get you a fence."

The aspens quaked overhead. Several flat golden leaves caught the drifting air and twisted to the ground. Knox smiled, then rolled his eyes at his own silliness. If Lee Bradley could hear him talking to the plants, it would just confirm his worst suspicions—he was nothing more than a tree hugger in a Forest Service uniform.

He remembered the bloodied calf and resumed his search. After an hour, he gave up. Colleen would be waiting for him at the cabin, anxious to get on the road and begin their weekend in Salt Lake. Knox drove to the station in Loa and called in two part-timers to continue the search for the barbed wire fence, with instructions to take photographs before they tore it down.

Chapter 13

The only person who looked more out of place than Sandy felt was Mitch. A bunch of people from the station planned to meet at the Xenon Dance Club, and Mitch had asked Sandy to go with him. Mitch liked country music and cowboy bars.

When Sandy told him the Xenon played nothing but Top 40 and alternative music, he'd shrugged and said, "Well, if you like that stuff, let's go."

She did like that stuff. And she loved to dance. But the only one she wanted to dance with was Mitch, and it was like his back was glued to the wall.

When she tried to pull him to the dance floor, he resisted. "I'm sorry, Sandy. That's a sight you never want to see."

After a few more attempts, she gave up and joined him at the wall, content to listen to the music and watch the others. She wondered why he'd come if he hated dancing that much, and when she asked him, he looked down at her in surprise and said, "To be with you."

Almost everyone not stuck on the overnight shift was there. Some had come straight from work. Others had taken the time to dress up. Sandy had lost a bet to Mitch—she owed him a beer at his favorite dive bar—that Jack Danielson would show up wearing a polo shirt, but Jack sauntered in, wearing double denim and complaining about the lack of booze.

"What do you mean they don't sell alcohol?" he'd shouted over the music.

"They don't have a liquor license," Jennifer explained. She'd organized the night out. When Jack slapped his forehead and turned on his heel as if to leave, she'd grabbed him by his jean jacket and said, "Don't be such a big baby." Then, she dragged him into a dark corner, dug into her purse, and shoved a mini bottle into his hands.

Sandy, leaning against a wall, watched him down it in one swallow under the strobing lights.

Mitch was standing so close she could feel his hip touching her arm. He hadn't left her side all night.

"That guy's a barf bag," Mitch said.

"He's a big swinging dick," she replied.

Mitch jabbed her in the side. "Hey, don't make me jealous."

Sandy stopped breathing, feeling the strong pull of the tall man at her side. They hadn't slept together. Yet. Her head buzzed. She wanted him, but she was also afraid. Sandy hadn't been with anyone in years, not after the panic attacks started getting worse. She hated the thought of anyone lying next to her as she shivered and quaked, slick with sweat, and she couldn't stand the questions that would follow, questions she didn't want to answer.

But Mitch was different. Patient. Empathetic. He *understood* her. Her therapist had asked if she had anyone special, and she'd said no, but she'd lied. Because she couldn't stop thinking about Mitch. The way his dirty blond hair curled so slightly over his shirt collar, his long, strong fingers flying over the satellite downlink controls.

"Hey," he said, "I'm going out for a smoke. Want to come with me?"

He wiggled his eyebrows suggestively, and she was tempted to say yes. She just needed a few moments alone to decide if she'd take the plunge and ask him to come over. And stay.

"I think I'll go to the bathroom," she said.

He leaned down and gave her a long kiss, so long she nearly forgot where she was, and when they pulled apart, several of her co-workers were staring. Mitch didn't seem to notice, and if he had, he wouldn't care. That was the beauty of Mitch. He had a quiet confidence she lacked. Maybe, she hoped, a little bit of it would rub off on her.

As she pushed through the crowd toward the bathrooms at the rear of the building, she felt a tug at her elbow. It was Jennifer. The reporter was wearing an army green jumpsuit with shoulder pads and black shiny boots with gold heels. She'd crimped her blond hair. Sandy wondered what she had to do to get that look. It took her nearly an hour just to style the bangs she kept meaning to cut.

"I saw the six from home," Jennifer said. "Great show."

Sandy blinked. She wondered why Jennifer was buttering her up—she rarely handed out compliments. "Thanks?" she said, caution creeping into her voice.

Jennifer snorted. "No, really. You're a good producer. If they ever let me anchor, I hope I get you. Seriously." She glanced at Jack, who was jerking his shoulders along to the music as he talked with Karl. "And I swear, I hope *he's* gone by the time that happens because that guy gets on my nerves. We all feel sorry for you, having to work with him like that. Babysit him, really. It's so lame."

"I appreciate that," Sandy said.

"So, what's with you and Mitch. Are you, like, a thing?"

Sandy swallowed. That was a complicated question. She was ready to take the next step with Mitch, but she wasn't ready to announce it to the newsroom. Telling Jennifer anything would be like writing a memo in all caps and sticking it on the bulletin board where the schedules were posted.

"We're just hanging out," Sandy finally said.

Jennifer threw back her head and laughed. "Well, if that's what you call hanging out, then I'm not going to let you near Karl. No, I'm kidding. We'd like to have you over one of these days. We got a new place in the avenues, and it has an awesome view of the valley. And you can bring Mitch too."

The invitation caught her by surprise. "That would be fun," she said.

The bathroom wasn't as crowded as she expected, just a few girls putting on lipstick. As soon as she sat down, she heard someone retching a few stalls over.

The retching continued, then the unmistakable sound of drunk vomiting. Whoever was in there was in a bad way.

"You okay?" she called. "Need any help?"

"Uh, I'm fine," replied a ragged voice. "Drank too fucking much. Can I ask you a favor? Can you tell my husband it's going to be awhile? He's probably still outside, wondering if I fell down and cracked my head."

Sandy stood and flushed the toilet. "Of course."

"Thank you. He's the tall guy with glasses," the woman said in a faint voice. "His name is Knox."

"No problem," Sandy said. After she'd washed her hands, she re-pinned her hair, then went out.

A man was pacing the narrow hall.

"Are you Knox?" she said.

He glanced up and gave her a tentative smile. "Have we met?"

Now that she was staring right at him, he did look familiar, but she couldn't place him. Sandy quickly explained the situation and introduced herself.

The man grimaced. "The no-alcohol thing bit us in the ass. We stopped at the Oyster Bar on the way in and had a bit too much."

"Tourists?" she asked.

"No. Well, we live here now. But we're from Texas originally."

Sandy smiled. "Well, what happened to your wife happens a lot to tourists. They're not used to the altitude, and when you order a drink, you get a mini bottle instead of a shot. People end up drinking way more than they're used to. The altitude and the liquor aren't such a good combination. We've done stories about it at the TV station where I work."

"You work in TV news?" Knox asked warily.

"Yeah. But behind the camera. As a producer."

The man nodded. He looked a bit older than most of the people at the club, but not by much. He was good-looking, with an interesting face.

"I can go back in and check on your wife," she offered.

Knox shook his head. "She'll be okay. Just needs to work it out of her system." She turned to leave when he added, "I think your station did a story down where I work."

There was something in his voice that made her freeze. A grievance. She sighed. Mitch would have to wait a few moments longer.

"Where do you work?" she asked lightly, hoping he didn't say the power company. The investigative reporter had done a hard-hitting series on the utility recently.

"I work for the Forest Service," he said. "Down in Central Utah, where the sheriff's deputy went missing. I'm a ranger."

Her heart thudded in her chest. The big story they'd covered a day late because Jack hadn't done his job and made his beat calls. But as far as she could recall, there was nothing in it he might find objectionable, no suggestion the search and rescue team had somehow fallen short.

"I remember the story," she said.

Knox bobbed his head and seemed to be considering his next words. "I met with your reporter. An older guy with a mustache. He did a good job and all. Got all the facts right. But I was a little surprised he went off the deep end at the end of the story."

Sandy remembered now. B. Knox. The man standing in front of her was the ranger Todd had interviewed for his story. "The deep end? What do you mean?"

"That stuff about the monster in the forest," he said bitterly. "Or whatever it's supposed to be."

Her breath caught. She'd forgotten about that. "It's a popular story. I mean, really popular. It would have seemed weird not to mention it. It would be like…" She paused, searching for an example. "Like someone seeing something scary in the Oregon woods and not talking about Sasquatch. Or finding a wrecked spaceship in Roswell and not mentioning aliens."

"I guess that's one way of looking at it," Knox said.

The ranger still looked unconvinced.

"I hope your wife feels okay soon," she said and scurried off in search of Mitch.

The talk of monsters and aliens reminded her. Halloween was just a few days away, and she was scheduled to cover assignments and produce the five o'clock newscast. She didn't mind working that day. In fact, she'd hated Halloween for as long as she could remember. But people in the newsroom went crazy for it, decorating their desks with cobwebs and jack-o-lanterns. Dressed up in costumes. But not her.

She spotted Mitch leaning against a wall, a knee pulled up in a pose straight out of a western. Her heartbeat quickened, and a delicious warmth suffused her body. There was no question how she felt about him now. She hurried toward him. When he saw her, a slow smile came to his face. His white teeth seemed to glow in the neon light of the club.

Chapter 14

Sandy left Mitch in her bed. Despite her misgivings about starting a relationship with someone she worked with every day, it felt right—even in the light of day, completely sober.

And it wasn't as if she'd suddenly jumped in. More like waded into a nice, inviting pool of warm water. Mitch had made it plenty clear over the last year he wanted more than the occasional drink. And her night with him had been even better than she could have imagined, not that she allowed herself to think that far ahead. Her psychologist said she invented many ways to punish herself, and denying her own needs was one of them.

Sitting in Celeste Munson's home office, Sandy relaxed in her favorite chair and looked out the window with its views of the Wasatch Front. The weather had taken a sudden but expected turn. The station's weatherman, Ron Blye, had predicted it

Steel blue clouds stretched across the sky, bathing the street in cold light. If Ron was right, and he nearly always was, the snowstorm would dump eight inches on northern Utah. The fun was expected to arrive the next evening, with heavy snowfall falling along the Wasatch range.

Before she'd left, Mitch had opened one hazel eye and said, "When the storm hits, I'll drive you to and from work. I don't like the idea of you driving around in that tin can of yours."

Mitch drove a red and white F-150 pickup truck, a much bigger Ford than her little Escort. Whenever she saw him in it, usually wearing a plaid shirt, he looked like he was posing for an ad.

Mitch looked even sexier as he stared up at her from the bed, dirty blond head resting on muscular arms crossed behind his head. They weren't due at the station for another two hours. She was half-tempted to cancel her early morning appointment with Celeste, but she hated being a flake.

"Thanks, I hate driving in snow," she said. And she meant it. Getting to and from work when it dumped snow was stressful. A couple of times, her car got stuck, and she'd had to wait hours for a tow truck.

"Can I see you tonight?" he said as she was pulling on her coat.

"You'll see me all day at work," she said.

He moaned. "That's not what I mean, Sandra. Am I seeing you tonight or not?"

"Yeah, yeah, yeah," she'd said, pleased.

Mitch took all the guessing out of a new relationship. No hanging by the phone, waiting to find out if he liked you as much in the morning as he seemed to in the heat of the night.

"And tomorrow night too," he yelled as she left.

She was so lost in her thoughts, thinking of Mitch, that when Celeste emerged from the kitchen and placed the steaming mug of tea next to her, she looked up, startled.

Celeste wore a cream-colored turtleneck dress. Her eyes twinkled behind her round glasses. "You look happy," she said.

Sandy blinked in surprise. "I do?"

Celeste nodded. "Yes. And relaxed."

Sandy squirmed in her chair. It was pathetic how long it had been since she'd had sex, and forever since it had been *good*, but she was still surprised it was so obvious.

Celeste studied her for a moment, giving her an opportunity to explain, but when she didn't, the psychologist smiled and said, "Shall we talk about your family?" There was no mistaking the expectant tone.

It was something Sandy had resisted. Celeste knew the big picture. Her brother's fatal car accident. Her father's fatal heart attack. It was the stuff before, in between, and after she had trouble talking about. Especially before.

It had taken Celeste just a few sessions to sniff it out, like a bag of rotten potatoes at the back of a pantry. Celeste hadn't said anything, of course. That wasn't her style. But Sandy could tell the therapist knew about her secret by the probing look Celeste sometimes gave her, followed by, "Go at your own pace. Take your time. We're in no hurry, here."

This time, though, she felt she had to give Celeste something. A nugget or two. She'd played this game before. Every psychologist she'd seen demanded a pound of flesh. Over countless sessions, she'd learned a quarter pound would do.

"I've been thinking," Celeste said, "that we might start with what happened after your father died. You said you turned down a college scholarship because that would have meant leaving your mother. That must have been very hard for you."

Tears welled in Sandy's eyes. Celeste handed her a box of tissues, and she accepted it gratefully, sitting it on her lap. It was going to be one of those sessions.

"Yes," she said into a tissue. "It was. But here's the thing. My parents didn't want me to go anyway. They didn't understand why I wanted to move away to go to school. My mom said I was abandoning them. She called me selfish. She's very old fashioned. My grandparents are from Mexico, and my family thinks girls should live at home until they get married. I think my dad would have been okay with it, but he couldn't go against my mom. When I got the acceptance letter, I was….so excited. But my mother threw a fit. My dad was pretty sick with diabetes by then. He was supposed to be on this strict diet, but he could never stick to it, and he wasn't supposed to drink, either, but he did. And then one day, he collapsed at work. He died right there on the factory floor."

"I'm sorry," Celeste said. "And that's when you decided you had to turn down the scholarship?"

Sandy sniffed and threw back her head, blinking back a new round of tears. "Yes. Because then, it did seem selfish. To leave my mom all alone after she'd lost her son and her husband. And I was already a disappointment to her because I refused to work full-time at the restaurant. She owns a Mexican restaurant on the west side. I mean, my brother did. But he liked working there. He thought it was fun, and the customers loved him. But I hated it, and when I went on a tour of a TV station in high school, I knew that's what I wanted to do. Work in TV news. So, I talked to my English teacher, and she was really nice. She had a friend who worked in the journalism department at the University of Utah, and she took me to see her. The professor explained what kind of classes I'd need to take to get a job like that. So, I went there instead, and it all kind of worked out."

Celeste nodded slowly and sipped her tea. "And what was your mother's reaction to your change in plans?"

"She didn't even notice," Sandy said with a sigh. "To be fair, she had her hands full with the restaurant and trying to figure out the insurance. We had to sell the house, and we moved into an apartment. Just the two of us, and…" Her words drifted off.

"And then you felt stuck?" Celeste offered.

"Trapped," she said. "We're really different. My mother and me. We've never got along all that well. My brother was her favorite. She adored him." She hesitated. The quarter pound of flesh wasn't hurting as much as she'd anticipated. In fact, the honesty felt almost good. Maybe Mitch's simple approach to life was already rubbing off on her. "My mom was really mad when I told her I was going to the U. She wanted me to help at the restaurant, and I said I would, as much as I could, but I wanted to do something different with my life. So, we started fighting. A lot. The professor at the U helped me fill out the forms for financial aid. I think she knew something was going on at home, and she kept telling me I needed to move into the dorms. Focus on my studies. And when I said I couldn't afford it, she found a special scholarship for students who were the first in their families to go to college, and I got it. It was enough for the dorms and my tuition, so it was kind of a miracle."

"And how did your mother react after that?" Celeste said.

Sandy lifted her mug and stared into her jasmine tea, its sweet fragrance tickling her nose. "Not good. She stopped talking to me for a while. Okay, for months, even after I moved into the dorms. When I'd go home to see her, or to the restaurant, she wouldn't even look at me. Pretended like I wasn't there. She's, like, an expert at the silent treatment."

Celeste set her mug on the side table. "Your mother didn't help you move into the dorms?"

A sob rose in Sandy's throat. She choked it back. It was ridiculous. All of that happened years ago. She should be over it now.

"No," she finally said. "She wouldn't even say goodbye."

"Sandra"—Celeste leaned forward and tapped her lightly on the knee—"some parents don't realize this, but the silent treatment is considered emotional abuse. Your mother was punishing you by withholding connection. It's a form of control, and it's very damaging. Now, this may be because your mother lacked the coping skills to deal with her disappointment, and no doubt she was in a lot of pain after the death of your father, but whatever the reason, the results are the same. The silent treatment is devastating to those on the receiving end. You must have felt abandoned. Did you?"

Sandy felt a tear slide down her cheek. She watched, helpless, as it fell into her mug, which she continued to clutch with hands that felt stiff and cold.

"Yes," she whispered.

"You mentioned you haven't had a relationship in a long time," Celeste said.

The memory of Mitch rolling over in bed and brushing the hair from her face flashed before her, and she felt her cheeks grow warm. She closed her eyes.

"That's right," she said. Which was technically true—up until the night before.

"The silent treatment has all kinds of consequences. Making people feel like outsiders. Like they don't belong. Lowered self-esteem. And another big one, impacting the ability to attach in future relationships because it's natural to worry the other person is also going to leave you."

Sandy felt herself flinch. "Sounds about right," she murmured. "All of it." Suddenly, she felt exhausted. That was the thing about early morning sessions—it was the one time that suited her busy work schedule, but showing up for work required a major mental shift. She set her mug aside, sat up straighter in her chair, and wriggled her shoulders. After all the talking they did, the session had to be nearing the end.

Celeste confirmed this by giving her a congratulatory smile. "Sandra, you've been through a lot. It sounds like you didn't get much emotional support after your father died, and you were grieving too. When you decided not to go to Missouri, you gave up a dream and received no acknowledgment for it. And when you deserved congratulations for getting a scholarship to the U, your mother cut you off. You've got incredible grit. You're a survivor. And you are every bit as worthy as that Jack character you work with—frankly a lot more. I want you to remember that when you go to work. You've more than earned the right to be there. You deserve to have that job."

The gush of unexpected words made her feel so lightheaded she had to grip the arms of the easy chair. Celeste had always been kind—emanating soothing support—but she'd never been so forthright before. Sandy felt so touched that she was close to tears again. Making the transition to work after this session was going to be tough.

"Thank you," she said in a small voice. "I'll try. I'll try to remember that."

Outside, the storm clouds seemed to hug the mountains a little closer, and the wind had picked up. As she drove through the neighborhood, she noticed all the Halloween decorations and smiled. There was nothing like a good snowstorm to put a damper on all that spooky nonsense.

Chapter 15

Eyes still red from her therapy session, Sandy holed up in a darkened edit bay, squirting drops in her eyes to get rid of the red and catching up on the stories she'd missed since her last shift. She'd darted past the Desk with a wave to the assignment editor, who was arguing with Karl over a story he didn't want to do, and avoided the cluster of desks where the producers sat. Jack was there, his feet propped up on her chair. She'd been tempted to kick them to the floor, but he'd take one look at her and ask why she'd been crying.

The glass door slid open, and she jumped.

Mitch stepped inside, filling the small space. He grinned and set down a bagel and coffee on the counter, next to the sign that read, "Absolutely No Food or Beverages." It was a warning he'd put up himself just the week before after a reporter spilled Coke on the tape deck's control panel.

Mitch must have showered at her place. The room smelled like her sandalwood soap.

She scooted her chair further into the gloom. The eyedrops hadn't worked their magic yet. If Mitch started asking questions, she'd be tempted to tell him the truth, and once she started, she might not be able to stop. Even Mitch had his limits. Now they'd taken that first step together, she didn't want to risk it.

She unwrapped the bagel. Cinnamon raisin, with a thick layer of cream cheese—her favorite.

"You remembered," she said, touched.

He leaned over, grabbed the sides of her chair, and rolled her toward him. "Do I get a reward?"

His face hovered near hers. It was a good thing she was sitting down because her knees weakened. Sandy looked past him. No one was nearby. They were safe for now, but someone could come barreling down the hall and around the corner any moment.

"Yes, but you'll have to wait. Anywhere but here," she said, stroking the side of his face.

Mitch straightened and shoved his hands in his pockets.

She eyed his chunky work boots. "Do you always wear those things?"

"You have a short memory. I don't think I wore 'em last night."

She burst out laughing. "That would be worse than wearing socks." She paused. "So, how is this going to go? You and me. Here." She gestured to the knot of people at the assignment desk. "You know how this place is. It's a newsroom. Nothing stays secret for long."

"Do you care what other people think?" Mitch asked, a slight frown coming to his face.

She shrugged. It was a tricky subject, one too early to raise since they'd only slept together for the first time the night before. It had been so long since she'd had a boyfriend, it was possible she was overthinking what might, for him, have been a one-night stand.

Mitch seemed to read her thoughts because he smiled and said, "You didn't seem that worried about them at that stupid dance club."

Her hands flew to her face, and she groaned.

Mitch peeled her fingers away and cupped her chin. "Hey. I've been waiting a long time for you to go out with me." He jerked the thumb of his free hand over his shoulder. "You think I care what those assholes have to say about it? No. Because it's none of their damn business."

"That's easy for you to say." She sighed before continuing. "Because you're Mitch Stevens, mister popular, and I'm Sandra Molina, bitch producer."

"No, you're not. Who says that?" he asked with exaggerated indignation. Then, he chuckled. "Well, yeah. I may've heard something like that from a couple of these jerks. But if you weren't the way you are, Sandy, those guys would run right over you. Remember what happened to Dana? She was too nice, and that was the end of her. She didn't even last three months, which was a shame because her shows were really clean."

Her stomach fluttered. "Do you think I'm a bitch? At work? That's what people say?" She was beginning to panic now. Is that how people saw her? Was she someone they sat around discussing? *That Sandy. What a bitch. A bitch with no balls, no news judgment.*

"No!" Mitch said, putting his hands on her shoulders. They felt heavy, warm, and comforting. "Sandy. Stop. You're not a bitch. You're a producer who has to get shit done with one hand tied behind your back and with all the double duty they throw at you. And hey, I've mentioned the crap you put up with to Brody more than a few times."

She gazed up at him in surprise. "You have?"

"I have. But that's between you and me, and that's all I'm going to say on the matter." He pulled her to her feet.

Mitch's back was to the tinted sliding glass door, so he didn't see Jack striding toward them.

Sandy moaned. "What the fuck does *he* want?"

Before Mitch could reply, Jack pounded on the glass. She reached past Mitch and opened the door.

"What's up?"

Ignoring Mitch towering over him, Jack pointed at the clock on the wall. They were everywhere in the newsroom. "If you're finished screwing around in here, Sandy, you're late for the sweeps meeting." He hurried off.

Mitch stared after him. "That guy is a piece of work."

The room suddenly felt warm. Face flushing, Sandy sped toward the conference room. She was never late to meetings. Ever. She was halfway across the newsroom when she realized she'd rushed off without a word to Mitch. Sandy glanced over her shoulder. Mitch was where she'd left him outside the edit bay, looking put out she hadn't said goodbye.

"All right, everyone," Brody said. "Listen up. November sweeps is around the corner, and I don't have to remind you, it's a biggie for us. We're closing the gap between us and the guys across the street, and we hear they're nervous. They're used to being the big dogs, and they've got us nipping at their heels. So, we've got special reports lined up to run twice a week all month." Brody turned to the executive producer, Monty. "Tell me all those stories will be ready to go."

Because Sandy had arrived late, she'd taken the last open seat, a chair against the wall. Everyone else sat at the conference table. Sandy watched Monty tap his pencil against a yellow pad. His job was to oversee the quality of the newscasts, but he spent most of his time on special projects.

"Absolutely," Monty said. "Mitch has worked his usual magic, editing the packages, and everything is in the can and ready to go. Well, almost. He's got two more to finish up for the last week of sweeps."

"If he has time," Jack muttered, with a glance over his shoulder at Sandy.

Everyone at the table turned to stare. A few people gave knowing chuckles.

Well, there it was. Sandy had no one to blame but herself. She'd thrown herself at Mitch at the Xenon Club in full view of her co-workers. Anything she said would make matters worse, so she returned an innocent smile and shrugged. That wasn't the reaction Jack had been hoping for because he scowled.

The meeting continued without further comment on her personal life. When Brody ticked off the final agenda item scribbled on a yellow pad, he clapped his hands. "And if there's breaking news, guys, we need to get there first, and we need to *own* it."

"I hope everyone heard that," Jack said, smirking.

Sandy stiffened, felt her chest tighten. She knew who that was aimed at, and if there was any doubt, there was Jack, twisted in his chair, staring at her again. Jack's comment got a few awkward laughs, but not enough to satisfy him. He slumped in his chair.

Brody acted as if he hadn't heard. "And I have two announcements before I let you get back to work. As you've probably noticed, Harbin isn't here today. His wife went into labor early, and there are some complications, so he won't be in for a while. Don is out too. There are network meetings up at Snowbird through the weekend. Gus has invited some of us managers to attend the meetings, too, so I'll be going up, and so will Monty."

Sandy blinked in surprise when she heard him mention Gus. The news director was never out during ratings, and neither were Brody or Monty.

Again, all eyes turned to her, and her heart sank.

Brody said, "So, Sandy will be handling assignments in Harbin's absence."

Jerry, the ten o'clock producer, opened his mouth to speak, then closed it after noting Brody's stern expression. Sandy couldn't tell if Jerry objected because he didn't trust Sandy, or because he'd wanted that job for himself.

The managing editor placed his hands on the desk and pushed himself to a standing position. "I think Sandy's more than earned the right to work just one job instead of the usual two we throw at her. While I'm gone, I want you to give her your full support." He glanced around the table, eyes resting on Jerry. "Got that?" He strode out of the room.

Sandy was as surprised as everyone else and wondered why Brody hadn't discussed it with her in advance. But that was just like him, to assume she'd be happy to do any job he gave her. Not that she minded assignments. She'd be working regular shifts staffed with full crews of reporters and photographers—nobody was allowed to take vacation time during sweeps—but still. It would be nice not to be taken for granted once.

"Try not to blow it this time," Jerry said, walking past Sandy settling in at the desk.

She put on Harbin's telephone headset, which would be hers for the foreseeable future.

"Fuck you, Jerry," she said mildly.

He was probably in a bad mood because he'd been asked to come in early for the sweeps meeting. His usual shift didn't start until two-thirty.

Sandy looked past him at the long bank of windows. Blue-gray clouds hung low across the sky. Which reminded her—they hadn't discussed a storm coverage plan, and if their weatherman was right, they'd need one. When she popped into Brody's office, he was packing up his briefcase.

"Harbin said there's a list of stories in the file," Brody said. He hesitated. "And hey, did I mention we want you on the desk through the weekend since it's sweeps?" When he noted her startled expression, he continued. "No? I'm sorry if that wrecks any plans." Brody snatched a beanie from a drawer and twirled it in the air. "I hope I can do some skiing. The powder should be excellent."

And then he and Monty were gone, and she was in charge.

Sandy had never worked the assignment desk without having to produce. It felt strange at first, to focus on one task instead of two. It was almost luxurious. She perused the notes Harbin left behind, and when reporters cruised up to the desk to talk through their stories, she was able to give them her full attention. Later, when they were in the field dealing with the inevitable setbacks, she offered help without snapping at them. The reporters seemed to like the more relaxed, supportive Sandy, and by the time the five o'clock newscast began, she was basking in a rare sense of camaraderie that had eluded her for all her years at the station.

She monitored the competition's five o'clock newscast to make sure she hadn't missed any big stories, and she hadn't, but when video of a familiar forest appeared on screen, her stomach did a somersault.

"What the fuck…"

Jack looked up from his computer, where he'd been typing furiously. He was producing the six. "What did you miss now?"

Sandy hugged her elbows and stared at the screen. "Shut up, Jack."

Had they found the sheriff's deputy who disappeared from Fish Lake National Forest? She'd checked in with Richfield just hours ago, and the dispatcher hadn't said a thing.

The anchor began, "That's right, Gene. We have a special report coming up tomorrow at five, and you're not going to want to miss this one. We're celebrating Halloween by rounding up Utah's scariest stories, including the legend of the Root Witch, a creature some people believe lives in an aspen forest in the central part of our state."

Relief washed through her, only to be replaced with a vague unease. Jennifer ambled up to the desk, makeup mirror in one hand and mascara wand in the other, getting ready for her on-set piece at six.

"People are going to eat that shit up," Jennifer said. "People love urban legends. It's too bad someone here didn't think of that. It's a great story."

Sandy watched as Jennifer wandered in the direction of the studio to finish her makeup in front of a well-lit mirror. Their brief exchange represented progress, of sorts. Jennifer hadn't given her a tough time about the Halloween story. She'd used the generic "someone," which technically meant Monty, the executive producer in charge of special reports.

"We can still do the story" Jack said. He'd taken to wearing long-sleeved polo shirts—more ridiculous than the short-sleeved versions, but at least they covered his skinny, hairy arms.

She could feel a vein throb at her temple. "We can't just copy them."

"Why not?" he demanded, voice rising. "That's how it's done, San-dee."

She snorted. "Not when I'm in charge."

It was dark out, and the windows turned into mirrors. Sandy caught a glimpse of herself. Her makeup was smudged, and her eyes were black holes in a pale, haunted face.

Chapter 16

Even with the water running at the bathroom sink, Knox could hear Colleen winding herself up in the sunroom.

"The library," she wailed. "I need to go to the library now!"

Which was what she always said when she got stuck on a scene in her latest book.

Over the past few months, he'd become quite familiar with her process. In her desperation to avoid staring at the typewriter, she decided the thing holding her back was some bit of research that could only be done at a well-equipped library or bookstore. The problem was, both were hours away in Salt Lake City.

Knox padded into the kitchen, his face still slathered in shaving lotion, heart sinking at the sight of his wife pacing in front of her desk. Both her hands were pressed against the sides of her head, as if she was trying to prevent it from exploding. The curtains were drawn. Soft morning light streamed in through a gap.

"Colleen," he said quietly, so as not to startle her.

Her body jerked, and she gave a little scream. "Jaysus, Knox. Don't sneak up on me like that." Her hands came down to her hips. "Did you hear me? I can't finish. I need to go to the library in Salt Lake, and yes, I know you're working this weekend, but I have to go. I'm perfectly capable of driving myself."

He shook his head. "Colleen. Remember what they said on the radio? There's a snowstorm up there. The roads are a mess. It's not a good time to go."

Colleen buried her face in her hands and groaned. "I swear, it's like the world is against me."

Knox hurriedly rinsed his face in the kitchen sink and dried himself with a paper towel. He had an idea. If only he could convince her.

"I think you just need to take a break," he said. "You've been writing nonstop for days. You just need a change of scenery."

"Oh, I do, do I? And where would that be? Because we'd have to drive hours to get the hell away from here."

"Let's do what everyone else does when they get cabin fever. Go out, take a walk, and get some fresh air. Clear our heads. Look, I have a few hours before I go in." He crossed the room in a few steps and yanked open the curtains. "Come on. People come from all over to see the fall colors, and we haven't been out there once." He made a sweeping gesture toward the wall of white trunks, topped with shimmering golden leaves.

Colleen's eyes wandered to the trees, and she let out a noisy sigh. "I stare at those trees all day, every day," she said without enthusiasm.

Fifteen minutes later, they were dressed, Colleen trailing behind him as he led the way into the forest. "I'd still rather be at the library," she grumbled.

"You'd never get there in a snowstorm," he said, stopping and waiting for her to catch up.

She was purposely dawdling, her arms hanging listlessly at her sides as she stared at the ground, instead of the blaze of fall color around them.

Knox took her firmly by the hand and pulled her along. When she resisted, he slipped an arm around her waist and half carried her a few yards, until her body began to relax and she giggled.

After another few yards, she relented. "Okay, it's pretty."

Not far into their walk, Knox was beset by doubts. He hoped they wouldn't come across a dead animal. That's all he needed. Colleen was still upset by the incident of the mutilated calf, and he'd stretched the truth to explain it away—saying the cow had stumbled onto a bit of old barbed-wire fence.

After a half hour, Colleen began to walk more vigorously and with more intention. She pointed to the ridge line. Grinning, Knox set out running, but she soon outpaced him. His wife had the feet of a goat, nimbly weaving around fallen trees and rocks, clambering over boulders.

The view from the ridge was breathtaking. Colleen wrapped her arms around his waist as they took in the display of vibrant, fiery leaves against a cloudless deep blue sky.

As they began to make their way down, they heard people shouting.

Tourists, probably, though they sounded upset. On the way down, Knox moved ahead, leaving Colleen to trail behind. He wanted to see what was going on before she did, just in case. The shouting stopped, but he could still hear voices.

He followed the sound to a clearing.

A knot of hikers gathered around a young boy wearing orange pajama bottoms. A woman with long red hair spilling out of a University of Utah cap knelt next to him, talking quietly into his ear. The boy was sobbing and holding his ankle. Knox felt Colleen grab his elbow.

"Oh my god, is he okay?" she whispered.

He patted her hand and stepped toward the group, clearing his throat. "I'm a ranger. It looks like you need some help." When the woman's head snapped up, he added, "Is he all right? Did he fall?"

She shook her head. "No…"

That was as far as she got. A man with the same eyes as the frightened boy came crashing out of the trees, wielding a knife.

"Whatever it was, it went into the ground," he gasped.

There was no stopping the tumble of words that fell from the man's mouth. His six-year-old son ran into the trees and started screaming. When he chased after the child, he saw an enormous shadow, and tree roots had come out of the ground and were dragging the boy away. The man had to use a knife to free his son. He'd chased after the shadow, but it vanished. An outrageous, unbelievable story, but told in such a way Knox believed him. Or believed the man was certain of what he had seen. The parents were accountants with their own practice in Salt Lake City and were staying at the lodge near the lake for the weekend. Knox took down the details of the incident in his notebook, as Colleen listened, biting her nails.

Knox examined the boy's ankle. Red welts lashed the pale, freckled skin. Above the Achilles tendon, the flesh had separated, blood spilling onto the ground. One of the onlookers rummaged through a backpack and handed Knox a scarf. He wrapped it around the wound as the child whimpered, clinging to his mother.

After Knox advised everyone to leave the clearing immediately, the boy's mother rose to her full height. She was as tall as Knox.

Her lips narrowed. "You can't just leave and not tell us what you're going to do about this," she said.

Everyone turned to stare. There was only one good answer.

"I'm going to get some help and conduct a search," he said.

The answer seemed to satisfy the group, and they hurriedly left by way of the road.

Even though that was the longer route, and probably the wisest, Knox was eager to get to his truck. Through the forest, the way they came, would save thirty minutes.

As they jogged to the cabin, Colleen kept a tight hold of his sleeve. The experience had spooked her. Badly. It had alarmed him too. He didn't know what to make of that improbable story, but couldn't imagine what had really happened.

When their cabin was finally in sight, Colleen stopped in the shade of the aspens, just short of the meadow.

"I hate this place, Knox," she said, face twisting. "I hate this forest. I hate all these fucking trees. And now, God only knows what the hell is in there. Did you hear that man? A shadow monster? Jaysus, Knox. And you expect me to stay here, by myself, all day long, while you go to work? With that fucking creepy forest in our backyard. Are you really okay with that?" When he didn't answer immediately, she grabbed him by the shirt and shook him. "It's just not fair, Knox. I didn't sign up for this, and I can't do it. I won't. I'm leaving. Now. I'm not staying in this place another night. No way, no how."

Tears streamed down her face. She was scared, and she had every right to be. But before he could take care of

Colleen, he had a job to do. He pulled her tight and felt her struggle a moment before she went limp in his arms.

"Colleen, listen. I hear you," he said. "I do. Loud and clear. But you saw what happened. I need to go to the station and get a search organized, and then, I'll be back as soon as I can. I promise."

The cabin sat a safe enough distance from the forest.

Colleen jerked free, chin jutting out in defiance. "If you leave, Knox, I swear to god, I may not be here when you come back."

He scraped a hand through his hair and groaned. "Colleen. Come on. Give me a break. Please. Can we talk about this after work? We can't decide something this important now."

With a wail, Colleen bounded toward the cabin and got there before he did. Doors slammed so loud the boards of the wooden porch vibrated under his feet.

Colleen had shut herself in the bathroom. He could hear her sobbing through the knotty pine door.

"Keep the doors locked, Colleen, and I'll be back as soon as I can."

He pressed his ear against the door, heart pounding in his chest. "Don't you want to say goodbye?"

In answer, she kicked the door.

Time was wasting. He needed to get to the station.

"I love you," he said, then walked out to his truck and left.

Chapter 17

Of course, two photographers would call in sick. Their boss, the operations manager, was at the conference with the news director and the managing editor, so it was up to Sandy to figure out what to do.

She eyed the list of available photographers, wondering how the newsroom would get through the day. Sandy hated to pull Mitch off his special report editing duties, but if she had to, she would. Hopefully with some juggling, everything would work out.

The Halloween snowstorm was the big story, but otherwise, it was turning out to be a painfully slow news day. Honestly, the snowstorm was all anyone would care about anyway. Widespread power outages, cars off the road in Parleys Canyon and on the roads to the ski resorts. Ron Blye came in to work early to work on his forecast.

"This storm is going to get intense, Sandy," he said, leaning over the desk. "I expect the National Weather Service to issue a warning any moment. We're in for some major wind, and that's going to mean whiteout conditions and slick roads."

She nodded. "The scanners are already going crazy with all the traffic problems. What if we send a reporter to do a live shot with someone at Highway Patrol. They can give us the latest info, and we can roll some video we get during the day?"

Ron drummed the desk in approval. "That's great, Sandy. Can I toss to the reporter?"

Glancing at Jack, his narrow back to them both, she said. "That's not my call. Jack's producing, but I'm sure he'd be fine with that."

Sandy knew Jack would hate that. He firmly believed only anchors should toss to reporters in the field, so she enjoyed the thought of Jack squirming when Ron asked. Jack was dressed as a Frenchman, in a black and white striped shirt, a black beret, and a skinny red scarf tied around his neck. He looked ridiculous.

When Karl passed by, coffee mug in hand, she waved him down. "Want the lead at five and six?" she asked, then explained the storm coverage plan.

His eyes widened in surprise. "I would, but I got called in to cover the commute on the morning show." He paused. "Do you want me to pull a double shift?"

She shot a grateful smile. "Nah. We've got enough reporters. There's no reason to torture you like that."

In the morning editorial meeting, the only reporter without a story pitch was Jennifer. Sandy suspected as much the moment Jennifer strolled in and slumped into a chair, staring at the table. When the other reporters had gone, she turned to Jennifer.

Keeping her voice as pleasant as possible, Sandy said, "And what do you have today?"

Jennifer rolled her eyes. "Nothing," she snapped. "And believe me, I've tried. I've been on the phone for the last hour, and either no one is available to talk on camera, or something was canceled because of the storm."

The obvious thing to do was assign Jennifer the weather story, but Sandy hated to reward her with the lead. Besides, she'd already decided to give it to the late shift reporter set to arrive at two-thirty. It made sense. According to Ron, the squall was expected to begin late in the afternoon and would remain in effect, conveniently, through the ten o'clock newscast.

With the number one weatherman in the market, the storm would be a ratings bonanza on the first night of sweeps.

"Well, it is Halloween," Sandy said reluctantly because she hated Halloween. "I mean, you could do a story about how the storm is going to wreck it for all the kids. Maybe there are some last-minute indoor events?"

Jennifer took a deep breath and pushed back her feathered blond hair. "Yeah, okay. But I was hoping to have something a little sexier. For sweeps."

Sandy held her breath. Jennifer's reaction was better than she hoped for. At least she wasn't rejecting the idea outright.

"I'll make some calls," Jennifer finally said, then drifted from the room.

Sandy was typing up a list of local stories for the day to distribute to the producers, one ear on the scanners, when the desk phone rang. Since they were still out a desk assistant, the receptionist at the front desk was screening calls to the newsroom. Sandy picked up the phone.

A breathless-sounding man was on the other end. He was talking so fast she could only pick out two words.

Root Witch.

Sandy stiffened. "Pardon me?" she said into the receiver.

The man continued to babble, and after a few moments, she said, sternly, "Sir, you are going to need to slow down because I can't understand you. Where are you calling from?"

"I'm calling from a phone at Lakeside Lodge in Fish Lake," the man said, still out of breath but at a slow enough speed the words didn't run together. "I'm down here for a family reunion. A bunch of us were on a hike in the aspen forest this morning, and my sister and I saw something. At first, we thought it was a bear, but it was too big for that. It was as tall as a tree. We've never seen anything like it in our lives. So, we ran. And it chased us, I swear. When we told them about it at the Lodge, the guy said it was the Root Witch. That it was coming alive again."

Her stomach dropped. In all the time she'd worked at the station, no one had ever called in with a sighting.

"Did you call the sheriff's office?" she asked.

The man snorted. "I sure did, but they didn't seem too interested in what I had to say. They said they'd send a patrol car and take a look around."

Something clicked in Sandy's head—the man she'd met at the Xenon Club, the one with the unusual name waiting for his wife to finish throwing up in the bathroom. Knox.

"Did you try contacting anyone at the ranger station?" she asked.

"It was closed when we went," the man said angrily. "They left a note on the door. For all the good that was going to do us."

The lights on the phone were all lit up. She covered the receiver with one hand and shouted at Jack to help out. After she'd returned Jack's middle finger, she rubbed the back of her neck and said, "Was anyone hurt?"

Sandy could hear an intake of breath on the other end of the line. "You believe me then?" the man asked.

"I don't know," she said quietly. "I mean, I don't even know your name."

"Kyle Howard," the man shouted. "My name is Kyle Howard. Now listen, I watch your station all the time, and I thought you'd appreciate a news tip like this. Aren't you going to do something? Investigate? Isn't that what you're supposed to do? That's what it says on those advertisements you play all the time. And all those billboards too."

He slammed down the phone.

It was impossible to concentrate after that. The man had sounded truly upset, but it was such a crazy story it had to be a prank. She wouldn't put it past someone at the competition to make a call like that. But it was easy enough to confirm. Kyle Howard had said he'd called the Sheriff's Office. She could too.

Sandy flipped through the cards in the Rolodex.

When the dispatch operator answered and heard Sandy's voice, she said, "Please do not tell me you are calling about that Root Witch baloney."

Sandy's heart jumped in her chest. Karl hadn't been lying about that much, at least. "So, you got that call too, Janelle?"

"You mean calls. Oh yeah. Several since my shift started an hour ago. H-E double toothpicks. I couldn't stand it anymore, so I sent an officer."

Sandy swallowed, thinking of the man walking alone through the aspen grove. "Did he find anything?"

"A lot of hysterical people is all," Janelle said. "Some of them have congregated at Lakeside Lodge. Some of the others are staying at Doc Creek Campground. It's mass hysteria, is what it is."

"And it's Halloween," Sandy added.

"Well, there's that too," Janelle said with finality. "Anything more I can do for you?"

Not knowing what else to say, Sandy thanked the dispatcher for her time and hung up.

Jack marched up to the desk. "Jesus, it's insane. I must have gotten four phone calls from people saying they saw something in the forest where that deputy went missing."

Sandy's chest felt like it was being squeezed. "What did they say?"

Jack rolled his eyes. "I don't know. They were yelling on the phone, so it was hard to understand them. Just that they saw some big boogeyman."

"Did you get any names, or phone numbers?"

"No," Jack snapped. "They were calling from pay phones."

Sandy pressed her fingers into her temples, trying to think through the possibilities. She wished Brody was around. Or any of the managers for that matter. The anchors weren't in yet and weren't due for a few more hours.

"Do you think the guys across the street are just having some fun with us?"

Jack frowned. "Would they do that?"

Sandy shrugged. They wouldn't have called the Sheriff's Office. It didn't make sense.

The phone rang again. Jack didn't move. He leaned on his elbows, staring at Sandy. His hairy arms stuck out from the sleeves of his striped shirt. They were so thin they reminded her of insect legs. Sandy picked up the call.

"Hello," a woman's voice said. "My name is Jonie Waite, and I'm calling from Lakeside Lodge in the Fish Lake National Forest. There was an incident down here earlier, and I'm hoping you can help me bring some attention to the matter."

Sandy mouthed "another one" to Jack and spoke into the receiver. "What incident?"

"This is going to be very hard to believe, but I swear it's true. I was out on a walk this morning with my husband and son. He's six. The weather is cold but nice down here. We got up early to see the fall colors in the aspen forest before it got too crowded. There are a lot of people down here this weekend. Well, we were walking, and our son got ahead of us, and suddenly, he started screaming. We couldn't see him, so we started running and found him lying on the ground. It looked like some tree roots, or something, had Jordan by the ankle. At first, I thought he must have caught his foot on a root or something, but then, it was like the roots were trying to drag my son down into the ground, and my husband had to use his knife to cut them off. By that time, some other people heard Jordan screaming because some hikers showed up. And then, when we got back to the lodge, other people were saying they saw the Root Witch. And I just thought someone should know."

Heart hammering in her chest, Sandy said, "Would you talk to us? On camera? We'll need to send someone, and it will take a while to get there."

The woman didn't hesitate. "Of course. That's why I called. My husband will talk to you as well, but I want to be clear, I won't let you talk to my son. He's still upset."

Sandy jotted down the number of the lodge on her legal pad and hung up.

"You're not really going to send a crew down there?" Jack said.

"Just last night, you were saying we should steal that special report on Utah's Scariest Stories, and now a story like this drops in our lap, you don't want to do it?"

"This is different," he said with a grimace.

"Different how, Jack? Exactly?"

"I don't know, but it is," Jack said, dropping his gaze.

Sandy stood, yanked the beret off his head, and sent it sailing toward his chair. "I can't talk to you when you're wearing that thing." She dropped her voice. A few of the reporters still at their desks were beginning to stare. "Jack, look. You were right about one thing. Their special Halloween story is going to get some serious eyeballs. We've got Ron and a storm, so that puts us ahead, but I can practically hear people tuning out to watch that Utah's Scariest Stories stuff. Now, we can beat them to it with a story about Root Witch sightings. And it's legit. It's an actual news story that just happens to be a great Halloween story. Do you get it now?"

Jack rolled his neck. When he'd finished, interest glimmered in his eyes, and Sandy knew she'd won him over. Jack might be annoying as hell, but he was a good enough producer to realize a story like this one could be ratings gold.

"Put like that, yeah, I get it," he said. "But isn't that pretty far? Can we even get a live shot from way down there?" Jack looked skeptical.

"Not with a regular truck," she replied, pushing her bangs from her face. "But we can send the sat truck."

Jack's eyes bulged. "The satellite truck. For a feature story? Satellite time is incredibly expensive. Isn't it reserved for big breaking news?"

Sandy shrugged, affecting a nonchalance she didn't feel. Inside, her guts twisted at making such a risky call—which told her it was the right thing to do. The other producers thought she didn't have the nerve to make tough calls, and now that's exactly what had presented itself. She had an opportunity to prove she had what it takes and help her station win the first night of the ratings period.

Sandy buried her face in her hands for a moment, drawing strength from the words of Celeste Munson. *You've earned the right to be there, in the job that you now hold.*

As assignment editor, that meant sending resources where they were needed.

When she looked up, Jack was staring at her, a puzzled expression on his face, but whatever he was thinking, he kept it to himself for once.

"We're going," she said.

Chapter 18

The Root Witch story was so good, Sandy was tempted not to give it to Jennifer. She didn't deserve it, not the way she'd strolled into the editorial meeting empty-handed, but since all the other reporters already had their assignments, Jennifer was the only choice.

When Sandy summoned her to the desk and told her about the calls they had received, that she was to interview a couple who claimed a shadowy creature had tried to make off with their son in the aspen forest, Jennifer let out a whoop and ran for her desk. Seconds later, she returned clutching a pink duffel bag and whipped off her dress—something she never would have done if the managers were around.

Sandy watched, shaking her head, as the reporter pulled on a red cowl neck sweater and tugged on a pair of jeans. She wondered what Jennifer used that made her hair slide back into place so perfectly.

"Are you finished with your striptease?" Sandy asked, frowning at the list of available photographers. Each had its drawbacks. One had already told her he couldn't work late because he had a Halloween event at his daughter's school, and the other was hobbling around with his foot in a boot. Hiking through the woods, lugging camera equipment, was out of the question.

When Sandy explained the problem to Jennifer, she said, "Karl can go."

"Karl's a reporter, not a photographer."

Karl, who'd joined them at the desk, attracted by the sight of his girlfriend standing around in her bra and panties, said, "I can do it." When he noted Sandy's doubtful expression, he added, "I worked as a photog for two years before I became a reporter."

"Do you even remember how to white balance?" she asked, tapping her nails against the desk. They were painted bright red, and like her hair, they were too long. If she didn't trim them soon, she'd have trouble typing.

Karl rolled his eyes. "Yes, I do. It hasn't been that long. And I was a pretty gnarly photographer, if I say so myself."

Sandy could feel herself relenting.

Jennifer bounced up and down and chanted, "Come on, come on, come on. He can do it, he can do it," like a demented cheerleader.

"But you worked the morning shift," Sandy said, thinking of the overtime and the long drive. "You'll be exhausted."

Karl shook his head. "I'll be fine. Jennifer can drive on the way down. I'll take a nap and be good as new. I don't sleep much anyway. And I really want to go. It's a great story. It'll be fun."

Sandy leaned back in her chair and felt her face relax into a smile. "Okay."

Karl sprinted down the hall toward the photog lounge where the camera equipment was stashed, while Sandy pondered her next problem. She'd need to send the satellite truck so Jennifer could go live at five and six, and that meant sending someone who knew how to operate the truck. Plus, that person would need to know how to edit. That narrowed down the list of options.

"You gotta send Mitch," Jennifer said, tugging on her hiking boots.

A heaviness settled into Sandy's stomach. She pinched the bridge of her nose and squeezed her eyes shut, thinking. Mitch was tucked away in an edit bay located in the farthest corner of the newsroom, working on a special report due at the end of sweeps. The executive producer wouldn't be happy if she pulled him, but it would only be for one day. He wouldn't lose *that* much time.

Jennifer leaned over the desk. "Our only other option is Ed," she said in a low voice. "He's not that good of an editor, and he's so slow. We'll never make air if you send him."

Everyone knew Ed was an excellent photographer who'd never mastered the art of editing, probably because he thought it was beneath him.

Jennifer was right. It had to be Mitch. He knew his way around the satellite truck, and he was one of the few who could fix the many things that seemed to go wrong with it. Plus, he was their best editor, and the fastest. But the idea of sending him made her feel funny all over, like she was coming down with something.

"I guess," she finally said.

Jennifer bounded across the newsroom and, seconds later, dragged a confused-looking Mitch to the desk. To make himself more comfortable in the warm editing room, he'd unhooked a strap of his overalls so the bib flapped open and removed his plaid shirt so he was now wearing just a thin white muscle tee. With his tousled dirty blond hair, he looked like he was posing for a cover of a cheesy western romance novel.

Her mouth went dry, and she struggled to find the familiar words.

I'm sending you on a story.

Why was that suddenly so damn hard? In fact, the idea of sending Mitch, Jennifer, and Karl filled her with unease. Images of the aspen forest stretching in all directions flashed before her. Where had her enthusiasm for the story gone? She'd learned nothing that would cause her to rethink the assignment. It was still a great story.

Sandy shook her head and blinked.

Jennifer rapped on the desk. "Hello, earth to Sandy. It's go time."

Sandy reached for her mug. The coffee was cold and stale, but at least it was wet. She explained the assignment to Mitch, pushing ahead even when his mouth opened and his eyebrows had disappeared under his thatch of hair.

"Okay," he finally said, sounding uncertain.

Jennifer brought her hands together in an ear-splitting clap. "I'm hitting the bathroom before we get on the road."

When she was gone, Mitch leaned over the desk until their faces were inches apart. "Are you sure you want to do this? Brody is pretty cautious about sending the sat truck out. And there's the weather." He gestured to the bank of windows. Snow was falling heavily.

"Ron says the weather's okay down at Fish Lake," she said.

"Yeah, but we need to get there. It's going to be pretty nasty out near Point of the Mountain."

She glanced past Mitch to the window. The news vehicles were lined up just outside the door, covered in snow. "Jennifer and Karl can take the Bronco. And the Sat truck should be fine. We've sent it up to the mountains in snow before." She hesitated. "You don't think this is a good idea?"

Mitch stroked his chin. His eyes drifted to the TV monitor tuned to the competition. The volume was turned off, but the screen showed the promotion for the special news report airing that evening—Utah's Scariest Stories. After a moment, he thrust his shoulders back and slapped the desk.

"We'll make it work," he said with a smile.

Sandy noticed the smile didn't reach his eyes, and she fought another wave of unease. It was like she'd lost control of her lips. They trembled and refused to pull upward in a return smile.

Mitch studied her for a long moment, then reached over the desk and squeezed her hand. "Don't worry. I've got your back."

Her heart sank as she watched him stride down the hall, whistling. She'd just wrecked their plans for dinner at the Oyster Bar after the six o'clock newscast. If Mitch was lucky, he'd be back by nine.

Chapter 19

From the ranger station, Knox called the district supervisor at home and related the story of the couple from Salt Lake City and the shadow creature that tried to make off with their son.

Bill Skeene had come running to the phone and was still out of breath. Knox could hear him panting on the other end of the line, though he wasn't saying much.

"What do you think it was, Knox?" Bill finally said.

"I have no idea. I can't think of a single animal that fits the description they gave. But I have to confess, I'm a little worried. They didn't seem crazy, and they weren't the exaggerating type. They were truly terrified. Something caused those wounds on that boy's ankle."

"He could have got his feet wedged under a root," said Bill. "Then panicked, and when he tried to pull his feet out, scraped them up. Some of those old roots are pretty rough."

Knox propped his elbows on the desk and stared absently out the window. One of the part-timers was pulling up in a beat-up truck.

"Maybe," he said. "But it's not very likely. I've got three people coming in today. Can you send some extra people over to help with the search?"

Bill sighed. "I can do that. But why don't you guys get going. I'll have someone raise you on the radio when they get there."

Knox straightened. He'd been expecting more moaning and complaining about the crazies who came out on Halloween, not the matter-of-fact cooperation he was getting. He hoped his next question wouldn't change Bill's mood.

"Do you think we should close the area to the public?" Knox asked, then winced in anticipation of the answer.

"Close the area!" Bill sputtered. "Like it's a shark attack in that *Jaws* movie? And what would we possibly cite as an excuse to close public lands in this case, Knox? Tell me that? I'm waiting."

Well, that didn't go well. Bill was more riled up than he'd ever heard him.

"Just out of an abundance of caution," Knox said.

"Ah hah. Gotcha. You didn't answer my question, did you? See? It's not as simple as you think it is. I know you're new and all, but we can't just go shutting down a forest because some kid thinks he saw the boogeyman. Now look, you get on out there and have a good look around, and if you see anything you're concerned about—and by that, I mean something with four legs and foam coming out of its mouth—then you call me back, and we'll talk again. Got that? Now let me go make those calls." Bill banged down the phone.

There was nothing to do now but search. Knox had only five minutes to wait before three part-time rangers arrived at work. He gathered them together with the two men assigned to maintenance duties and explained the situation as succinctly as possible, careful to avoid the words "shadow monster" and "tentacles."

When he was done, the crew exchanged glances that were hard to read, and Knox heard a burly man named Dave say something loudly on the way to the vehicles. "Didn't I tell you the Root Witch was back?"

Dave was nearly twice Knox's age and prided himself on handling some of the heaviest and dirtiest work in their service area. Knox caught up with him at his truck and asked what he meant, but Dave merely shrugged. He had more hair on his neck than his head, with round black eyes that reminded Knox of a bird.

"I was just joking," Dave said, staring down at his thick work boots.

Knox ignored that. "I'm new around here. Every place has its stories. I think I mentioned I'm from Houston. Over where I used to work, we had swamp ghosts and unexplained floating lights. I'm guessing the Root Witch is kind of like that and—"

Dave's face lit up. "That's exactly how it is."

The man's answer caught Knox by surprise. "How so, Dave?"

Dave continued beaming. "Well, you may not believe this, but it's true. My son is a bit of an expert on the Root Witch. We live over in Koosharem, and he grew up hearing the stories. He's real smart, my son. He's up at the University of Utah now. I can never remember what he's studying, but his team is doing a project on the Root Witch. I've got some copies with me if you can hold on just a moment."

Knox waited impatiently as Dave rooted around in the glove compartment and watched the other men get into their vehicles and race down the street. Any excuse to drive fast.

After a few minutes, Dave waved around a newspaper clipping. "Got it!" With a flourish, he handed it to Knox. "That's an extra copy. You can keep it. The Neil in that report is my son. I'm going to take off, boss. See you there."

Knox was the only one remaining in the parking lot. He ought to get moving, but he was overcome with curiosity. And the others didn't need to wait for him to begin searching. He'd told them to look for anything unusual, and if they found something, leave it alone and alert him immediately.

The sheet of paper was folded in quarters. He opened it and read:

"The Root Witch: A Legend Examined"
By Neil Keller, PhD candidate at The University of Utah

Summary
Reports of shadows in rural forests are nothing new. Legends have existed for centuries to explain them. But there is one legend notable for its recent origins: the legend of the Root Witch, associated with an aspen forest in Fish Lake National Forest in central Utah.

The story of the Root Witch is not only remarkable for how quickly it has spread, but how firmly it has taken hold in the public's mind.

As with many legends, it is difficult to pinpoint the exact moment it began, but it appears to have gained traction in the early 1970s. Research into the single-organism forest of quaking aspens, which reproduces using vegetative propagation, or sending up shoots to regenerate, began to make its way out of scientific journals and into popular media.

The forest is not dangerous in its terrain, but based on the stories shared about the Root Witch, there is a strong connection between the sightings of the giant shadow figure resembling a tree and the unnerving sound of fluttering aspen leaves, which happens in the slightest of breezes.

The Root Witch was typically spotted by visitors to the forest, not by the Forest Service employees who worked there.

Those who claimed to have seen it have described it as the forest coming alive.

The stories have evolved beyond merely an entity roaming the forest and frightening unsuspecting visitors. According to interviews with people who've claimed to have seen the Root Witch, the legendary creature is blamed for the disappearance of off-leash dogs.

By the early 1980s, the tale took on an even darker tone, and forest rangers began to report evidence of the being. One ranger, formerly associated with the area, claims the Root Witch killed mule deer and elk on behalf of the aspen clone forest, perhaps using the bodies as an additional source of nutrition.

In a soon-to-be-published paper based on research conducted at the University of Utah with Matthew Swan and Laura Bittner, we examine the reasons this contemporary folklore story continues to evolve and keep its grip on the public's imagination.

Knox's heart slammed against his ribs. He stared at the clipping for a long time, until the words began to blur together. Knox thought of the lacerations on Lee Bradley's calf, the mutilated mule deer. And the boy with the bloody legs. The father he met that very morning insisted something had pushed through the earth and curled its tentacles around his son. He'd had to hack away at them with a knife to free his child.

There had to be an explanation. For all of it.

The Root Witch was pure fantasy.

Dave Keller's son had called it a "folklore story." Neil Keller didn't give any real credence to the sightings. But at least one of his former predecessors had—and then taken it even one step further, proposing a theory.

The forest was hungry.

It was also waiting to be searched. Knox shook himself, tucked the folded paper in a vest pocket, and hurried to his truck.

When he parked at a pullout along Highway 25, he could hear the voices of his men calling to each other as they searched the forest. A breeze blew the sound toward him. The leaves rustled overhead. That paper had done a number on his head. His brain didn't feel attached to his body, and several times, he had to grab a white tree trunk for support. Knox laughed, startling himself. He was being ridiculous, spooked by a ghost story.

Knox glanced anxiously around for any signs of movement. All was still. His stomach rumbled since he hadn't had breakfast. There'd been no time, not with Colleen acting up and threatening to leave. He wished he'd brought a water canteen and a granola bar, or even better, some beef jerky. Anything to quiet his stomach.

When he reached a clearing, he stopped. It looked familiar. He recognized the saplings he'd seen before, the shoots he'd talked to. Was he imagining things, or did they seem taller? Maybe by as much as a foot or so. Did aspens grow that fast? It didn't seem possible. But he was certain they were the same new growth he'd come across before. He took a good look around. There was the same boulder with lichen. The white trunk with black bulges indicating canker disease.

"Look at you," he said, crouching next to the shoots.

Knox imagined blood oozing slowly down to the ground from the tender stalks. He squeezed his eyes shut, and when he opened them again, there was nothing. Just leaves fluttering in time with the rustling canopy overhead.

His radio came to life. Bill had come through. Extra help had arrived, and he hurried to meet them.

Knox summoned his men, and everyone met by the side of the road. His guys reported they'd found nothing unusual so far. Knox pulled out a map of the aspen forest and opened it on the hood of his truck. His men pointed to the ground they'd already covered. With the extra help, they'd be more methodical. They'd cover the entire forest. It wasn't that big—less than 110 acres.

Knox told the crew to watch for anything that might have frightened some hikers that morning. He described the shadowy creature but left out the part about the boy being attacked. Then, he sent the men off.

"Watch out for the Root Witch," Dave Keller called with a forced chuckle before crossing the highway. He and a group of six men offered to search the other side of the forest, the one farthest from the morning's incident, Knox noted.

When it was nearing one o'clock, Knox handed one of the men a hundred-dollar bill he'd taken from a petty cash box in his desk and asked him to buy sandwiches for everyone. They were eating lunch at the side of the road when someone said, "I think that's a news truck."

A white Bronco with a television camera painted on the doors slowed. A young woman with lots of blond hair was at the wheel. The window lowered. Someone appeared to be in the passenger seat, a coat over their face.

After squinting at his badge, the female flashed a gap-toothed smile. "Hi. Whatcha guys up to, Mr. Knox?" She rapped the door with the station logo. "I'm Jennifer Rowlin, reporter."

Before anyone else could answer, Knox stepped forward. He hadn't thought to ask Bill what to tell the media if they showed up, because the possibility hadn't occurred to him. The station, he knew, was based in Salt Lake. He wondered what brought them so far south.

"I can ask you the same," he said lightly.

The woman gave a little laugh. "Oh, an interesting Halloween story. We're off to meet some parents at the lodge who said a shadow monster, or something like that, came out of that forest you're standing in front of and tried to take their boy." She paused for dramatic effect. "Or kill him." The smiled had disappeared.

His throat tightened. The family must have tipped off the station.

"Is that right?" Knox finally said. He could hear the murmurs of the men behind him. They'd heard her, even from a distance. She had the kind of voice that carried.

The woman peered around him at the men finishing their lunches. Knox could feel their reproachful eyes boring into his back.

"I'm assuming you're conducting a search. How about we do a quick interview, and you can explain what you're looking for."

The person next to her sat up, the coat falling away. A young man with a healthy head of glossy brown hair blinked sleepily in his direction.

"What's going on, Jen?" the man said, yawning.

"We need to shoot, Karl," she said, eyes fixed on Knox.

Knox shook his head and scowled. Bill Skeene would have a thing or two to say if he talked to the media without permission, and he wasn't about to incur Bill's wrath twice in one day.

"I did not agree to an interview," he said, adopting a stern tone. "And since I'm the ranger responsible for this area, I'm going to have to ask you to leave."

The reporter's eyes widened. "Huh!" she said and drove a short way down the road before turning off the engine.

Knox watched as she swung her long legs out of the vehicle. Her companion hopped out and pulled a camera from the back, hoisting it onto his shoulder.

"I told you to leave," Knox called, hands balling into fists.

The woman made a big show of looking around. "The road isn't closed. Is it? Because I don't see any signs."

Behind him, the men chuckled.

"I like 'em feisty," one said.

Knox could feel the situation spinning out of control. The woman was pushy and obviously accustomed to getting her way in her position as a reporter. She was right about one thing—he hadn't closed the road because Bill Skeene had refused to consider closing the forest. If the forest remained open, so did the road.

"Okay, guys, let's get back to work," he barked over his shoulder. "And if Miss Rowlin approaches any of you and asks any questions, the answer is no comment." Then, he turned back to the reporter and said, "Just stay out of the way, miss."

The young man named Karl already had the camera pointed in his direction and was probably recording. It wouldn't do to look angry, or like he was hiding something. So, he forced the muscles in his face to relax and acted the role of a busy professional coordinating a search. The cameraman scurried after them.

When he was just yards away and stepped off the pavement. Knox said, "If you can please remain on the road, sir, I'd appreciate it."

Jennifer ran up carrying a tripod and snapped it open. The photographer screwed the camera onto a plate on the tripod and lowered his eye to the viewfinder. Knox could imagine the footage—his team of men weaving through the aspen trees until they disappeared. A powerful image. No interview required. She'd got what she'd needed. Video of the search for whatever attacked the boy.

There wasn't much he could do about it. After issuing one final warning to the TV crew to stay where they were, he joined the search.

Chapter 20

When the search ended at five o'clock, Knox hurried back to the ranger station and called Bill Skeene at home. He let him know they'd found nothing that would account for the boy's injuries. Then, he told Bill about the news crew from Salt Lake and listened to another tirade. He made no mention of the Root Witch paper soon to be published by the university.

As he drove down Main Street, he saw a cluster of parents with young children dressed in costumes, heading to the cafe for dinner. He wished there was a place to pick up a couple of pizzas, but Loa's offerings were limited to typical American fare and a tiny Mexican restaurant, which was closed. The chilly wind had picked up. Dirt from the fields blew across the road. Dried leaves flew in the air and caught on chain link fences.

When he reached Highway 25, he scanned both sides of the road for the van. There was still enough light left in the sky for him to peer between the gaps in the trees, but there was nothing. No vehicles. No people.

As expected, the campgrounds were full. It was dinner time. Kids would be running around as parents cooked over camp stoves. Smores. Scary stories around the campfire, and then an early bedtime for the children. That, he hoped, was the extent of Halloween.

As he pulled into the long gravel driveway leading to the cabin, he wondered how Jennifer Rowlin's reports had turned out. He'd hear from Bill soon enough, who said he'd watch the newscasts.

The cabin was dark, not a single light on.

The beam of his headlights illuminated the meadow. Colleen's small car was gone.

If she left, she'd closed the gate for once. She always forgot. His hands didn't seem to be working right. They shook as he unlatched the gate, and he hit the gas so hard the truck lurched forward. Knox threw open the door and pounded up the steps, yelling, "Colleen," but there was no answer.

The cabin was empty.

He stumbled to the bedroom and flung open the wardrobe. The bag she used for their weekend trips to Salt Lake City was gone, and some of her clothes seemed to be missing. The bed was neatly made. She'd taken all her makeup from the bathroom and her little packet of birth control pills. He staggered like a drunk man, looking for a note. She wouldn't have left without a note. Nothing. Not a scrap of paper with a scribble.

Colleen had left him.

He'd pushed her too far. She tried telling him she wasn't happy, and he'd ignored her, went to work and forgot all about her. And she'd had enough. Drove off in her little car to who knows where. He'd warned her about the bad weather in Salt Lake. Colleen wasn't used to driving in snow. But where else would she go? Las Vegas? She'd mentioned Las Vegas.

Knox flicked on the lights, fetched a cold beer, and sat on the top step of the porch.

A cold wind was blowing through the trees. The trunks of the aspens creaked and groaned. Like it always did in cold weather, his nose had begun to run, and when he swiped it with the back of his hand, he discovered his entire face was wet. He'd started crying and didn't even know it.

The sky was a dusky gray. Yellow light spilled out of the open door onto the porch.

There was something on the grass just beyond the gravel driveway. A small, shiny clump. He set down his beer, walked to it in a few long strides, and picked it up. The keys to the cabin. Colleen never got around to attaching them to her car keys. It seemed significant somehow, a sign of her refusal to commit to the place. He imagined her throwing the keys out the window as she drove off.

Knox wasn't ready to go back inside. He was too restless, too worried about Colleen driving alone at night. Would she call him? Let him know where she'd gone? His heart twisted, thinking of all the things that had gone wrong between them. How he'd blown it.

He began pacing, his thoughts racing. Maybe she hadn't left him for good. Maybe it was just temporary. A few days away to teach him a lesson.

Knox tripped, pitched forward, and landed on all fours. There were clumps of dirt where the grass should have been, and the ground was all churned up.

Pushing himself to his feet, he wiped his gritty hands on the front of his jeans. It looked like someone had come through with a rotary tiller. He walked backwards until he could get a better view. Maybe Colleen, in a huff, had made a big circle and driven through the meadow, instead of backing up a bit and turning around where the driveway widened. But that wouldn't account for the mess. Knox took a few giant steps back, noticing the disrupted area formed a gentle mound. That was new too. There was no way Colleen's tiny car and puny tires were responsible.

He stood with his hands at his side, hearing the mad fluttering of the trees in the wind. His skin prickled, and his breathing quickened. He stared at the wall of trees, heart thudding in his chest. Knox knew the roots of the clone forest stretched under the highway, connecting with the grove on the other side. Then, he noticed saplings had sprouted in the meadow close to the cabin next to the sunroom, where Colleen had worked.

The shoots were everywhere.

Chapter 21

Jennifer and Karl missed their live shot at five o'clock. They'd missed the six o'clock too. Jack was furious. Sandy was frantic. In the time she'd worked with those two reporters, they had never missed a live shot. Sandy had gone from fantasizing about what she'd say to Jennifer when she finally appeared, breathless and defensive, to being genuinely worried.

What if they'd had an accident?

Sandy hadn't visited the aspen forest since she was a kid and only had a vague memory of the terrain. It wasn't anything extreme. Not like some places in Utah, like the Shafer Trail in Moab with its terrifying drop-offs, or Delicate Arch where you could tumble hundreds of feet head-over-heels into a giant red rock bowl.

Still, the forest made her clammy just thinking about it. All those trees and shadows. A place she'd rather forget.

Sandy was hunched over the phone, talking to Mitch. He'd arrived at Fish Lake National Forest in good time, around 2:30, parking at the campground closest to the forest so they'd have access to a pay phone and a bathroom. Sandy had booked a short satellite window so he could run a quick test. Everything worked.

Karl and Jennifer agreed to meet Mitch at the truck at three o'clock to begin working on the story for the early evening newscasts. But they hadn't shown up. Mitch wasn't worried at first. Sometimes interviews ran long, or maybe there were new developments to chase. But when four o'clock came and went, Mitch started getting nervous. He'd called Sandy and asked if she'd heard from them. She hadn't. There was no way to communicate directly with the crew, not in a regular news truck. That required a phone, which they didn't have, or the satellite truck. Sandy called Lakeside Lodge and talked to a woman at the front desk. Yes, the tall woman with the blond hair and the cute young man had been there. She'd seen them interviewing a family outside. No, they weren't still there. She'd seen them drive off but hadn't noticed the time.

"They took car number four, didn't they?" Mitch asked.

Children laughed in the background.

"Yeah, they did," Sandy said. "And it was gassed up too. I checked the log."

"They should be fine," Mitch said. "It's four-wheel drive and has good clearance. Even if they had to go all the way down to the valley floor where it twists and turns, they should be fine."

"Maybe that's where they are," Sandy said, heart skipping. "Maybe they had car trouble or something. Can you go check?"

Mitch snorted loudly. "Not in the satellite truck. That thing is top heavy and underpowered. It's made for pavement and can't handle much else."

"We have to do something," she hissed into the phone, glancing at the wall clock. It was 6:10.

Jack was pacing nearby, glaring at her as if what had happened during his five o'clock newscast was her fault. Jennifer missing her live shot meant chaos in the control room.

"Why don't you call the police and explain the situation?" Mitch said. "Have 'em send a patrol car and cruise around. See if they can spot the Bronco."

"It's the Sheriff's Office. Not police. But that's a good idea. I should have thought of that myself. Thank you."

"That's why we're a team," he said. "Okay. You got the number. I'll be waiting here, and I'll do my best to keep people off the line."

The only way for them to communicate was by booking a window of satellite time, which was easy enough but expensive and mostly used for feeding video and for live shots. Not for talking. She'd made a questionable call using a resource usually reserved for breaking news. Racking up extra charges was the last thing she wanted to do.

Sandy remembered meeting a ranger from that area at the Xenon Club in Salt Lake—the guy with the throwing-up wife. After scrutinizing the wall map of central Utah, she decided Loa was the closest town and flipped through the Rolodex until she found the right card. She punched in the number and got a recorded message. Sandy recognized the man's voice immediately. The station was closed for the evening and would reopen at 8:30 Saturday.

"If you're having an emergency, please call the Richfield's Sheriff's Office," it said.

Sandy hung up and called dispatch. A woman answered, sounding tired and irritable. Janelle.

"Aren't you working late?" Sandy asked in surprise.

Janelle had the most seniority, so she usually worked days. She sighed heavily. "I switched shifts so the gal who works nights could take her kids out trick-or-treating. Something I didn't think through, because I'm also filling in this weekend."

"That was nice of you," Sandy said. "But listen. I need to ask a favor. We sent a crew down there to do a story, but we're not hearing from them." She rattled off the rest of the details.

Janelle groaned. "Does your story have anything to do with that incident in the forest this morning? The one with the kid who said the Root Witch tried to get him?"

"That's it," Sandy said.

"Well, I can't hold that against you," the dispatcher grumbled.

Sandy told her what she knew and described the reporters and the news car.

"I'll send somebody right away," Janelle said. "I'll call you as soon as I hear something."

When the six o'clock newscast was over, people began to wander in from the studio and control room. The word was out that Jennifer and Karl had not only missed their slots, but hadn't contacted the newsroom.

Joe Martin paced in front of the desk. The anchor looked orange under the fluorescent lights with his makeup still on.

"Have we considered this might be a hoax?" he said. "What if those people calling about the Root Witch were just having a little fun on Halloween?" Like Sandy, Joe was one of the few Hispanics in the newsroom. Unlike Sandy, he kept it a secret. Joe was Puerto Rican. He'd shortened his surname. When they'd first met, he'd whispered, "Utah is not ready to accept a Martinez reading the news."

Sandy rubbed the back of her neck. As much as she hated to admit it, the thought had occurred to her throughout the day.

"It's possible," she conceded. "But that's a whole lot of trouble to go through. And it doesn't explain why we haven't heard from Jen and Karl."

Joe's shoulders sagged. "True."

The assistant director, who rarely missed an opportunity to voice his opinion, said, "What if it's something else? Maybe a plan to get us to send people down there and kidnap them or something. For ransom?"

Joe saved her from answering. "Oh, come on. That's a bit far-fetched."

Most everyone wandered off for dinner. Only Joe and Jack remained.

Joe had stopped pacing and was watching her with worried eyes. "Have you called Brody?"

"Not yet," she admitted.

Joe glanced over his shoulder at Jack hovering nearby. "I wouldn't put it off," he said in a quiet voice.

She nodded and shot him a grateful look. Joe could be short-tempered on the set when problems arose, but off air, he was surprisingly coolheaded.

The card for the hotel at Snowbird wasn't in the Rolodex, and she cursed. Sandy hated when people borrowed them and didn't put them back. She snatched up the phone, preparing to punch in the number for directory assistance, when Jack dangled a card in front of her face. Her eyes bulged as she read it. He had the card, which could only mean one thing. He beat her to it. And God only knew what he'd said, how he framed it. The fucker.

"You already called Brody, didn't you?" she said through gritted teeth.

Jack plucked the receiver from her hand and returned it to the cradle. "I did," he said, not sounding the least contrite.

"But the phone lines are down. Due to the snowstorm. There's full-on blizzard conditions up there, so no one is expecting a fix anytime soon. And look, I wasn't trying to call Brody to snitch on you. I saw you had your hands full, so I thought I'd be proactive and see if I could reach him for you."

Sandy flopped back in her chair. "Yeah right," she said.

He untied the red scarf dangling from his neck, balled it up, and threw it on his desk. "Seriously, I wasn't. But listen, whatever is going on with Jennifer and Karl, this is something we're going to have to deal with on our own."

She bolted upright, eyes narrowing. "What do you mean?"

"You didn't watch the weather, did you?" he asked, lifting his bushy black eyebrows. "They closed the canyons. No one is getting out. All the managers are stuck up there, probably for the whole weekend with the way it's snowing, so as far as I can tell, you're in charge." He ambled over to his chair and sat. "But don't worry, I'm not about to abandon you. I'll stay until we figure out what's going on."

There was that "we" again. For Jack, that translated to sitting around, hoping she screwed up even more than she had already by sending three people hours away for what was, essentially, a feature story. The ten o'clock producer marched over and demanded to know where in his show he could expect to slot Jennifer's story, and Sandy bit down on her bottom lip hard until the urge to scream in his face had passed.

"Wherever you think it should go," she said. "But since we haven't heard from them yet, I'd make a plan B."

Jack snickered. "So much for the Root Witch making us a ratings winner."

Sandy was too distraught to answer.

The next hour dragged by. Someone brought pizza, but she just nibbled at her slice, staring at the phone, willing it to ring. Jack had taken to pacing the newsroom, opening the back door several times and sticking his head out.

"It's really coming down out there," he announced.

The reporter assigned to the evening shows called in to say his photographer had got some great footage of weather-related accidents, and he'd be back in a half hour to edit his story.

One crew accounted for, the other still missing.

Sandy began to imagine the worst. A bear or mountain lion attack. Ted Bundy escaped from prison, back again and on a killing spree. Another half hour passed without a single call to the newsroom. She picked up the phone and hit nine. There was a click, and then the drone of the dial tone, but the familiar sound brought no relief. The phones were still working. Her chest felt like something heavy was sitting on it.

Finally, Janelle called.

"Did your officer find them?" she asked breathlessly.

Janelle sighed on the other end of the line. "He found the news vehicle on a forest road that leads to the valley floor. It's narrow and windy and goes down to the east edge of the valley. It was quite a ways in. The doors were closed but not locked, and there's no flat tire or anything obviously wrong with the truck. No sign of your crew, though."

Sandy didn't like the sound of that. She imagined Jennifer falling down a steep embankment. Maybe she'd broken her leg. Or maybe it was Karl who'd fallen. They could be out there in the cold, hoping for someone to find them.

"Did your officer *look* for them?"

Janelle cleared her throat. "Well, we have a bit of a situation there. Wesley—that's the deputy—came back real spooked like. He said he was walking around with his flashlight when something chased him through the woods, and he nearly broke his neck trying to get away in the dark. Swears it was nothing like an animal. Too big for that." Janelle hesitated. "He's refusing to go back out there 'til the sun's up."

Sandy blinked, feeling dizzy. "He can't just refuse to do his job, can he?"

"That's a personnel matter, and I'm not going to say any more," Janelle said briskly. "And if you please, keep that to yourself, along with what I'm about to tell you. The sheriff is making some calls, trying to round up a volunteer search team, but as soon as people hear the forest is involved, there's some excuse or another." Silence followed, then a long-drawn out sigh. "Something's not right out there."

Sandy stood up and pressed a hand to her forehead. "Isn't somebody going to do something?" she cried.

"The sheriff's working on it, but I'll tell you what. You said you had another guy down there at Doctor Creek Campground. The ranger lives just up the road. I can give you his telephone number. His name is Knox. Maybe those two can get together and start looking until we can get some more people to you. How does that sound?"

It sounded like the only practical thing to do, but imagining Mitch walking around in the forest at night sent chills up her arms. But someone had to find Jennifer and Karl, and Mitch was an outdoorsy guy. And big and strong. And he wouldn't be alone. He'd be with a ranger.

Sandy jotted down Knox's telephone number and hung up.

The ranger picked up immediately and at first confused her with his wife. Sandy had to identify herself several times before he finally remembered meeting her at the Xenon Club. He sounded distracted and had trouble understanding what she was asking him to do.

Knox asked her to repeat parts of her story, interrupting with questions several times, before he said, "Wait, wait. Yeah, I saw them earlier. Tall blond lady and a guy with a lot of brown hair? I saw them on Highway 25 earlier today. You're saying they're missing?"

Sandy kneaded her forehead. She'd already gone through it, but she explained it all again, and finally, Knox seemed to fully grasp the seriousness of the situation and, most importantly, what she wanted him to do.

He took a deep breath. "I'll leave now," he said. "And you said this Mitch guy is at Doctor Creek Campground, right? Okay. I'll run over there, and we'll call you if we find your crew."

When he'd hung up, Sandy called the pay phone at the campground to let Mitch know the ranger was headed his way, but a boy picked up the phone and said the tall man with the TV station truck was in the bathroom. When she called again five minutes later, no one answered.

Her bladder was going to burst if she didn't go to the bathroom herself. The ranger was probably already halfway to Mitch. She'd try calling the pay phone again as soon as she was back. After yelling at Jack to watch the phone, she raced out of the newsroom and down a long hall, muttering curses at whoever decided to put the women's bathroom at the back of the building. When she returned, panting from her run, Jack stuck his head out from the feed room, where he'd spent the last hour watching some TV show.

"Hey, Mitch just called," he said. "Good news. He said he met some guy who's letting him borrow his Jeep, and he was gonna drive around and look for Karl and Jen."

She blinked at him, confused. "You mean the ranger? That wasn't the plan. The ranger was supposed to go *with* him. Did you tell him that?"

Jack ignored her question. "He didn't say anything about a ranger. It sounded like it was just some nice camper who was going to loan Mitch his jeep."

"Alone?" she shouted. "Mitch was going alone?"

Another nonchalant shrug. "I guess. He didn't mention anybody else." Jack disappeared back into the feed room.

Sandy pressed her palms into the desk and took deep gulping breaths, fighting a wave of panic.

Chapter 22

Colleen was gone. He knew she had walked out, but his mind was playing tricks on him, torturing him for the way he'd treated her.

What if the stories were true? What if some ghost or monster lived in the aspen forest and had taken her?

For one wild moment, it seemed not only possible, but probable. He'd stood just inside the front door to his cabin, peering nervously at the meadow. Dark had fallen, and he could no longer see the churned-up earth, but he knew it was out there. What could have done that? The Root Witch. It was all in the name. The name provided the explanation for so many wild stories he'd heard. It explained, possibly, the dead and mutilated animals that had been munching away at the saplings and roots.

All of that flashed through his mind as he was trying to make sense of what the TV producer was trying to tell him.

Her crew was missing. She needed his help.

That snapped him back to reality. There were things to do. People to find. His deranged notions of a shadow creature with roots for arms receded into the dark corners of his mind.

Tomorrow, he'd figure out what to do about Colleen, if he hadn't heard from her.

He splashed cold water on his face and made a pot of coffee. As much as he hated to do it, he called the district supervisor at home. Bill Skeene started by saying it was up to the Sheriff's Office to mount a search effort, as it was off-hours, but ended by asking Knox to assemble his own team, a change of heart Knox attributed to the fact the two missing people were members of the media.

"But listen, Knox, under no circumstances are you to go out searching alone," Bill said before he hung up.

Which quickly presented a quandary because he couldn't reach anyone. Either no one answered, or a message machine picked up, or, in two cases, wives said their husbands had gone hunting for the weekend.

Knox filled a few canteens with water, grabbed some granola bars and beef sticks from a cupboard, crammed them into a backpack, then made his way to the truck. The wind was blowing hard. The rustling of the aspen leaves had turned into a roar, sounding more like an ocean than a forest.

When he got to Doctor Creek Campground, there was no sign of Mitch. Knox was too restless to go back to his empty home. There was nothing else to do but look for Mitch.

He'd never driven the road to the valley floor before. It was something Dave Keller and the maintenance crew usually did. There were no facilities, just a dirt lot where the tourists parked and hiked into the forest.

The dark road narrowed. Knox gripped the steering wheel as he navigated the sharp hairpin turns. White tree trunks loomed like ghosts in the headlights.

Finally, he spotted the Jeep, and just beyond it, the news car. But no people. So, Mitch had gone looking for his friends.

That meant three people were out there in the forest.

"Mitch," he shouted, trying a few more times.

Knox doubted anyone could hear him over the wind and the roar of the leaves. He aimed the beam of his flashlight on the path leading into the grove—all around was impenetrable darkness.

A shadow sped across his path. He was so startled he stumbled, and his flashlight jerked upward. When he regained his balance, he saw a small animal scampering away.

His heart pounding, he bolted to the truck. Instead of going home to the cabin, he headed for Loa. Maybe Colleen's words got to him. He couldn't remember being so spooked. Sleeping on the old, lumpy couch in the lunchroom at the ranger station was suddenly far preferable to the isolated cabin and that massive wall of shaking trees

If Colleen decided to call home and put him out of his misery, the machine would record her message, and he'd listen to it first thing in the morning. But he had a bad feeling about Colleen. It roosted in the pit of his stomach next to his concern for the missing TV news crew.

It was going to be a long, miserable night.

Chapter 23

The ten o'clock newscast aired with the snowstorm as the lead, without Jennifer and the Root Witch story. Jerry, the late show producer, threw his scripts at Sandy as he blew past the assignment desk.

"Happy fucking November sweeps," he said.

She was too numb to respond. Waiting and wishing for news of the missing crew had left her limp. Every time the phone rang, hope bloomed in her chest, then quickly shriveled and died.

Hands covering her face, she sensed someone hovering nearby. She pulled her fingers away. It was Jack, eyes staring.

"Are you going home?" he asked, glancing at the clock. Their shifts had ended at six-thirty.

Sandy felt a muscle twitch in her jaw. "No, I'm not going home. I'm the one who made the assignment. I need to stay until I hear from the crew."

Which now included Mitch. He'd borrowed a stranger's Jeep to look for Karl and Jennifer, and nobody had heard from him either. If she'd had a chance to talk with him before he left, she'd have ordered him not to go anywhere alone— standard safety protocol—but he'd called in the four minutes it had taken her to run to the bathroom.

"What if there's no word until morning? Will you stay all night?" Jack asked.

Sandy thought of the aspen forest. All those trees so close together. And tall. They were so tall.

The snowstorm was confined to the Wasatch Front. In central Utah, the temperatures had dropped but were still well above freezing. If Jennifer and Karl hadn't found a place to shelter, they'd be miserable, but at least they wouldn't be wet. And both had taken warm coats and thick-soled boots. Still, they'd have to contend with the high winds Ron had forecast for the area. She liked to think of Mitch driving around, nice and safe in the Jeep, and not out there in the dark.

"Yes, I'll stay all night," Sandy said. "It's the right thing to do. The only thing to do. Besides, we don't have a morning newscast on the weekends, so we're not staffed overnight today or tomorrow…" Her voice drifted off.

Surely, the crew would be found by then. Someone would find them. Jennifer and Karl would be tired and cranky, probably blame her for whatever happened, but they'd come back, and she'd take them out for drinks at the Oyster Bar to make it up to them. And Mitch, too, of course. The story they came back with would become the stuff of station legend.

"I'll stay too," Jack said. "In case shit goes down and you need help."

As much as she didn't relish having to work another overnight with him, it was better than spending the night in the newsroom alone.

"Okay," she said.

Jack didn't seem to notice her grudging tone. He gave her a thumbs-up. She watched him cross the newsroom and go outside, and she wondered if she'd misunderstood him. He reappeared, carrying a paper bag. Straddling the chair next to her, he pulled out a bottle of red wine and opened it with a tool hanging from his keyring.

"I don't want any," she said, shaking her head.

Jack ignored her and poured several inches of wine into her empty water glass. "Well, you need it because you look like shit. And since we're stuck here, with not a lot to do, we might as well have a drink." He pushed the glass at her.

It smelled strongly of rich, dark fruit. She studied the label on the bottle. It was expensive—not the usual cheap white wine she had at home. Leave it to Jack to just happen to have a bottle of Cabernet Sauvignon in his car.

Lunch was a vague memory. Had she eaten? A bit, she recalled. The director had gone out for lunch and brought her back a barbecue beef sandwich and French fries. It was so messy, she'd only managed half, eating at the assignment desk. Dinner had been a slice of pizza. The longer she eyed the glass of wine, the more tempting it was. Anything to take her mind off her crew.

"Thank you," she said, then took a cautious sip. The wine tasted slightly bitter and made her mouth tingle. It slid down her throat with a pleasant burning sensation.

Jack chugged his wine and tilted his head at her. "What do you think happened to them?"

Sandy set down her glass. "Really, Jack? How am I supposed to know?"

"Come on, you must have some theory,"

She squeezed her eyes shut and shook her head slowly. 'No, Jack. I don't."

The last of the staff said uneasy goodbyes and good lucks, and Jack downed most of the wine. Then, he announced he was going to take a nap on the couch in the reception area, and Sandy waved him away, getting up to make a fresh pot of coffee. She had to stay awake in case anyone called.

Just after midnight, the phone rang, and her heart nearly burst out of her chest.

It was Janelle, who sounded as worn out as she felt. "Well, I've got some news at least. The sheriff called in a few favors and rounded up some deputies from some other counties, and they're going out to look for your people. The sheriff is going to get that new ranger involved too."

"What about Mitch?" Sandy interrupted. "Has he turned up yet? He can help."

"Not that I know of," Janelle admitted. "But I'm sure he will. Now look, I'll call again as soon as I hear anything more. I just wanted you to know we've got people looking. And a search dog too."

By two o'clock, she was so exhausted she had to lie down. It was either that or fall off her chair. She went into the darkened feed room, turned down the volume of the TV monitors, and stretched out on the floor. One of the editors had left behind a jacket, so she bunched it up and used it as a pillow.

The uncertainty was unbearable. She used the tactics Celeste had showed her to regulate her breathing, but her mind kept wandering back to the forest. To Mitch, Karl, and Jennifer. She listened to the sound of the scanners, trying to get comfortable on the hard floor, wondering if she would ever be able to sleep.

Eventually, her eyelids closed.

Chapter 24

The phone rang at the ranger station in Loa not long after Knox arrived. Bill Skeene had tracked him down after calling the cabin and getting no answer.

"There you are!" he said, in a tone implying Knox had been hiding from him. "Don't worry about putting together a search team to look for those TV people. The sheriff's got a group together, so you can join them. That way, they can't say we didn't have a presence. And here's another thing. I told 'em they can set up a command center at your cabin, since you've got all that space out front for parking and facilities if anyone needs 'em." He hesitated. "I hope your wife don't mind. My wife overheard me talking to the sheriff and gave me an earful."

"It's not a problem," Knox said, voice strained. "She's visiting friends this weekend." If Colleen showed up, the use of their private home as a command center would be just another strike against him.

When he got back to the cabin, the meadow was overflowing with four-wheel drives and men in uniforms. Vehicles had parked on the churned-up soil in the meadow. One deputy, blinded in the headlights of an incoming car, tripped over a clod of dirt and cursed.

Knox introduced himself to the sheriff and opened the front door. Sheriff Wagoner had a small mouth and close-set eyes that affixed a permanent look of suspicion on his long face.

The wind had not abated. The men had to raise their voices to be heard over the roar of the aspen leaves. Sheriff Wagoner stopped on the front porch and stared in the direction of the trees.

"I don't know how you can stand it," he said. "You couldn't pay me to live out here."

Knox's own opinion about the cabin had undergone such a radical change over the last few hours, he didn't feel compelled to defend it. "It's not for everyone," he said.

Making straight for the wooden table, Knox smoothed out a detailed map of the aspen forest he'd brought from the station. The deputies trooped in, and everyone gathered around it. The man next to him smelled of stale beer. Knox wondered how many had been drinking on what had been their night off.

Only a few said they were familiar with the forest. The men—who ranged in age from mid-twenties to late fifties— looked more resigned than enthused.

"Those TV people had no business wandering around where they could get in trouble," a deputy said. The man's tag said he was from one county over.

The man didn't elaborate, but everyone seemed to agree with the gist of his complaint, which explained the desultory start of the search. Knox hoped they'd summon a bit more enthusiasm once they began looking.

It wouldn't hurt to remind them those were real people out in the dark, and not just talking heads from the big city. "Their names are Jennifer Rowlin and Karl Olson," he said. "I met them earlier today. They're both tall and in good shape. She's blond. He's got movie star hair. And they're young. Not even thirty. There's a third man. I've not met him, but he's described as a big guy, six-foot-three, so it's going to be hard to miss him. He's got a big production truck parked at Doctor Creek Campground, and he borrowed a Jeep to look for his friends when they didn't show up. I found the Jeep near the news vehicle on the road into the valley, but no sign of him. So that's who we're looking for."

The night and the wind seemed to conspire against their efforts.

Not long after starting the search at the valley floor, just yards from the very path Knox had fled hours before, a deputy said, "I can't see shit."

The officers carried flashlights that were extremely bright and focused, but beyond the narrow beam of nearly blinding white light, the woods surrounding them seemed even darker in contrast.

Knox was the only one carrying a flashlight that provided a broad beam, but he hadn't thought to bring extras from the station. The wind rained down branches on their heads, and he could hear men cursing as they stumbled along the uneven ground.

The howling wind and flying debris made every yard feel like ten. Sheriff Wagoner proved himself a hesitant walker, slower than the rest, mumbling about a bad case of Achilles tendinitis. The other men, younger and with better feet, moved quickly in pairs, eager to find the missing crew and get out of the miserable weather.

Knox stuck by the sheriff. If he weren't surrounded by men in all directions, he couldn't have brought himself to stay in the forest for long. He thought about the academic research into the Root Witch and shivered. Knox had a sudden urge to warn the man walking beside him. Sheriff

Wagoner would think he was crazy, and Bill Skeene would hear all about it. How he'd acted like a nervous nelly, afraid of his own shadow, spooked by a story meant to frighten children.

Wagoner's flashlight swept across a steep embankment. Dirt had fallen away, revealing a web of roots. They coiled around each other, reminding Knox of snakes.

"Nature is kind of ugly sometimes, isn't it?" the sheriff said after a moment. He shook his head and walked on.

After a few minutes of silence, both men aiming the beams of their flashlights in opposite directions, Sheriff Wagoner cleared his throat. "So what story was so important it brought them all the way from Salt Lake to this damn place?" he shouted over the trees swaying and creaking in the wind.

Using as few words as possible, Knox told him about the parents from Salt Lake who claimed the Root Witch had attacked their son.

Sheriff Wagoner stopped. "If something like that was out here, someone would have taken a picture or a film of it by now. Like Big Foot. And I'll tell you something else, there's nothing more unreliable than eyewitness accounts."

After another hour of fruitless searching, they decided to break for the night. They'd need to start again in the morning, when their chances of finding the missing crew improved with light, but for that, they'd need some sleep. The sheriff radioed instructions to his team. Due to the sheriff's hobbling, he and Knox hadn't made it very far from where they'd started, and they reached the meeting point first. Knox was getting seriously worried about not finding Jennifer, Karl, and Mitch. He couldn't imagine where they could be, or why the reporter and photographer had decided to drive down to the valley floor, so far from the spot where the boy had been injured. Knox set a few lanterns on the roof of his truck and flicked them on.

In pairs, the deputies checked in, confirmed they'd found nothing, then headed up to the cabin. Knox and the sheriff were waiting for the last of the deputies to check in when Knox spotted two men running toward them through the trees. As they got closer, he could see there was something wrong. They looked disheveled and wild-eyed and kept glancing over their shoulders. Just as they were about to emerge from the trees, one of them tripped and went sprawling.

Wagoner turned and said, "What in god's name…"

Knox swung his flashlight in their direction. As the second deputy ran toward the light, panting like he'd crossed a finish line, the fallen man writhed on the ground, staring up into the trees. Then, he froze. His face was twisted with terror. Knox felt a powerful rush of adrenalin as he followed the man's gaze.

Something was up there, swinging.

And then it fell, hurtling to the ground, landing on the deputy with a horrible thud.

It was a deer. A buck. The trees thrashed in the wind, leaves rattling. But despite the unrelenting assault on his ears, Knox could only hear his pounding heart.

He crept forward, a hand to his mouth. At first, he had trouble making out the shapes on the ground. Then, the hairs on his arms went up. The animal had dropped, antlers first, penetrating the man's neck. The buck—a big one—had then toppled to its side, its weight lifting the officer off the ground, face staring directly at Knox. He stepped back, colliding with the sheriff.

The deer's body had gone soft with decay, and the smell made him gag. It must have been in the trees for days, just like the cases he'd read about. But bucks didn't just fall from the sky.

His paralysis broke. Knox staggered forward, kneeling in front of the officer. So much blood. The man's eyes fluttered open, then closed. His fingers twitched. The ground was smeared with blood, and more was pouring down the man's neck.

Behind him, Knox could hear the other officer blundering around. "Oh Christ. What…just…happened?" he panted.

A moment later, Knox felt a strong hand grip his shoulder. "Let's get out of here," Sheriff Wagoner yelled into his ear. "I'll have my guys keep watch until the ME can get here."

Chapter 25

At sunrise, a group of eight men retrieved the body of Deputy Henry Stewart. The medical examiner had arrived, and one officer took photographs before they began the gruesome and difficult task of separating man from animal. The officers who had them tied bandannas around the lower half of their faces to filter out the stench of the decomposing buck. Some gagged. Others retched.

When they were done, the officers gently lifted the dead man onto a stretcher, picking their way across the ground strewn with fallen branches, and put it gently into the medical examiner's van.

Then, they turned their attention to the buck.

Knox handed out thick yellow gloves and spread a heavy-duty tarp on the ground next to the mule deer.

The wind had calmed down, leaving behind a steady breeze. Golden leaves rustled overhead. It was a beautiful crisp fall morning, the first of November.

"This buck has to be two hundred pounds," said an officer. "Maybe two fifty. Somebody want to explain how it got up in that tree?"

Sheriff Wagoner squinted warily at the canopy overhead. "I sure can't. And those branches don't look strong enough to hold it, even if someone hauled it up there."

Knox squeezed his eyes shut. He'd only seen it swinging above for a millisecond, and he had the impression the animal had somehow been affixed to the tree. How, he didn't know and couldn't guess.

The speculation continued as they hoisted the animal into the back of Knox's flatbed. He planned to dump it in the maintenance yard at the station.

Before he left, Knox pulled the sheriff aside. "Did you have a chance to talk to the officer who was with Stewart last night?"

The sheriff frowned, pulling his small eyes even closer together. "I tried, but I couldn't get much sense out of him. He just kept saying something big came at them from behind a tree, and they started running. Then, it was ahead of them, so they turned around and ran the other way and got lost. When I asked him to describe the thing that chased them, he couldn't. The man was on the verge of a breakdown, so I sent him home." He hesitated. "He didn't say anything about a witch, though, if that's what you're asking."

Knox supposed he was, if he was being honest. "Considering what happened, do you think we should handle the search any differently?"

The sheriff looked past him at the trees, swallowing. "I do. Groups of four instead of two."

"Sounds about right to me," Knox said. He watched the sheriff hobble off and give instructions to his men before climbing into his truck and driving off.

The deputies didn't seem to be in any hurry to get started. They hung around their vehicles, shoulders curled forward, talking quietly amongst themselves. Not that he blamed them. He didn't want to go into the forest either. When they noticed him, they slowly headed toward the path leading into the trees, steering clear of the spot where Deputy Stewart had been killed.

Only when the last men disappeared from view did Knox leave.

He was five minutes into his drive before he remembered Colleen. His thoughts toggled between dead certainty she'd left him and was at that moment asleep in some cheap motel in Las Vegas, to....

To something horrible. Something to do with the Root Witch.

But it was just a story, a folk tale. Colleen had walked out of his life. Jennifer and Karl were out there, somewhere, waiting to be found, as was Mitch, who was probably very sorry he'd taken it upon himself to look for them in the dark. They were young, healthy, and fit. They'd be embarrassed when they turned up, but they'd be fine.

Knox slowed to navigate a tricky hairpin turn, then slammed on his brakes.

A tall man was crossing the road. He wheeled around to face the truck, eyes widening, leaves stuck to his jacket and dark blond hair. The man stared at the truck, then noticed the Forest Service emblem on the door and broke into a grin. He jogged toward Knox.

Knox stuck his head out the window. "Please tell me you're Mitch from the TV station," he called.

Mitch held up a hand. "Guilty. Can I get a ride?"

Knox leaned over and hit the latch on the passenger side. "I'm Knox. We've been out looking for you and your friends. You okay? Did you find the others?"

Mitch slapped the dashboard. "Shit. That means you didn't find them either," he said with a slight drawl. "I'm fine. I had a bad night, is all."

As he drove, Knox studied the man sitting next to him. He was so tall his head pressed against the roof. With broad, powerful shoulders, Mitch had the build of a linebacker with the cadence of a cowboy. Colleen, he was sure, would find him so good-looking she'd forget she was married and start flirting, as she sometimes did.

"We found the news car down the hill," Knox began. "I met your reporter yesterday. Jennifer. She told me what they were up to, but I can't figure out why they were headed down into the valley. The people they wanted to talk to are at Lakeside Lodge."

"I don't know either." Mitch's jaw hardened. "I wish we never came down here."

For several minutes, Knox concentrated on driving the winding road.

"I just missed you at the campground last night," Knox said, breaking the silence. "A guy said he loaned you his Jeep so you could look for those reporters."

"Yeah, the satellite truck I'm driving is worthless off-road, so I borrowed a Jeep to see if I could find Jennifer and Karl. And I did find their news car, so I stopped and had a look around."

Mitch paused and glanced over at Knox. "Can I tell you something crazy?" Mitch asked.

Knox took a deep breath and nodded.

"I called their names and poked around the edge of the clearing but didn't see anything, so I was just about to get back in the Jeep when there was all this noise behind me. I turned around and saw this giant black shadow in the trees, coming fast. Scared the shit out of me. I didn't wait around to see what it was. I hauled ass up the road, and I kept running. Whatever it was stayed back in the woods. I got turned around in the dark and ended up on a skinny trail.

Finally saw an old cabin, so I stayed there for the night." He gave a grim laugh. "Better inside than out."

Knox nodded. Forest Service land was full of abandoned buildings like the one Mitch stumbled upon. It couldn't have been a comfortable stay. The red-tagged structures were often covered in mold and rat droppings.

Mitch cleared his throat and continued, his eyes never leaving Knox's face. "I had all night to think about what happened back there. My mind kept going back to this one weird spot I saw while I was out. There was this clearing, not too far from the news car. I don't know how to describe it, really, but the dirt was all churned up. It reminded me of the way we used to till the fields at my family's ranch, except there's no reason to do that out here. And then…" He paused and chewed his lip for a moment.

"Then what?" Knox prompted.

"There's this little hill with a bunch of tree roots sticking out of it, and I thought I saw something in there. I got a weird feeling somebody was watching me, and I got a bit spooked. All I had was a flashlight, and the battery was going fast. So, I decided to leave and come back later."

Something Mitch said struck him. Knox gripped the steering wheel so hard his knuckles turned white. "You said the dirt was churned up?"

"I can show you," Mitch said eagerly. "In fact, I'm hoping we can go back and take a look. Together."

Knox's breath came a little faster. "We can do that. I have some unpleasant cargo I need to drop at the station in Loa first, though."

"Okay. And if you can drive me back to the campground, I want to get my camera from the satellite truck. Just in case we find something."

"Like what?" Knox's chest heaved in anticipation.

"If I knew, I'd say," Mitch said. "But whatever it was, it felt like it didn't belong there."

In Loa, Knox dropped the carcass of the buck behind the office. He gave instructions to the staff coming on duty and checked the machine for messages, but there were none.

Then, they drove to Knox's cabin to get some breakfast. Mitch used the bathroom while Knox made coffee and scrambled egg sandwiches, which he wrapped in paper towels.

Before they left, Mitch asked to use the phone to call the TV station. Knox waited on the porch, half-listening, one eye on the trees. Even from where he was standing, he could hear a woman's voice coming from the receiver. When Mitch appeared, filling the entire doorway, Knox said, somewhat enviously, "Someone was sure excited to hear from you."

Mitch surprised him by blushing. "Yeah. My girlfriend works at the station. She's the producer who sent us down here. She wasn't too happy with me going rogue last night."

Knox's eyes widened. It was a small world. He'd met the pretty producer at the Xenon Club, and she'd called him at the cabin last night, asking for help.

Mitch stopped in front of the truck and stared at the meadow. "What happened there?" he said, pointing at the mound of churned earth.

Knox's hand froze over the door handle. "I don't know. I left for work yesterday, and it was fine. And when I came back, it was like that. My wife and I had a bit of a fight, so her car might have done that."

Yesterday felt like a hundred years ago.

"Maybe," Mitch said, but not as if he believed it.

As the Forest Service truck bounced over the dirt road to Highway 25, they ate their sandwiches. When they had finished, Knox told Mitch about what happened to Deputy Stewart.

Mitch let out a low whistle. "There's something wrong with that forest."

They'd reached the abandoned news car and the parking lot. The old Jeep Mitch had borrowed was still there too. Mitch hoisted the camera onto his shoulder as if it weighed nothing. Knox contemplated radioing Sheriff Wagoner to request a few men to accompany them but decided against it. His men were still searching for the reporters, so Knox decided it was best to let them continue.

The sun was out. There was plenty of natural light to see where they were going, and he was too anxious to see whatever Mitch had found to wait for help.

He followed Mitch as they headed south into a thick aspen grove. They walked in silence, Mitch occasionally stopping to get his bearings.

After ten minutes, he came to a sudden stop. "This is it," he said.

Something had disturbed the ground just ahead. Like the meadow in front of his cabin, the earth had been churned up.

Knox watched the tall man slip between two trees, then jump down.

Knox stared. His heart felt as heavy as a brick inside his chest. There was a faint buzzing in his ears. Erosion had cut away into the soil, exposing the roots of the aspens and creating a hollowed-out space underneath, giving the impression of an entrance to a cave.

Mitch turned his head to look back at Knox. "You won't be able to see anything up there," he said, frowning.

Overhead, the leaves fluttered. The canopy was so dense it was like standing under a golden dome. Despite the thick tread on his boots, Knox found himself sliding down the steep embankment.

Mitch produced a square of white paper from a pocket and handed it to him. "Unfold that for me and hold it front of the camera, will you?"

"What are you doing?" Knox asked. He knew nothing about video cameras.

"It's called white balancing," he said. "Okay, ready. You want to go first, and I'll shoot?"

Knox swallowed. He felt a sudden urge to run, but his desire to see what was down there was stronger. Something was in the hollowed-out space behind the roots. It was probably a piece of trash. A jacket dropped by a hiker.

Knox bit down on his lower lip, squatted, and peered into the hollow.

It was a body—a man wedged deep in the dark space, turned on his side. The clothes were ripped and shredded, revealing a round white belly. Roots penetrated the fleshy skin, blood covering the twisted stems. The man's neck was at a strange angle, the head covered in something brown and fibrous, like a burlap bag. Knox's halting mind churned through the possibilities. It wasn't a bag. That wasn't it at all. A mass of root fibers blanketed his skull.

His stomach rolled, and his legs shook. He could hear Mitch's ragged breathing just behind him.

Black spots bloomed before his eyes.

"It's not Jennifer or Karl," Mitch said.

Knox shook his head. The movement made him feel dizzy. "No. It's got to be the deputy who disappeared. Lane Carroll. It's got a uniform." It. He'd stripped the man of his humanity and reduced him to a corpse. "We need to show this to someone. I need to call the sheriff."

Both men scrambled up the embankment, eager to put some distance between them and their hideous discovery. They sprinted across the uneven ground back to the truck, panting. Mitch pulled ahead, the camera handle gripped in one strong hand. And then he stumbled, the camera swinging wildly. Knox heard a *crack* as it smacked into a tree.

"God dammit," Mitch shouted. He sank to the ground and pulled the camera onto his lap. After a brief inspection, he raised his head and sighed. "A few scratches, and the viewfinder's busted, but it's not as bad as it sounded…" His voice drifted off as he stared past Knox's knees. "What the hell?"

Mitch set the camera down. Still on all fours, he scrambled past Knox and began furiously digging through a pile of golden leaves and twigs. Seconds later, he was holding a TV camera that looked identical to his own.

Knox stared. He didn't need to ask if the camera Mitch found belonged to the missing crew—that he could tell just by looking at the man's stunned expression. Crouching next to Mitch, he said, "That was lucky."

Mitch brushed dirt off the camera. "It looks fine. Hopefully, there's something on the tape that will tell us what happened to them." He hit a button on the side of the camera. Nothing happened. "The battery's dead."

Knox watched Mitch press another button. A panel popped open, revealing the tape inside. Mitch slid out the tape and pointed to the writing on the sticker.

"The Root Witch, Tape 1."

Chapter 26

After she heard from Mitch, Sandy walked on wobbly legs to the bathroom, shut herself in a stall, and cried with relief.

"I love you," is what nearly escaped her lips before they hung up.

It had been a close call. Once said, there was no unsaying it. Sleeping together, once, hardly qualified them as a couple. Saying the L-word would have landed her in crazy girlfriend territory.

Sandy washed her face in the sink. Without makeup, and without much sleep, she looked pale. What she needed, desperately, was a hot shower, but she didn't dare go home. Janelle, the dispatcher down in Richfield, said the search for Karl and Jennifer would continue, and she needed to remain at the desk in case they called with updates. She hurried back to the newsroom.

Jack had reappeared. He swiveled in his chair and looked her up and down with a grimace. "You look like shit."

Her eyes narrowed as she took in his wet hair. He looked awake and suspiciously freshly scrubbed. "Did you go home to take a shower?" she asked, voice rising.

"No. The sales department has showers. They get all the perks. There's one for women in there too."

She dithered for a moment. Leaving the desk for any amount of time felt like abandoning her responsibility as assignment editor, but there was no telling how long she'd be at the desk. The storm was still full force in the mountains. Brody and the others would be stuck at Snowbird, probably for the remainder of the weekend. A shower would wake her up. She needed to be alert.

"Don't you dare leave the desk until I get back," she said.

In the studio where the on-air talent put on their makeup, she found a rust-colored blouse hanging on a rack that looked like it would fit her.

She was surprised to discover a well-equipped shower stall in the lady's bathroom upstairs in the sales department. There were even bottles of shampoo, conditioner, fresh towels, and a blow dryer. She used them all quickly and emerged feeling like a new person. The hot water had performed miracles on her stiff neck and back. Avoiding the assignment desk, she cut through the control room and back into the studio, where she helped herself to the makeup strewn across the counter. When Mitch stayed over, he'd said she looked beautiful without makeup and asked why she bothered using it. Which was nice to hear, but she felt naked and vulnerable without it.

She was applying eyeliner when her right hand began to tremble. A wave of heat coursed through her. The vanity lights were bright and hot. She flicked them off. Her heart had begun to race, and it felt like an iron band encircled her chest. Her temples throbbed, and the pain caused her to double over and gulp in air.

A panic attack. At the station. While she was in charge. Hiding in an edit bay was not an option. Leaving wasn't either. She had to get back to the desk, and soon.

The studio was dark, quiet and empty. She paced, stepping over cables, breathing in through her mouth, releasing the air from her nose, shaking out her arms.

After several circuits, the terrible squeezing eased, and she sagged with relief. The panic attack had crested, and she was on the downhill side now. It had come out of nowhere. She hadn't been thinking any particular thoughts that would trigger it, she told herself. But she was lying. Again. Her thoughts kept returning to the aspen forest where Mitch had been forced to stay the night. He'd explained he'd gotten lost, but Sandy was sure there was more to that story. Mitch had sounded uncharacteristically tense, even evasive, which wasn't like him. It had plunged her into a miasma that even a hot shower hadn't been able to disperse.

She'd visited the forest, just once as a child. White trunks. Heart-shaped leaves that never stopped shaking. The forest was full of light and flickering shadows and one shadow bigger than the rest. Enormous.

That's what she'd desperately wanted to tell Mitch. More than "Good luck finding Jennifer and Karl." More than "I love you."

Run.

That's what she'd wanted to scream.

Chapter 27

On the two-way, Knox told Sheriff Wagoner they'd found the body of Deputy Lane Carroll. Then, he and Mitch settled into Knox's truck, doors locked, and waited for the sheriff to come back from his search.

Mitch stashed the video camera in the back seat and covered it with a raincoat. "Do me a favor," he said. "Don't tell the sheriff about the video. There's a good chance he'll try to get me to turn it over, and there's no way I'm going to let him."

Knox opened his mouth to protest, but he was too numb to get the words out.

Nearly an hour later, Sheriff Wagoner hobbled out of the forest, wincing with every step, flanked by two burly deputies. The men's faces drooped with exhaustion.

A deep groove had formed between the sheriff's black eyes. "Let's see him," he said dully.

Mitch led the way. They trooped through the trees, dead leaves and twigs crunching under their boots.

When they arrived at their destination, Mitch helped the sheriff down the steep embankment. Sheriff Wagoner accepted the assistance without protest.

Knox hung back. He'd seen enough to feed his nightmares for the rest of his life.

One of the officers, nimbler than the sheriff, crawled close to the partially hidden body. Seconds later, he jumped back. "God almighty," he cried.

Knox watched as Mitch provided a steadying arm to the sheriff as he bent his head to peer into the darkened space.

When the sheriff straightened, his eyes were wet and red. "All right. We're leaving him there until we can get someone from the ME's office out here." He looked around, frowning. "We need to secure the scene." Turning to Mitch, he said, "I'm not sure what the hell is going on here, but this is a criminal investigation, and as such, I'm going to ask you nicely to keep this to yourself, and if you don't, you'll be hearing from me."

When Mitch nodded his assent, the sheriff's eyes slid to his two officers. They'd turned their backs on the atrocity in the earth, arms folded across heaving chests, faces frozen into grimaces.

"You two stay with him until I can figure out some shifts," Sheriff Wagoner said.

"The sheriff needs to know about the video tape," Knox whispered.

Mitch nodded reluctantly.

When they finished explaining what they'd found, and where, Sheriff Wagoner rubbed the back of his neck and turned to Mitch. "Well, that's the first good news I've heard since we started looking for your crew. Let's just hope it tells us something useful. I'm assuming you have a way for us to watch the video?"

Mitch cleared his throat. "I do, but the viewfinder on my camera broke, so we're going to have to go back to the satellite truck at Doctor Creek Campground."

Sheriff Wagoner clapped his hands. "Okay. Let's get to it then. You go on ahead, and I'll meet you there after I sort a few things out."

When Knox started the engine, he turned to his companion. "Mind if we stop at the cabin first? I need to make a few phone calls, and we can get some more coffee." Calls about Colleen. Act like a husband who wanted his wife back.

Mitch was watching the sheriff talk on the radio with a worried expression. "Fine by me. As long as I can use the phone to call Sandy and let her know we found a tape."

Knox stared ahead at the road. "You going to tell her about the deputy?"

"Just that we found the body so she can start making calls to get it confirmed and on the air. I wouldn't even know how to describe what we saw, and she's already a mess with Jennifer and Karl missing. Too much detail might push her over the edge, and besides, the sheriff wouldn't like that. You heard what he said."

They drove the rest of the way in a silence driven by equal parts fatigue and avoidance, but as they approached the cabin, Knox said, "There's a man who works for me. His son is some kind of folklore expert up at the University of Utah. He's writing a paper about the legend of the Root Witch. I read a summary of it. It's weird stuff. Unbelievable, really. I mean, what do you expect with a folktale, but there's this theory the Root Witch kills animals to help the forest. As in, using the animals as nutrition to help it survive. The way things are going, with the deer and cows overgrazing and eating the roots, and tourists allowed to trample over the new growth, the forest will eventually die."

Knox could feel the man's eyes boring into the side of his face.

"You're kidding?" Mitch finally said.

"I'm just saying what was in the article," Knox said. A defensive note had crept into his voice.

"Do you think there's anything to it?"

Knox shrugged. "I didn't at the time. But that would explain what we saw back there."

Beside him, Mitch shifted. He was so tall his knees were jammed into the dashboard. Knox was struck anew by the man's size.

"I don't think either of us are thinking too straight at the moment," Mitch said. "But isn't that something you should know? As a ranger? You must know all about forests. If a body is out there for a long time, in the ground, isn't that something trees do? Consume it?"

Knox gave a grim laugh. "Not like that. At least, not that I've heard of anyway. And here's another thing. What was the deputy doing way down there? His car was found on the highway, just down the road from my cabin. It doesn't make sense."

"Not much has since I got here," Mitch said. "A good-sized buck fell out of a tree and killed a man, and we just left a guy with roots sticking out of his gut."

Knox flinched as the truck hit a pothole. "What do you think's on that tape?"

"Your guess is as good as mine." Mitch rubbed his hands on his thighs. "We'll find out soon enough," he said without enthusiasm.

In the short time he'd known him, Knox had come to like the guy. Mitch was easy to be around. He reminded Knox of a friend he left back in Texas. Didn't talk too much. Made smart observations. The kind of man he wouldn't mind knocking back a few beers with under different circumstances. Having someone around of his size didn't hurt either, all things considered.

At the cabin, Mitch stood staring at the meadow for a long time, tugging on his bottom lip. When he finally dragged his gaze away from the disturbed ground, he said, "That looks awfully familiar, doesn't it?"

Knox was standing on the front porch. His hand shook as he inserted the key into the lock. "It does. I don't know what to think about it. My brain feels like it's about to break."

"I think I'll stay out here while you make your calls," Mitch said, kicking a dirt clod.

Knox went inside, used the bathroom, and began rummaging around in Colleen's desk. The green leather address book was in the top drawer. He carried it to the table in the living room and flipped through it until he found the first number.

Colleen's best friend in Houston picked up on the third ring. There was no way around it. The only way to get useful information was to tell the truth. Sherry was happy to hear from him, then shocked when he explained Colleen had left him after a fight and hadn't contacted him since.

"That's really awful, Knox," Sherry said. "I'm sorry. But I don't know a thing, I swear. If I did, I'd tell you. I mean, I knew she wasn't happy about living way out there, but she's crazy about you. Will you call and let me know when you find her? Because now you've got me all worried."

"Thank you, Sherry. I will. I promise."

"And Knox? When she turns up, you ought to sit down and have a serious talk. Those books of hers are taking off, and she deserves to choose where she lives and works, just like you."

Her words hit him like a slug to the chest.

Two more phone calls to Colleen's closest friends ended with the same result. Surprise, followed by a scolding.

He was waiting for Colleen's brother, Cameron, to pick up when he saw Mitch walking near the trees, neck bent, studying the ground. His heart sank. He hadn't thought to look for those odd clumps of earth elsewhere on the property.

Cameron finally answered. He sounded breathless. "Oh, hi, Knox. Sorry, I was outside. Everything okay?"

"Not really," Knox admitted, then explained the situation.

A long silence followed. Colleen's brother was younger by two years. He and Colleen had had a rough, unstable childhood, and they had always been close. "Oh man, I'm sorry to hear that." He sighed. "Well, Colleen did call me. She was really pissed off after you guys got into it. She said she was thinking about going to Las Vegas or someplace for a few days, to teach you a lesson."

"Have you heard from her since?

"No," Cameron said without hesitation. "And I didn't really believe she'd go. You know how she gets. Kind of hysterical, and she rants and raves, and then she's over it. How long has she been gone?"

Knox squeezed his eyes shut. A headache was coming on. "A day maybe. She was gone when I got home from work last night. She hasn't left a message. Did she mention where she'd stay?"

"No. Just Las Vegas."

After promising to call if either of them heard anything, Knox hung up. He stuck his head out the window and yelled,

"I'm off the phone," then retreated to the bathroom, where he took a quick shower and changed into fresh clothes.

When he padded into the living room, toweling his wet hair, he heard Mitch groan. He was sitting at the table, phone receiver pressed against his ear. "Okay, okay. I get it. I understand. I'll do it. No, I promise, but that doesn't mean I have to like it. All right. I'll talk to you soon." He replaced the receiver with a heavy sigh.

"Was that your girlfriend?" Knox said as they walked into the kitchen.

"It was. She doesn't want us to watch that video without her. Which is a bad idea because who knows what's on it, and if it's something bad, I don't think she's going to handle it too well. And I'm down here, and she's up there." Mitch knocked the side of his head. "I blew it. I should have watched it first and *then* told her."

Knox opened a can of coffee and gave it a sniff. It still smelled fresh. The last one he bought had dried out, and he hated stale coffee. He measured out the grounds and poured them in. "So, why did you? Tell her, I mean."

Mitch leaned against the counter. "It's a long story, but all the managers are out. They're stranded up at Snowbird, and Sandy's in charge. She's got a right to know and to make the call. No question. It's just that, I'm worried about her. She's under a lot of stress, and she's working with a Class A douchebag."

"How's she going to watch the video all the way up there?" Knox asked, rummaging in the cupboards for another thermos. Sheriff Wagoner had looked like he could use some hot coffee.

"Satellite link," Mitch said. "She books a window of satellite time. That allows us to talk in the truck, and when we play the video, she can watch in real time at the station and record a copy as it plays back too."

Knox watched the coffee drip into the pot. After a moment, he said, "I saw you out by the trees. Did you find anything?"

"No. But I didn't walk in far. Any word about where your wife went?"

Knox swallowed. "No."

Chapter 28

Sandy paced the feed room, waiting for Mitch to get to the satellite truck. From what he'd said, the drive wouldn't take longer than fifteen minutes. Thirty minutes had passed, and she was starting to get worried. People had a way of disappearing in the aspen forest.

And there was what happened to the boy visiting with his parents from Salt Lake—the reason she sent a news crew more than two hours south, along with Mitch and two vehicles, one costing more than a house.

Jonie Waite, the child's mother, had called several times, asking why the story hadn't aired. She felt the lie leave her lips a little too easily. They'd encountered unexpected technical difficulties, and the story would hopefully air soon. She'd taken down the woman's number and promised to call when she knew more.

That hadn't been the only difficult phone call.

News of the missing crew had leaked out. First, she fielded calls from reporters with the newspapers, then the other TV stations, and finally the all-news radio station. Without the news director, Brody, or the general manager to issue an official statement or offer guidance on what she could or could not say, she said as little as possible. Just enough to confirm what Janelle, the Richfield dispatcher, had revealed. A search was underway for two reporters from the station who disappeared while on assignment.

"What story were they on?" asked one persistent newspaper reporter she'd dated two years before.

"I don't see how that's relevant," she said, then banged down the phone. Which the jerk probably attributed to the way things ended between them.

And then there was Jack, listening to her conversations, bombarding her with advice on how to better phrase things, and speculating on what kind of trouble she'd be in once the managers got back. He sat sipping coffee, talking with the weekend producer as if she hadn't been sitting a few feet away.

"She could get off easy, I guess," Jack said. "Write her up and stick her on the overnight shift again. Or they could suspend her. But if they find Jen and Karl and they're dead, then she's really screwed. We're talking see-you-later-you're-fired screwed. It's possible they could even file charges against her."

Finally, she couldn't stand it anymore and yelled at him to book the satellite window. As soon as she had, Sandy remembered he'd never done it before, so she walked him through the steps, staring down at his hairy neck, wondering why his barber didn't shave it.

She'd retreated to the feed room, ordering Jack to stay at the desk until it was time to view the tape. Jack had insisted on watching it too, and she hadn't been able to think of a good reason for him not to. The feed room editor wasn't due in for several hours, so she had it to herself. She was too restless to sit, so she paced, one eye on the satellite receiver.

Chapter 29

Sheriff Wagoner was waiting for them at Doctor Creek Campground. He'd come alone.

The sheriff dispatched the curious campers, who kept a respectful distance behind the row of cones he'd put down a few yards from the satellite truck. He scowled when Mitch told him the assignment editor, Sandra Molina, would be watching the video in Salt Lake, and the sheriff mumbled something about not enough time for a court order.

Inside the truck, a dizzying array of equipment lined walls from floor to ceiling—TV monitors, consoles, and panels with switches and knobs. There was enough room for all three of them inside. Mitch headed toward the far end and sat at a built-in counter facing the largest screen. He pushed some buttons, and Knox could hear the roof-mounted satellite dish moving around outside.

Then, Mitch picked up the phone and punched in a number. His long fingers flew over a control panel, and seconds later, he pushed the tape into a machine to his left.

Color bars appeared on the screen, and Knox could hear a woman's voice on the other end of the phone.

Mitch hit a button on the tape machine, and a blur of images flashed on the screen as the tape rewound.

"Ready on your end? Are you rolling?"

Sandy's disembodied voice came through one of the overhead speakers. "We're good."

Sheriff Wagoner sat in the only other available chair, absently rubbing his ankles as he stared at the color bars on the large screen. Knox stood behind him, battling that feeling he used to get as a kid when a friend talked him into riding the tallest and fastest roller coaster. That moment he found himself at the front of the line, confronted with the terrifying reality of those wood and metal hills, and it was too late to chicken out.

Mitch hit play. Knox felt his stomach drop.

Chapter 30

Sandy's breath hitched in her throat as the color bars appeared on the screen. Her pulse skipped.

Jack glanced her way. "Calm the fuck down over there," he muttered.

As usual, he was standing too close.

She hit the bright red record button. Whatever was shown in the satellite truck would be recorded on the three-quarter-inch tape in the feed room.

Jennifer appeared on the screen. She was wearing the same thing she'd left in—a bright red sweater and jeans. Karl could be heard off camera, telling Jennifer and the couple where to stand. The three were outside what appeared to be a hotel, a large lake in the background.

"All right, can you tell me your names please?" Jennifer asked, holding the mic up to the woman.

For once, Jennifer was interviewing someone taller than herself. The woman, Jonie Waite, identified herself as an accountant from Salt Lake City, visiting the area for the first time to see the fall colors with her husband and six-year-old son. The mic moved over to the husband, who introduced himself as Ben Waite.

Jonie explained she'd heard her son screaming in the distance and hadn't seen what happened, but she believed his story.

"My son doesn't make things up or lie," she said. "He said something tried to drag him toward a tree, and I believe him. I saw what it did to his ankles. My husband was there. He can tell you more."

Sandy gripped the back of a chair to steady herself. The whooshing of her heart was so loud in her ears, she turned up the volume on the tape deck.

Ben Waite nodded, a bit reluctantly, Sandy thought. "Our son had got ahead of us, and when I found him, there were tentacles wrapped around his legs. They came out of the dirt." He ran a hand through his hair, a faraway look in his eyes. "I've never seen anything like it. I tried pulling them off, but they just pulled tighter—"

"You said tentacles," Jennifer interrupted. "Were they slippery?"

Ben shook his head. "No. They were dry. And hard to the touch, but they could bend. Like I said, it's hard to describe. I couldn't get them off, and then I remembered I had a knife, so I started hacking away at them, and that got them to loosen up, so I kept slashing, and then the tentacles disappeared into the ground. I could see the ground moving, like something was under there, so I chased it a bit. I don't know what I was thinking, because my son was screaming at me, begging me to stop. So, I did."

The man was visibly shaking as he finished his story.

"Did you see a witch?" Jennifer asked. "The Root Witch?"

The man closed his eyes. "I don't know. I don't know what she's supposed to look like, and after what happened today, I hope I never do."

The tape paused. Mitch's voice came over the speaker again. "Should I fast forward a bit?"

Sandy debated for a moment. It was a thirty-minute tape. If there was something significant, they should get straight to it. If there was nothing, they could rewind and pick up where they left off.

"Yeah, that's a good idea," she said.

The interview with the Salt Lake couple lasted another several minutes. In the background, a man came running down the steps of the lodge, waving his hands over his head. The camera swiveled toward him. Karl, acting as photographer, aimed the camera.

"Are you here about the Root Witch?" he asked, trying to catch his breath. He was a small, beak-nosed man in his fifties.

"We're looking into reports of some sightings," Jennifer said. "Do you have something for us?"

The man nodded. "Yes. Yes, I do. My sister and I were hiking in a part of the forest we hadn't been to before. Someone told us about it. Said there were fewer people down there, and so we went. We were walking, and my sister tripped. Something came out of the ground and was crawling up her legs. And then my sister started screaming that something was behind me, so we ran. The road wasn't far, thank goodness."

Jennifer did her best to extract more specific details, but the man said it happened so fast it was all a blur. When the reporter asked if he and his sister would accompany them to the spot for an on-camera interview, the man refused.

"Oh, heck no," he said. "We're not going back there."

When Jennifer asked if he'd repeat what he'd just said, one more time on camera, he readily agreed, then gave directions to the lower part of the forest. The tape came to a stop.

Over the speaker, Mitch said, "That explains why we found Jennifer and Karl's truck down there,"

"They must have gone to get B-roll," Sandy replied.

The sheriff cleared his throat. "What's that?"

"Extra footage," Mitch said. "In this case, shots of the forest they'd use to illustrate the interview they'd just shot."

Jack closed the gap between them and clutched Sandy's arm, blasting her with stale coffee breath. "This is good shit."

Sandy jerked free. Their crew had vanished, and not once had he expressed any genuine concern for the two missing reporters. To him, they were simply a story—a good one he could slot in a newscast.

She ignored him and stepped closer to the mic. "I'm ready if you want to keep fast-forwarding." Her voice quavered.

Mitch hit play, and the video continued rolling. She watched, hardly daring to breathe, as Jennifer fluffed her hair, wriggled her shoulders, and counted down. "Three-two-one. I'm standing where Ben Waite found his six-year-old son screaming for help…"

When she'd finished, the screen flickered, and a new image appeared. They were still in the aspen forest, but the trees were closer together, the ground more uneven, the light dimmer—everything cast with a strange, murky gold.

Karl could be heard giving directions to Jennifer. "Okay, just keep walking. I'll follow as you point to what we're looking at."

Jennifer traversed the ground easily in her boots, with long, confident strides. She glanced over her shoulder with an expression that promised interesting things were ahead.

Stopping next to an enormous boulder, she came to abrupt halt and said, "The dentist from Provo who shared his strange and terrifying experience was unwilling to return, but this is where it happened…"

When she finished repeating the man's story, the camera tilted down. An orange scarf lay on the ground. It was covered in clumps of dirt. To Sandy, it looked as if a team of over enthusiastic gardeners had spent the morning turning over the earth. The disturbed patch stretched for yards in all directions.

The camera bounced.

Sandy watched as Jennifer flashed an uncertain gap-toothed smile at her boyfriend. "What's wrong? Why are you looking at me that way?"

Jennifer looked beautiful in the soft, perfect light. Her red sweater stood out against the chalky whiteness of the tree trunks. A few golden leaves fell, one landing on her shoulder.

"What's that sound?" Karl asked.

Over the speaker, Sandy heard a rushing, a roar like a distant ocean. The aspens quaking.

Jennifer opened her mouth then closed it again. The light was changing. The entire shot darkened. Had the automatic iris on Karl's camera malfunctioned?

Sandy watched, pulse quickening, as Jennifer's eyes widened in surprise. Karl could be heard cursing off camera, and then there was a swift intake of breath, a hissing, and the camera swung upward over Jennifer's head. For a second, Sandy saw the tops of golden trees and blue sky. When the camera tilted back down, something that hadn't been there before loomed into view.

An enormous, black shadow behind Jennifer.

Every muscle in Sandy's body tensed. She wanted to look away, run from the room. Anything to avoid watching.

The shadow began to stretch in all directions, growing taller as it spread wider. Jennifer's mouth opened, her arms reaching out, like a child pleading to be held.

The scene played in silence. Sandy wondered, for a moment, if something had happened to the audio. No one was talking. Even the leaves had stopped shaking.

The silence seemed to drag on forever, although the red numbers on the tape deck told a different story. Seconds, not minutes.

Behind the camera, Karl shouted, "Jennifer, move, move, move!"

Jennifer dropped the microphone. It thumped on the ground. Sandy watched, a hand pressed against her mouth, as Jennifer ducked her head, dropped to her knees, and scrabbled toward Karl. Her eyes were wide with terror. And all the while, the camera held steady enough to show the shadow behind Jennifer coming together, edges solidifying, until it resembled a strange and twisted tree. Something both monstrous, and yet, vaguely human.

A limb reached out and grabbed Jennifer by the waist, lifting her high into the air as if she weighed nothing, as if she were a small child and not a woman of five-feet-eleven.

"No!" Karl cried.

Somehow, Karl kept the camera trained on Jennifer, who was screeching now, arms and legs flailing, hair whipping.

In one giant sideways arc, the shadow slammed Jennifer into a tree with a terrible thudding sound. Her screams stopped. The shadow monster slammed her into another tree. The second impact seemed to break her. She went as limp as a rag doll. The great dark figure continued to smash Jennifer's body against the surrounding trees, each strike accompanied by the sounds of bones cracking—her legs, her spine, her skull.

The enormous shadow shriveled, swirling into the exposed roots of an aspen tree.

Jennifer's body lay broken and twisted on the ground. Off camera, Karl could be heard whimpering.

Roots slithered out of the soil, uncoiling with the fluid and mesmerizing movement of tentacles. They snaked toward Jennifer until they had encircled her ankles and began tugging her into the loosened, churned earth.

The aspen trees resumed their terrible fluttering.

Karl began to scream, and the camera hit the ground.

Sandy had a brief glimpse of a deer, frozen, in the distance. Karl grunted. It was all happening out of sight from the camera lens, but the sounds suggested Karl trying to crawl away. A wail filled the air.

The video ended.

Chapter 31

Sandy's wall of denial collapsed into a pile of bricks, dust, and death. The horrifying video had brought it down with stunning finality. For the entirety of those few minutes on the tape, Sandy had been there with Jennifer and Karl as they tromped through the quaking aspen forest.

Long ago, she had been there too. Experienced the terror of that enormous black shadow, then doubted her own memories because no one believed her. Not the authorities. Not her father or brother. Not even her own mother.

The rumors of the Root Witch had stirred a faint recollection, pulled strings as if she were a puppet. She'd known the forest was dangerous, but she needed proof, and she'd taken the one opportunity given her to show—as only video evidence could—the Root Witch wasn't just a legend, but a terrifying reality.

This time, she wasn't the only one to see it. Others had too. Jack, Mitch, a Forest Service ranger, and a sheriff.

No one could call her crazy now.

She was no longer alone to carry the burden of knowing the impossible, the unbelievable, existed, that a great looming behemoth lurked in the forest.

Over the speaker, she heard voices shouting. Something to do with the ranger's wife, Colleen, then the sound of a struggle,

In the feed room, Jack lunged for the tape deck. His hairy hand turned the rewind knob. The bastard intended to watch it again, watch the Root Witch smash all the bones of his co-worker, then pull her into the earth. Or maybe he wanted to see if there was any more video that would show how the creature had killed Karl.

She shoved him aside and screamed, "No!"

The door to the feed room flew open. The weekend producer appeared, eyes wide with alarm.

"What's going on?" he demanded.

Sandy screamed at him to get out as she shoved Jack aside, but not before he'd popped out the tape.

When she snatched it from him, she heard Mitch say, "Sandy? Sandy!" into the speaker.

Jack tried to pry the tape from her fingers, and she tightened her grip. His hands were surprisingly strong, but still she refused to let go.

"I need to see it again," he cried, as he pulled up on her fingers, bending them the wrong way.

She grunted in pain, then dug her fingernails into the back of his hand.

Jack yelped and relinquished his hold with a cry of frustration.

Sandy jumped away, losing her balance and falling to the floor.

Suddenly exhausted, she allowed herself to lay there, panting, clutching the tape to her stomach. She squeezed her eyes shut and felt a shudder roll through her body.

"Is she okay?" the producer said from the doorway. He sounded far away and worried.

Jack sank down beside her. She could feel him staring at her.

When she didn't respond, he said, "Sandy, are you trying to freak me out?" He sounded like he was talking from the far end of a tunnel.

Her eyelids felt heavy, so heavy it took all her effort to pry them open. Jack's dark eyes were wide and frightened. It felt like her brain wasn't attached to her body, and she was having trouble understanding what Jack was saying. Mitch's voice continued to blare over the speaker, but she couldn't understand him either. Even lying down, she was dizzy, and her face had gone numb.

I'm having a stroke.

With great difficulty, she forced herself to form the words, "Feeling weird."

Jack bit his lip but nodded. Then, he stood up and lurched to the mic connected to the satellite receiver. "Hey, Mitch, your girlfriend is having some sort of episode. She's totally lost it. I think I'm going to have to call an ambulance."

Sandy listened. Even if she'd wanted to protest, she couldn't have formed the words if she tried.

Chapter 32

Once he reached the cabin, Knox surveyed the expanse of churned-up meadow, and for several seconds, he could do nothing but breathe in the rich, loamy smell of the earth.

Mitch had tried to stop him, but Knox had broken free. Mitch was preoccupied anyway—his producer girlfriend had collapsed. Sheriff Wagoner yelled at Knox to stop, but he was too hobbled by bad feet and shock from watching the video to do much else.

They'd come soon, and if they didn't, the sheriff would send his officers.

He had to hurry.

Knox ran to the shed and grabbed two shovels. Ignoring the rustling of the aspen leaves, his heart thudding, he plunged the point of a trench shovel into the disrupted soil. The dirt was soft and loose, almost inviting him to dig deeper.

The rush of adrenalin made him breathless and dizzy.

Roots appeared in the dirt, thick and brown. Aspen roots. He raised the shovel high and brought it down with a grunt, cutting through the growth.

The mass of roots formed a solid mat. He paused, panting, leaning on the shovel.

That root spread wasn't normal. The meadow was too far from the line of trees for the roots to be so thick. He'd been trained to turn to science for answers, but nothing he'd learned could explain what was beneath his feet. Just as it couldn't account for the horrors he'd witnessed on the video tape.

His intestines writhed, and he continued hacking away.

The tip of his shovel struck something hard. Something harder than roots or soil. Leaning into the hole he'd created, stomach pressed into the ground, he brushed aside the dirt, revealing a patch of blue steel that glinted in the sun.

Knox frantically cleared more dirt. The roof of a car.

No.

Colleen's car was buried under feet of roots and soil. The horrific video crash-landed into his thoughts, roots tugging Jennifer's broken body toward the base of an aspen.

He'd brought his wife to this place, walled-in by a forest she detested. And when she tried to leave, it had stopped her.

It. The Root Witch.

In the distance, he could hear the rattling of aspen leaves, louder than before. When he glanced down, he was surprised to see his hand clutching a root stretched across the car's roof. Knox could imagine it pulsing under his touch. He gasped, the faint rhythmic throbbing soothing his beleaguered mind. His thoughts of Colleen began to drift.

A noise roused him. Tires rumbling on the road.

He snatched his hand away, and almost immediately, the strange sensation passed.

"Fuck you," Knox shouted in the general direction of the wall of trees, then frantically resumed his task of shoveling dirt and roots from the top of the car.

A shadow loomed over him.

"What the hell?" said a familiar voice, and a moment later, Mitch had joined him in the pit.

More faces appeared. Glancing up, Knox spotted Sheriff Wagoner and several of his deputies, eyes bulging.

"There are more shovels in the shed around the back," Knox shouted.

With six men working, dirt flying, they soon reached the car's windows. Knox's chest heaved. The same fibrous mat that covered the face of the deputy in the forest covered the windows.

The men worked faster now, clearing enough space around the doors to open them. A metal door handle emerged. Knox was clawing at it when Mitch knocked him aside with a thunderous, "No!"

Knox hunkered up to the edge of the pit and watched as Mitch helped the sheriff into the hole.

Sheriff Wagoner regarded him with pity. "I can't think of any reason for you to see this, young man."

Knox hardly heard him. He was listening to the aspen leaves fluttering madly, as if trying to get his attention. Covering his ears, he shook his head. "I'm staying."

Sheriff Wagoner gave a curt nod, then pulled the handle. The door swung open. Dirt spilled out.

The car's interior gaped darkly, revealing its hidden secret. A tumble of brown hair. A patch of bare shoulder.

Slender roots lashed Colleen's head to the steering wheel. A thicker one bound her to the seat, its end disappearing into her stomach. Blood pooled in her lap.

Bile rising in his throat, Knox felt himself topple sideways, and as he did, he saw her hands, torn and split.

He leapt up, racing for the forest, shovel in hand. Only when he'd nearly reached the line of aspen trees did Mitch catch up and tackle him. The shovel Knox carried as a humble weapon went flying into the air. A deputy skidded up, panting. The two men hauled him to his feet.

Knox felt his face contort. He had no control over his muscles. A scream rose in his throat, but all that came out was a croak.

The aspen leaves quivered.

Knox cast a venomous glance at the aspen clone. He'd deal with it later. Lifting his chin, he said, "Colleen didn't leave me," then turned away from the men and the trees and collapsed.

Chapter 33

The hospital room smelled of antiseptic and the chicken soup an orderly had delivered for dinner. The doctors determined she'd not suffered a stroke and gave her a sedative for work-related trauma. Now, all she had to do was wait for her psychologist to arrive and Mitch to come pick her up.

One sympathetic doctor suggested she stay the night, but she'd refused. Mitch promised to drive back to Salt Lake as soon as he could and take her home.

Calling her mother was not an option. Sandy couldn't bear another scolding, especially now that she knew the truth.

A truth she was finally able to share with Celeste.

She watched the six o'clock news with the crisp white sheet drawn up to her neck. There was a brief mention of the missing news crew—their names, ages, and where they were last seen. The other TV stations did the same. There was no mention of incidents involving the monster in the quaking aspen forest.

The video tape documenting the horror that had befallen her co-workers was in her patient belongings bag hanging in the closet. Somehow, she'd managed to keep it clutched in her hands through the ambulance ride.

After the six o'clock newscast ended, she called the station to check in.

"It's a slow news night," Jack reported. "Not much going on. And by the way, you being out of commission means I'm the newsroom manager." If Jack had suffered any ill effects from the horror of the Root Witch caught on tape, he showed no signs of it. His voice hummed with barely concealed excitement.

Brody and the other managers were still snowed in at the conference. When she glanced out the window of her hospital room, the storm showed no signs of letting up.

"I'll be back tomorrow," she said through gritted teeth.

"Take your time!" Jack hung up.

"Fucker." Sandy banged the receiver into the cradle.

Celeste appeared in the doorway, eyebrows raised. "Your friend at work?" she asked mildly.

Sandy had hoped to talk on the phone, but her psychologist said no, left home on a Saturday, and drove across town on hazardous roads to see her in person.

"Thank you for coming," Sandy said.

"Of course," Celeste replied, as if she made house calls all the time.

With Celeste staring at her expectantly from behind round hippy glasses, Sandy began to cry. Celeste pulled a tissue from a box on the bedside table and handed it to her.

"Bad day?" she said.

Sandy coughed, then laughed. She'd never known Celeste to crack a joke during their sessions. "Very," she said. Everything she'd planned to say was forgotten, and now she didn't know where to start.

Celeste pulled up a chair and gave her an encouraging smile.

"My mother told me to keep the story to myself," Sandy said. "That's how it all started, I guess. She warned me if I didn't, everyone would think I was a liar."

Celeste nodded, as if what she'd just said made perfect sense. "Does this have something to do with what's been triggering your panic attacks."

"It has everything to do with it." Sandy stared down at her hands. They looked strangely colorless. "Have you heard of the legend of the Root Witch?"

Celeste frowned. "It's a ghost that haunts an aspen forest, isn't it? Up at Mount Timpanogas?"

"No. In central Utah. Next to Fish Lake."

"That's right," Celeste said, nodding. "It's a rather scary story, if I remember correctly."

Sandy leaned back against the pillows. "It is. Terrifying, actually. I went there with my cousins when I was a kid. I was ten. I'd never been camping before, and I was kind of nervous about it. In the middle of the night, I had to go to the bathroom, but I couldn't get anyone to go with me. So, I went alone." She hesitated. "I was attacked. Almost killed. I don't remember what happened exactly, but I remember something picking me up and hitting me against a tree."

Like Jennifer.

Celeste's eyes widened, but she said nothing.

Sandy continued. "It was too big to be a person. Way too big. I saw it before I passed out. It didn't look human. But I was only ten. Anyway, whatever it was, it broke my arms and legs and almost my back, and they had to operate, several times, actually, to fix everything. And I had a concussion. At first, the swelling was so bad they thought I'd be left with brain damage, but I was lucky."

Celeste leaned over and squeezed her hands. "That's terrible."

"It was, but that wasn't the worst part," Sandy said dully. "The worst part was when the police asked me to describe who did it, and I told them. I could tell they didn't believe me. My mom got so mad. She said I was lying. And when I swore I was telling the truth, she said I'd go to hell for making up a story like that. The police said a man had kidnapped me. Except they never found him."

"That must have been painful, for your own mother to say those things," Celeste said. She hesitated, head tilting, peering at Sandy through half-closed eyes. "Did all of this come back to you today?"

Sandy ignored that, determined to tell the story her own way. "On Friday, I was handling assignments. The bosses weren't around. We were getting a bunch of calls from people saying they'd seen the Root Witch. But none of them sounded like they'd be credible enough to interview. And then a lady called, an accountant, and I knew if there was anyone people would listen to, it was her. So, I sent a news crew to do the story."

Celeste's eyes snapped open.

"Two of the people I sent went missing. I told myself it was a great story, an important story. One we had to cover. Except that's not what I was really doing. I..." Her voice drifted off.

"Wanted proof you hadn't imagined it," Celeste prompted.

"Yes," Sandy said bitterly.

"And bottling up what you recall of that traumatic event has caused your panic attacks over the years," Celeste said. A statement. Not a question.

Sandy pressed a hand to her mouth and nodded.

"Did you ever receive any treatment for the trauma you experienced as a child?"

"No."

Celeste blinked owlishly behind her glasses. "And why is that?"

Sandy stared out the window at the falling snow for a long time before she answered. "I'm not sure, exactly. I guess we didn't have any money for stuff like that. And when someone from the school district came to the house, my mother said I wasn't crazy, and she wouldn't let them talk to me. And for the most part, I was fine at school. I never got into trouble, and my grades were good, so they left me alone."

"Alone to deal with an assault that almost killed you," Celeste said, frowning.

She nodded. Whatever drugs they'd given her, they'd zapped her strongest emotions, including anger. She felt a flicker of resentment. When the sedation wore off, it would still be there, and with time, it might threaten to engulf her. But she'd be prepared. No more doubting her sanity. She'd go broke paying Celeste before she let that happen.

Celeste studied the ends of her long blond hair, then said, "Well, that's something we should talk about, but you haven't finished your story. Did they find the news crew?"

Sandy had no intention of telling Celeste the truth. She wanted to, desperately. But that would mean giving voice to the ghastliness of the Root Witch, and she wasn't ready to do that yet. She couldn't relive those awful moments in the feed room, witnessing death. And even psychologists had their limits. Without seeing the tape for herself, Celeste might not believe her.

Instead, she lied. "No. They're still missing. The guy I just started going out with went down there too, but he's fine. Honestly, I'm afraid the reporters are dead. And whatever happened to them is my fault. One hundred percent."

Celeste's eyebrows shot up. "Sandy, there's another way to look at this. One that better reflects the reality and complexity of the situation. You were at work. This happened on Halloween. You sent reporters out on a perfectly suitable story for the occasion. The Root Witch is a well-known local legend, and presumably, your reporters understood that. You were a child when you were abducted, and you'd been forced to deny the experience. The logical, busy professional Sandy wasn't connecting with something that happened to the little girl Sandy, what, sixteen years ago?"

"Yes," Sandy said, eyeing the IV pouch. The drip contained a solution for dehydration, but she suspected it was also pushing a nice, calming drug into her veins. That would explain why she felt a curious lack of agitation.

"Sixteen years is a long time," Celeste said, sounding sterner than her usual self. "While it's perfectly normal to feel bad for what may have happened to your co-workers, you don't need to carry the extra burden of blaming yourself. It's unfortunate your job duties intersected the way they did with your history, but it's something we're going to need to work very hard to decouple. Okay?"

Sandy pressed her palms to her eyes. They were wet with tears. She hadn't realized she was crying. "Okay." That simple word of agreement came out with a long, wobbly breath.

For a moment, she was tempted to tell Celeste everything, death tape and all. But despite what Jack said, she was still in charge of the newsroom, and she wasn't free to share what she'd witnessed with an outsider. Even her psychologist.

Chapter 34

Before Sandy left the hospital, the nurse warned Mitch Sandy might be unsteady on her feet due to the sedatives and advised a quiet evening at home. So, Mitch insisted on going to his house, but they stopped at Sandy's apartment in the avenues, where she picked up a change of clothes and her makeup bag.

Mitch's roommate was out of town, so they had the place to themselves. The house was a nondescript brick bungalow with a long driveway on a busy street near the University of Utah. Mitch rented the upstairs, and his roommate had the basement.

The storm had dumped several inches of snow on the driveway. Sandy was sliding out of the truck when Mitch ran around the side, scooped her up, and carried her and the plastic bag with her belongings across the white expanse and through a side door leading into the kitchen.

Every room had wood paneling and exposed brick, except for Mitch's bedroom, which was covered with blue and brown striped wallpaper. The house was simply but comfortably furnished. The blond wood furniture looked new and modern. The whole place was, she decided in her fuzzy state, very Mitch.

He deposited her on the couch in the living room and collapsed next to her. His hands were clean, but his clothes were thick with grime that gave off an earthy smell. All that dirt told a story, but she wasn't sure she was ready to hear it yet. Her mouth tasted sour.

"Do you have any wine?" she asked hopefully.

He glanced down, hazel eyes wide. "Should you be drinking with what they gave you at the hospital?"

"Probably not, but I could use a glass. Just one."

Mitch stood, pressed his hands into his lower back, and went into the kitchen. She heard the refrigerator open, then a cupboard and glasses clinking. He returned a few minutes later, carrying a glass of white wine and two inches of amber liquid in a tumbler.

She accepted it with stiff, cold fingers and a note of surprise. "Thank you. You had white wine? Really?"

He gave a tired smile. There were dark circles under his hazel eyes. His dirty blond hair was disheveled. "Well, sure. I was hoping I'd get you over here some time." He remained standing. "Is it okay? If not, I've got beer."

She sipped it. It tasted like citrus and summer. "It's perfect, thank you."

Mitch eased back down with a heavy sigh. The time for small, quiet, ordinary moments had passed. The looming conversation about the video tape had created its own atmosphere, heavy and oppressive, disturbing the air between them.

He took her small hand in his large one. "We didn't find them—Jennifer and Karl. The sheriff has people looking."

"Did he tell them what was on the tape?"

"No. He doesn't seem to know what to say about it, exactly, so he's telling his men to be careful out there, that a dangerous animal might be prowling around the woods."

Sandy wanted to scream. "You're kidding?"

"I don't blame him," Mitch said. "Can you imagine if the sheriff started talking about monsters?"

"But the tape—"

"The sheriff is up for reelection on Tuesday," Mitch said. "It's bad enough, with one of his deputies found dead and two reporters missing in his district. He said everyone is going to think he's lost his mind if he starts talking about the Root Witch, like it's real."

"But the tape…" Sandy trailed off. Her head was still too fuzzy to explain why she found the sheriff's response so appalling.

"We talked about that," Mitch said and sighed. "Sort of. He asked if it could have been faked." He waved his glass in the air. "I know, I know. I told him there was no way Jennifer and Karl could have done something like that with what little equipment they had. But I could tell by the way he was looking around in the satellite truck that he wasn't convinced. Maybe he thinks we can do special effects in there."

Sandy threw her head back and groaned. "That is so stupid."

"Well, he's feeling a little desperate because not even a faked video would explain what else we found." Mitch pulled her closer. "God, I hate telling you this."

She swiveled to face him. "Tell me."

"You know that deputy we found?" Mitch said. "He somehow got wedged into the side of the hill. Tree roots were growing into him." His hands came up to his face. "I thought that was the most horrible thing I'd ever seen, and then I saw worse. We found the ranger's wife. She was in her car, buried in the ground. Same situation with the roots."

"The ranger's wife!" she cried. "I met her at the Xenon Club."

She listened, heart pounding wildly, as Mitch recounted the shocking discovery in the meadow outside Knox's cabin, a short distance from the edge of the aspen forest.

When he finished, she whispered, "You didn't see it yourself, did you? The Root Witch?"

He shuddered. "I'm pretty sure I did while I was looking for Jen and Karl."

"Good," she said, and she didn't realize she'd said it out loud, because Mitch was looking at her, mouth slightly open.

"Good?" he repeated.

Sandy had planned on telling Mitch, but now that the moment had arrived, the words stuck in her throat. She drained the rest of her wine for courage.

"If you saw it, you'll believe me then," she said. "The Root Witch almost killed me when I was ten years old."

Now that she'd confessed the story to her psychologist, Celeste, the telling of it came easier and faster. When she finally finished, he rubbed her ankles and said, "So, it's been around since then."

They sat in silence, staring across the room, each lost in their own thoughts. After a few minutes, Mitch shook his head and looked at Sandy.

"I've got some more bad news. Sheriff Wagoner confiscated the video tape in the satellite truck. I pushed back as much as I could, but he said it was evidence in a criminal matter, and if I didn't hand it over, he'd arrest me. We'll have to let Brody sort that out when he gets back."

And that was it. No questions, no doubts. Mitch's belief in her story made her take a deep breath in relief. Sandy patted the white plastic bag next to her. The forest, and its horrors, felt very far away.

"I've got the copy here," she said.

"What are you going to do with it?" Mitch asked.

Sandy shrugged. "It's not mine. It belongs to the station. I'll give it to Brody when he gets back. He can see it for himself. The news director, too, and probably the general manager. It's their decision. But Mitch, what are we going to do? About the Root Witch?"

"We're going to stay the hell away from it, for starters," Mitch said. "It's not our problem."

"Someone has to do something," she said stubbornly.

Mitch drained the rest of his beer. "That someone doesn't have to be you. You've already been through enough as it is, and we've both seen what that thing can do. I'll call Knox tomorrow and see what he has in mind. The sheriff might not be willing to act, but Knox might. After all, that monster killed his wife."

Now that she'd stopped denying the Root Witch, she felt a responsibility to alert the public. That was her job as a journalist. But one glance at Mitch's tired face and the hard set of his jaw told her this wasn't the time to talk to him about her responsibility. But that wouldn't stop her from coming up with a plan when her brain wasn't on overload and the sedatives wore off.

After a long, hot shower together, they watched the ten o'clock news in bed. Mitch was asleep, snoring gently, before the second commercial break. The weekend weatherman, gesturing dramatically at the radar map, predicted a midnight end to the storm system over the Wasatch Front, with warmer temperatures Sunday and Monday.

As Sandy tried to sleep, her thoughts kept returning to Jennifer's final screams and Karl's anguished wail, punctuated by images of Knox's wife trapped in her car, stabbed through with roots. What the Root Witch was, or why it killed, was something she and Mitch hadn't had the energy to discuss, but she supposed it didn't matter.

What mattered was the Root Witch existed. They'd caught it on video tape.

Chapter 35

It was Sunday, a bright and beautiful morning, but the improvement in the weather had done little to lift Sandy's spirits.

The three-quarter-inch tape, with the gruesome images that haunted her through the night, was stashed in the top drawer of her desk, unlabeled. Sandy sat at the assignment desk, where the managers had left her.

Jack came scurrying in, showered and wearing a long-sleeved polo shirt in maroon and yellow. He'd raced home the second she walked in, and now he was back, fidgety with too much coffee.

He sat down next to Sandy, leaned over, and whispered, "Can you believe it? What we saw? It's incredible. I mean, that tape has got to be worth a million dollars. Jennifer's dead, for sure, but do you think Karl survived? We didn't see him die. Mitch said they're still looking for them, so it's possible, right? That he's alive? It would be amazing if we had a survivor to interview."

Sandy stared at Jack, her reaction dulled by the blue tablet she'd taken earlier—the one from the little plastic bottle she'd picked up at the hospital pharmacy.

"I don't see how that's possible, Jack," she said.

She watched as he rubbed the side of his face, frowning as his fingers encountered stubble. In his eagerness to get back to the station, he'd forgotten to shave.

"This is bigger than the Big Foot film," he said. "Way bigger. Huge. There's never been anything like it."

No, there hadn't. And whatever that thing was, it was still down there among the trees. Her only comfort was the Root Witch was confined to the aspen forest, hours south.

Jack snapped his fingers inches from her face. "Hello? I don't need to call another ambulance, do I? You scared the crap out of me with that fainting fit you threw yesterday. Mitch is around, isn't he? Do you want me to find him?"

That was as close to an expression of concern as Jack had ever voiced. Before he could act, she said, louder and sharper than she intended, "I'm fine."

Jack smirked. "Fine for now, San-dee, but you're about to get your ass handed to you. If I were you, I'd be packing up my stuff so you're ready when they escort you out of here. We have a bet going. Me and the other producers. You're not going to last 'til noon."

Someone cleared their throat behind them. It was Brody, the managing editor.

Jack whirled around.

"You're back," Sandy said, glancing up in surprise.

"They cleared the roads sooner than we thought." Brody gave a weary smile and wiggled the back of Sandy's chair. "Let's talk about what happened over the weekend. Jack, can you cover the desk until we're done?"

Jack drummed his fingers on the desk. "Yes, sir. That's what I've been doing for the last twenty-four hours, but I'm sure Sandy will tell you all that."

Despite the sedative, Sandy felt her jaw muscles spasm. Leave it to Jack to start in the first chance he got.

Snatching the video tape from the desk, she followed Brody into his office and hovered just inside the door as he shrugged out of his ski jacket.

"Aren't you going to sit down?" he asked, pulling off his beanie.

She perched on the edge of the chair, back straight, clutching the tape to her stomach. Then she waited, feeling her sluggish heartbeat start to speed up.

Brody scraped a hand through his hair. "Jesus, Sandy. I can only imagine what you've been through. Do they have any idea what happened to Karl and Jennifer?"

Sandy started to reply. Instead, she leaned over and placed the video tape on his desk and slid it across the wood. "It's on here."

Brody stared at the tape as if it might sprout teeth and bite him. "What's on there?"

"I sent Jennifer and Karl to the aspen forest near Fish Lake," she said. "We were getting calls from hikers saying they'd seen the Root Witch and—"

Brody held up a hand. "Why did you send two reporters?"

Sandy pressed her hands into her thighs and took a deep breath. It was going to take a long time to explain the complicated events of Friday and Saturday, to answer all the questions Brody would have. And she'd probably have to do it all again when the news director showed up.

"We were down a photographer," she began. "Karl was done with his morning shift, and he offered to go as Jennifer's photographer. I really wanted the story for our shows on Halloween. I thought it would be a ratings winner."

Brody picked up the tape and squinted at the label. "I'm assuming Karl shot this tape. Where was it found?"

"At the bottom of the forest," she said. "Not far from where they found the dead body of the deputy who went missing."

Brody pushed the tape into the deck on the low credenza. As soon as Sandy heard the familiar *kerchunk*, she lurched to her feet.

"I can't watch it again," she said. "I'm sorry." Before waiting for a reply, she fled the room, closing the door behind her.

Chapter 36

By Sandy's calculation, Brody had viewed the video twice from start to finish, and then the last three minutes at least a dozen times. He'd watched with the volume turned up, and Jennifer's last words and screams penetrated the plate glass separating his office from the newsroom.

He finally emerged, gray-faced, and called for Sandy to join him again.

"Jesus H. Christ, what did I just see?" he said, collapsing into his chair.

She swallowed. Words were bubbling up in her throat, and there was no way to stop them. "I knew it was there," she said.

Brody's head snapped up.

"The Root Witch," she added, looking at him to make sure he understood. "I knew it was there, and I sent them anyway."

The story came out in a jumble, as Brody stared with widening eyes. She explained what happened to her as a child in the forest, the attack that left her nearly dead, the years thinking her memories were defective, and finally, her big confession. She had sent Jennifer, Karl, and Mitch to the forest, not just because the Root Witch was a story worth ratings gold, but because she wanted to prove she hadn't imagined it.

"If I were you, I'd want proof too," Brody said. "I saw it on video, and I still can't believe it. What the hell is that thing? How come we're just now finding out about it?" He sounded shaken.

"I don't know," she said. "Mitch has more tape. Of what the Root Witch did to that deputy. They found another body too, belonging to the wife of the ranger. I haven't seen the video. I don't think I want to."

"There's more tape?" Brody gasped. "This is unbelievable. Listen, the news director should know what's going on. I need to call Gus at home. Can you give me a few minutes?"

She was back at the assignment desk for less than five minutes when Jack hunched over the phone and began talking in a loud voice. "No, you're really going to want this as an exclusive," he said. "I'm telling you, I've seen it myself, and I am not exaggerating. Oh, it's way better than the Patterson-Gimlin film. You can actually *see* something. Of course, man. Of course. I'll talk to the news director myself as soon as he gets in. We're tight. Okay, bye."

Enough of the sedative had worn off that Sandy felt her eyes bulge. "Are you talking to the network? Didn't Brody tell you never to do that again?"

Jack swung his legs up onto the desk. His pants hiked up, revealing thin hairy ankles. "Someone had to do their job and tell the network," he said. "I have a buddy on the desk in Los Angeles. They're all over it. The executive producer is going to call Gus as soon as he gets in."

His eyes drifted upward and widened. "Oh hey, Brody. I was just coming to see you."

When Sandy turned, she saw Brody standing behind her, jaw working, arms crossed across his chest. How long had he been there?

Brody said, "Jack, I need to see you in my office."

Jack turned to Sandy. "He's giving me your job now," he whispered, then strode confidently toward Brody's door.

The conversation lasted twelve minutes. Sandy knew this because she marked the time when Jack entered the managing editor's office. When he reappeared, he brushed past her and threw himself into his chair, scowling.

The blinds in Brody's office were halfway open, and she could see him on the phone. There was no telling how long he'd be, and she had to pee. On the way to the bathroom, she stopped to talk to an editor who just arrived for his shift. He asked for an update on Jennifer and Karl, but she lied and said she didn't have any news.

The first thing she noticed when she returned to the newsroom was Jack's desk. The top was clean and clear. The usual pile of scripts and wire copy was gone. Not even a coffee cup, and no sign of Jack. She peered inside Brody's office, but Jack wasn't there either. An envelope addressed to Brody was taped to the door.

She pulled it off, knocked, and went inside without waiting for a reply.

"I think this is from Jack," she said, passing the envelope to Brody.

Brody's eyebrows shot up. After he read the note, he slapped it face down on his desk and said, "Well, well, well. It looks like Jack has left us."

The announcement made her start. "You mean he quit? But why?"

She could tell by the look on his face—pinched lips and narrowed eyes—that Brody was furious.

"Because he overstepped and called the network about the Root Witch tape," he said. "Now they're all over us, and we haven't decided what to do with it yet. It's not like we catch monsters on video every day, so this one requires some serious discussion. Jack's too much of a liability, so I sidelined him to overnights. And I really, *really* didn't like the way he was talking to you when I came in today. So, I made him associate producer on the morning show. Guess he couldn't hack it."

Jack would have hated that, she knew. His ego couldn't withstand the demotion. Not when he imagined himself the hot new producer.

"Won't that be a problem?" she asked worriedly. "Jack said his dad is a general manager in San Francisco who's friends with our GM. Won't he be angry?"

Brody scoffed. "No. Not at all. Jack's here because his father knows he's a spoiled brat. He sent him here for some tough love."

That took a moment to register. Then, Sandy remembered Jack standing next to her in the feed room as the video played. "But Brody, Jack saw the tape."

Brody shrugged. "He did, but that doesn't mean anyone is going to believe him." He frowned. "Sandy, let me worry about Jack. To be honest, I'm more concerned about you at the moment. You went to the hospital. Should you go home? Get some rest?"

His solicitousness caught her by surprise. She had expected to be fired. Or suspended without pay, at the very least. But not this.

When she didn't answer, holding back tears, Brody came around the desk and stood in front of her. "The news director and the GM are on their way in. They'd like to talk with you, but only if you're feeling up to it."

"I can stay," she said, legs weak with relief. She still had a job. Brody wasn't angry. And if he wasn't, the news director wouldn't be either. Everyone knew Brody really ran the newsroom.

"Good," Brody said. "Can you do me a favor and ask Mitch to see me? And tell him to bring all the video he has."

She found Mitch in the darkened control room, sitting at the graphics machine, working on a special report. No matter what, even a Root Witch, the news machine kept churning. After she'd relayed Brody's message, Mitch pulled her into his arms. There was nobody around at that hour to see them.

Mitch felt warm and solid. "How did it go? With Brody?"

"He hasn't fired me yet, but the day isn't over," she said.

"If he was going to, he would have by now," Mitch replied with a grim laugh. "Brody doesn't play cat and mouse. He just goes in for the kill."

Chapter 37

Without the video tape to show Bill Skeene, Knox had no proof of what he'd seen in the satellite truck.

Sheriff Wagoner had confiscated the tape.

Once the sheriff considered his re-election, his attitude toward the incident had taken a rapid and dramatic turn. How he viewed the events privately, Knox didn't know, but the sheriff was now blaming the deaths on an enormous bear he said wandered into the forest from the mountains. It didn't seem to matter the monstrous shadow they'd watched on the video didn't begin to qualify as an animal, never mind a lumbering bear, or that the victims had suffered none of the telltale injuries of a bear attack. But that was the sheriff's story. He'd keep repeating it to his dubious officers, and if they wanted to keep their jobs, they'd keep their opinions to themselves. After all, none of the deputies had seen what was on the tape, and they probably never would.

The lies stoked Knox's fury.

He drove to Bill's office in Richfield, hardly remembering how he got there. Knox pounded Bill's desk. Kicked the walls. Threw a chair.

"How do you explain what happened to my wife?" he thundered.

Bill shook his head sadly. "Sinkhole. We're having a geologist from the university come take a look."

"We have to close the forest," Knox demanded. "Or this will keep happening!"

Bill repeated his condolences about the loss of his wife, but still, he refused to budge. "You take as much time off as you need, Knox. We've got a generous bereavement policy, so don't come back until you're ready. You let me handle things for a while."

Knox gripped the edge of the table, as if Bill meant to eject him from the room. "No, I don't want to do that. The Root Witch killed her, and you know it."

Bill shook his head sadly for a second time. "Now, see? That's what I'm trying to tell you, Knox. That's the grief talking. The Root Witch is just a story, and now that Halloween's come and gone, all that nonsense is going to die down until next year. You haven't been around long enough to know how it works."

So, Bill knew something was amiss in the forest and had even come to mark the strange cycles of the Root Witch, but when Knox pointed that out, Bill went red in the face.

"It's no big mystery, Knox," he said. "Most visitors come in the summer and Halloween, and so many of 'em come because of that darned story. The first little noise they hear, here we go again. Someone says the Root Witch tried to get them."

"But what about the deer?" Knox said. He was so angry his voice shook.

Bill's face had almost returned to its normal shade of beige. "We're overrun with them, Knox," he said. "They got all kinds of diseases, and not enough to eat some years."

In the end, Bill made two concessions. He couldn't force Knox to take a leave of absence, and, somewhat grudgingly, he agreed to let Knox post a warning to visitors about a predator in the forest. Knox compromised by agreeing to take the rest of the week off.

Returning to the cabin was out of the question. Not with all those people still there, investigating Colleen's death. He'd probably never return, but he didn't have to think about that now. Not knowing what else to do, he drove to Loa.

It was a small town, and word of Colleen had spread fast. When Knox pulled into the cafe on Main Street for a cup of coffee, Becky, the young waitress, rushed over to say how sorry she was to hear about what happened.

Lee Bradley walked in a few minutes later and joined him at the counter. The man looked shaken. "What the hell is happening around here?" he said. "First that deputy. Then those news people. Now your wife? And what's this about a sinkhole?"

Luckily, Bradley had no expectation of an answer, because Knox had none to give.

Bradley waived Becky over. "Get this man a hamburger. He looks like he's about to keel over." When Knox shook his head, Bradley raised his hand in the air. "Scratch that. Make it a piece of that apple cobbler, will you?"

When Becky had her back turned, Bradley removed a flask from his pocket and splashed amber liquid into Knox's coffee mug. Knox drank it gratefully, feeling the burn in his throat.

They sat in silence for a long time, Bradley watching as Knox picked at the cobbler. When he finally finished, a bit of energy had returned.

Bradley cleared his throat. "I'm really sorry about your wife. If there's anything you need, just let me know."

"You know of any place to stay around here?" Knox said. The one motel in town had a No Vacancy sign out front. With his luck, he'd have to drive twenty miles to find a room.

Bradley stood. "Sure do. My place. I've got a nice big guest room, and you're welcome to it for as long as you like."

Knox was a wreck, and he knew it. His back ached where Mitch had rammed into him, and he wasn't thinking straight. His thoughts jumped back and forth between Colleen and the ways in which he might avenge her death.

He nodded and followed Bradley to his ranch, their trucks rumbling over dirt roads into the backcountry. Bradley grabbed a bottle of whiskey, and the two of them sat in chairs next to the creek. A cold breeze swept past them, stirring the tall grass. Bradley lit a fire in the pit and pretended not to notice Knox's shoulders shaking as he silently cried into his glass.

"You going to stay on the job?" Bradley tipped his head back and watched the circling birds.

"Don't know yet," Knox said finally, pulling himself together.

"What the hell, Knox. A sinkhole? I've lived here all my life and never heard of such a thing. This isn't Florida."

"Or Texas," Knox said glumly. "Happens there too."

"I don't get it. You want to tell me what happened?"

Knox drank his whiskey, anger tensing his body. "You wouldn't believe me if I did."

"I might," Bradley said, raising his glass. "Especially if it has to do with that damn Root Witch. You know, I didn't used to believe in it, but after that incident with my calf, I started walking out there in the forest. I was determined to find that fence you said wasn't there. I never did find it. But something found *me*." He bent over and lifted his jeans, revealing a thick red scar around his ankles. "It came out of the ground and grabbed me. Thought I was going to have a heart attack. Luckily, I never go anywhere without a knife, so

I hacked at it. Managed to do a number on my leg anyway. Luckily, I wasn't far from the truck. I haven't been back since. So yeah, if you say you think the Root Witch got your wife, I'd be inclined to believe you."

Knox slumped in his Adirondack chair—physically and emotionally exhausted. It took him a moment to register the full impact of the rancher's admission. Another local had encountered the creature in the forest and wasn't afraid to admit it.

Bradley topped off his whiskey, regarding Knox with a hard to read expression. "What does your boss say?" he finally said.

Knox sighed heavily. "The usual bullshit. There's no such thing as the Root Witch. That's the sheriff's line too. I've got to do something because they won't, and putting up a bunch of warning signs about a bear isn't enough."

"Have any ideas?"

The rancher's words penetrated Knox's tired mind, straight to the back where a plan had begun to form. A crazy plan. One that would require guts and the means to carry it off.

"I do," he said, then laid it all out to Bradley, who listened quietly as he stroked his red beard.

"That's not a problem," Bradley said. "I can help. You just have to keep your mouth shut, is all."

For a moment, Knox doubted he'd heard the rancher correctly. "You're going to help me?"

Bradley turned to face him, eyes glinting in the firelight, hands braced on his knees. "I don't see anybody else lining up. If you have any objection to us working together, now is the time to say it. But the way I see it, your plan is better than no plan, and that thing, whatever it is, needs culling."

All that was too much for Knox to digest. He wished he could express his gratitude properly but was too overwhelmed by the unexpected offer from a man who, not long ago, didn't seem to like him much. That's what happens when you have a common enemy.

Chapter 38

On Monday, the news director announced to the entire staff that authorities presumed Karl and Jennifer were dead. The search for their bodies would continue.

Behind closed doors, in a meeting with Gus Durham, the news director assured her no one at the station held her responsible for the assignment that ended in the brutal deaths of her co-workers. His face still had a stunned look about it. Gus got his start in news as an anchor, and he still looked the part, with a chiseled jaw and dark helmet hair.

"You were just doing your job," he said several times. Then, Gus had a surprise. "We're not going to air the video on any of our newscasts. It's too violent, for one thing, and it requires context, for another. Instead, we've decided to make a documentary, and we'd like you to be a part of it. As a producer." He hesitated. "And as a subject, if you're willing to share your story about the Root Witch."

Sandy had no experience working on a documentary or talking in front of the camera, but she understood both would require dredging up painful episodes in her life. There would be no getting away from the monster for a long time.

"Can I have some time to think about it?" she said.

"There's an Emmy in it for you," Gus said. When he saw her expression, he rushed to add, "If you choose to do it, of course. You'll also need a more regular schedule than you have now. Brody's shuffling some people around and making you producer of the noon show."

She nodded, hardly hearing him. "What are they doing down there to protect people? Have they closed the forest?"

"Not that we've heard," Gus said. "It's business as usual, with some new signs warning people about a bear in the area."

Same as Mitch had told her the night before. But now she was stone cold sober, and the words hit her like a slap across the face. She leapt to her feet.

"The sheriff saw the tape," she cried. "He was in the satellite truck and watched the whole thing. How could he say *that* was a bear?"

Gus shook his head. "When we do the documentary, we'll get him in front of the camera and demand an answer."

"But that will be too late," Sandy said.

Too late. Too late. Someone else will die.

Those were her thoughts as she waited in Mitch's truck. The station had given them both the rest of the week off to recuperate from the travails of Halloween weekend. Both had readily accepted. Except for two weeks for vacation, the station rarely gave anyone paid time off, but Brody had insisted.

Sitting alone in the truck, feeling the weak autumn sun on her face, had given her time to think. About the Root Witch, and how much she hated it. Hated it as much as she feared it. And the sheriff—sworn to protect the public—every bit as self-serving and stubborn as the mayor in *Jaws* who refused to close the beaches.

She didn't know if the ranger planned to do anything. Mitch hadn't been able to reach Knox. That morning, she called Janelle, the dispatcher in Richfield, and asked if she knew anything, but for once, Janelle clammed up, then said in a business-like tone, "No comment."

If the menace in the forest was a dangerous animal, she'd ask Mitch to teach her how to use a rifle, then hunt it down. If it was something like a demon in *The Exorcist*, she'd find a priest who could send it back to hell. But the Root Witch was something else entirely.

For all its mysterious power, it belonged to the aspen forest far away—danger as remote as great white sharks or Nile crocodiles. If she kept her distance, the Root Witch couldn't hurt her again, except in her dreams.

But the forest remained a beautiful and dangerous place, especially in the fall when the leaves turned to gold, luring tourists unaware of the danger that lurked within its groves.

A cold tingle ran down her spine. If no one else was going to do anything, she could.

There was only one way to deal with an evil forest.

Chapter 39

On Wednesday, after a fierce debate Sandy eventually won, they were on their way to central Utah. An old army chest filled with beer and liquor bottles, cushioned with towels, sat in the bed of the truck. Before they'd left, Mitch installed the camper shell he used on his weekend getaway trips.

Mitch's eyes darted in her direction, and when she asked him if anything was wrong, he said she looked like a teenager. Without makeup, her hair in a ponytail, and a green sweatshirt with rainbow stripes, she supposed she did. It was no accident. If a cop stopped them for any reason, she wanted to look as innocent as possible. Mitch was wearing his usual jeans and a nondescript brown shirt, less conspicuous than his usual plaids.

Sandy was quiet on the first part of their journey, fighting an eruption of nerves that flared as soon as they'd pulled out of the driveway. She'd never gotten a traffic ticket and now was committing a criminal act that could lead to serious consequences. Everything she'd worked for would be lost. Her mother would be right—Sandy would be going to hell. If they were caught.

Despite the familiar anxiety building in her chest, she was determined to end the Root Witch once and for all. Lives were at stake.

Their first stop was the west side of Salt Lake to buy bottles of a potent grain alcohol. Sandy stayed in the truck. In Provo, Mitch purchased a few quarts of kerosene and heavy-duty tape at a hardware store, while she walked down the street to a Kmart and bought cotton dish towels and a pair of scissors because they forgot to bring them from home.

As they approached the forest, Sandy was first to spot the bright yellow sign:

> *WARNING*
> *BEAR IN AREA*

The signs were all over the place, and as far-fetched and ridiculous as they were, they seemed to have had some effect because they didn't see a single hiker or car parked in the turnouts along Highway 25. They turned into Doctor Creek Campground, which was nearly empty except for two RVs. No sign of people.

"They probably went fishing," Mitch said.

"That's good," Sandy said. The fewer people, the better. She sounded more confident than she felt. It was impossible to breathe normally, surrounded by the trees, knowing something was out there. The Root Witch could ambush them anytime. Mitch's solid presence was comforting, but he was every bit as vulnerable to the killer that lurked in the forest as she was.

Mitch parked at the far end of the lot, the furthest away from the RVs. In the camper, curtains closed, they assembled the Molotov cocktails. It was cramped inside and an awkward business sitting on the hard truck bed. Sandy held the bottles as Mitch did the pouring. She mopped up the spilled liquid with a towel.

Sandy didn't know the first thing about Molotov cocktails, but Mitch did. He and his brothers made them as teenagers to lob them at an old barn that needed demolishing. A Vietnam vet who worked on the ranch taught them how to make them and swore a grain and kerosene blend worked best.

"I imagine just using gasoline works fine, but I don't want to take a chance," Mitch said.

When the fumes made their throats itch and eyes run, Mitch cracked the windows, and they sucked in the fresh air. Sandy cut the dish towels into strips, and Mitch stuffed them in the bottles to use as wicks, taping them into place. When they were done, they returned the bottles to the crates, stuffing dish towels between them to prevent them from clinking together.

Mitch wasn't sure if they'd made enough to burn down the forest. He didn't know how to do that calculation. And there was no telling how far they'd get before someone caught them or fire crews arrived.

As agreed, Mitch drove down the winding road, to the forest floor where Jennifer and Karl were attacked, where the deputy's body had been found, and where a deer had dropped from a tree. They didn't know if the Root Witch had a special place it called home, but it seemed most active there, so that was as good a place as any to start.

It was also the most remote and isolated part of the forest. There were no cars, no people. The news vehicle that Jennifer and Karl had driven was gone, collected as evidence. The owner of the old Jeep Mitch borrowed must have finally got around to retrieving it.

Turning around in the dirt lot, Mitch headed back the way they'd come and, after a hundred yards or so, stopped in the middle of the road. Neither dared risk straying too far from the truck in case the Root Witch suddenly appeared and they needed to make a fast escape. They didn't need to be in the middle of the forest to accomplish their goal, surrounded by trees and dry brush, and Mitch had a good throwing arm.

"I can't believe we're doing this," Mitch said, staring at the box of matches in his hands.

For one awful moment, Sandy feared he might change his mind, but then he shook his head and gave a grim laugh. "I guess this makes me Clyde to your Bonnie."

He had a point. She'd talked him into it, made him her accomplice. If Mitch had his way, they would have stayed in Salt Lake, far away from the forest, hoping Knox would eventually figure out a way to deal with the monster.

But she couldn't trust Knox or anyone else to do the right thing. The only thing. It was her responsibility, and there wasn't any time to waste. After so many sightings, attacks, and deaths, she believed the Root Witch was just getting started.

Sandy joined Mitch a distance from the truck and its gas tank.

"This is crazy, you know," Mitch said.

Sandy said nothing, listening to the dry branches rattle in the trees, the constant rustling of the leaves. The same sounds etched into her brain sixteen years ago, her child's voice screaming as she was lifted into the air. And then, the indescribable pain as her small body slammed into a tree.

"I know," she said.

Many times on the long drive, she wondered if she'd lost her mind. But now that she was surrounded by all those ghost trees with their terrible white trunks, she knew she wasn't crazy at all. Just desperate.

Somewhere, deep in the grove, twigs snapped. Her heart thudded wildly, and she heard Mitch's swift intake of breath. A moment later, a deer stepped out into a clearing and froze.

"The animals," she whispered. Her blood ran cold. She'd forgotten the deer and elk.

"They can run," Mitch said. "Let's get this over with."

Sandy watched the deer race away, then retied her hair. It had come loose during the long ride, and she needed to see what she was doing. Mitch held out the first bottle while she lit the wick. Then, he hurled it toward a pile of brush at the base of an aspen.

Time seemed to slow as Mitch threw one Molotov cocktail after another, aiming where the trees were most densely packed. Only when she saw the flames shoot up the trunks and the air began to thicken with smoke did she think their plan had a chance of working.

Mitch's face was pale in the golden light, sweat glistening on his forehead. He was staring behind her, mouth slightly open. Then, he lunged.

"Get in the truck!" he shouted.

She spun around. An enormous shadow was hurtling toward them. It looked more human than she remembered, a misshapen tree, limbs distorted, eyeless. She could smell wet dirt and a sickly, musty stench of death.

"Get in the truck!" Mitch yelled again, and that time, adrenalin flooded her legs.

She raced toward the cab.

Sandy was halfway there when the ground under her began to move, roots rising through the dirt. She tripped and fell, skidding forward on her stomach and scraping her chin. Sandy scrambled to her feet. But just as she'd taken the first step to run, roots began to circle her ankles. One slithered up her leg and wrapped around her waist, the roots pulling her back and down, into a hole of loose earth.

"Mitch!" she gasped, but he couldn't hear her pitiful cry for help.

He was already in the truck, waiting for her to join him—he couldn't see the Root Witch's silent attack. Sandy began to hyperventilate, chest heaving, panic paralyzing her muscles.

She had to move. If she didn't, she'd disappear forever into the earth. She pictured herself wedged next to a tree, dirt filling her nose and mouth. Sandy whimpered, wondering how long it would take to die, smothered by the Root Witch.

She thought of Colleen. Mitch said she'd fought back. And she died. Sandy would just have to fight back harder.

The Root Witch was not going to win a second time. Little Sandy was helpless. Grown up Sandy was anything but.

The Root Witch could go fuck itself.

Sandy grabbed the sinewy tentacle around her waist, pried it off, then ripped it away. She kicked her legs, bashing them together until the roots around her ankles lost their hold. Heart slamming in her chest, she pushed to her feet, ran to the truck, and dove in, pulling the door shut. And then the truck was speeding up the road. When she looked into the side mirror, the Root Witch had vanished.

The smoke was just beginning to reach the upper part of the forest, but still, they heard no fire engines, and so far, they hadn't seen a single official vehicle.

Mitch sat gripping the wheel, breathing through gritted teeth. She'd never seen him look so tense.

"I can't believe you fought it off. While your useless boyfriend was twenty feet away."

"You didn't know," Sandy said quietly. "Another few seconds, and I'm sure you'd have figured it out."

Sandy still sensed the monster's presence, just as she had all those years ago, watching her. Waiting. The thing her mother said didn't exist, a thing she'd made up, had attacked her twice. But this time, she wasn't helpless, and she wasn't alone. She had Mitch. And she had fire.

"Let's finish up and get out of here," she said.

Before I lose my nerve.

Before all her courage drained from her body. Before the Root Witch could hunt her down again and kill her.

There weren't many safe, out-of-the-way places to park and throw their crude firebombs, so they stopped along the main road, waited for a few cars to pass, and began tossing Molotavs in both directions, expecting to see a Forest Service vehicle appear any moment. Sandy prayed if one did, Knox would be at the wheel.

As she scanned the highway in both directions, insides like cold jelly, she felt a rumble deep inside the ground. And then the pavement was cracking, and roots slithered out, snaking toward them. The trees moaned and leaned across the road, nearly blocking out the blue sky. The roar of the rustling leaves filled her ears. The monster made the earth groan as it sent its roots to take them.

She lit the bottle Mitch held, snatched it from his hands, and threw it at the approaching roots. When the bottle hit, exploding, the thick tendrils snapped back, charred, curling in on themselves. From behind those blackened bits, more pushed through the broken asphalt. Heart racing, she collided with Mitch at the crate as they both grabbed for the same bottle. Mitch was shouting at her to get in the truck, but she needed to stay. She had a job to do. Sandy counted three more bottles. Big ones. Liquor bottles.

"Aim for the cracks," she shouted.

Mitch lit the wick himself and hurled the bottle at the widening fissure. Sandy watched, hands thrown in front of her face against the heat, as the ball of flame expanded. Two more bottles quickly followed.

The ground heaved beneath her feet, as powerful as a violent earthquake, knocking her to the ground. Mitch yanked her to her feet, and together, they stumbled to the truck. Mitch threw the truck into reverse, and they shot backwards into the smoke. As they raced away, Sandy could see flames engulfing both sides of the forest. When they finally reached the campground, a small group of people were clustered at the pay phone. A man was gesturing wildly as he spoke into the receiver. The others were watching the fire in the distance, hands pressed to their mouths.

Mitch sped away from the highway, down a dirt road toward the blue water of the lake.

Sandy was half laughing, half crying as she looked in the rearview mirror. The flames had reached the upper canopy of the forest. She thought she could see twisting black shadows. Strange noises penetrated the closed windows.

The sound of the Root Witch screaming, she hoped.

Chapter 40

Knox woke, confused, head pounding. The bed wasn't familiar, and he was alone. Then he remembered. He'd slept over at Lee Bradley's house, and Colleen was dead. The tears he'd shed in the middle of the night accounted for his sticky face, and the liquor explained the hangover.

He swung his legs over the side of the bed, the top of his skull throbbing so hard it felt like it was about to pop off. Knox stared at the clock on the nightstand, but the numbers didn't register. Was it one in the morning, or one in the afternoon? He never slept late, and if he had, surely Bradley would have pounded on his door to rouse him.

A large glass of water was on the table. It hadn't been there when he'd stumbled to bed. Knox drank it down thirstily. The guest room had a large en suite bathroom, so he took a long hot shower and tried to remember everything that happened the day before. Before he drank away his short-term memory. By the time he was dressed, he recalled the rancher's offer of help and wondered if Bradley would change his mind now that he'd sobered up.

Knox went into the hallway. Voices and the aroma of meat on a grill came from the other side of the house. He crossed the living room with its high open beam ceiling, through a dining room filled with knotty pine furniture, and into the kitchen. A middle-aged woman with a pleasant brown face glanced over at him and smiled.

"Well look who's finally up," Bradley said, sitting at the far end of the table. He pointed at the chair closest to Knox. "Gloria's making us lunch. Breakfast for you. And you're in for a real treat because she's the best cook around for a hundred miles. Sometimes, I don't know why I bother going into the café in Loa. Well, probably because of that pretty Becky, if I'm being honest."

Knox sat, rubbing the side of his face. "Half the day is gone," he said in wonder.

"Well, one of us has been busy," Bradley said. "Once we've eaten, we got shit to do. I've got everything ready. All we need to do is get ourselves to the airport."

Gloria set a steaming mug of coffee next to him. Usually, he drank it black, but she'd added cream, sugar, and cinnamon, and on that morning, it tasted perfect.

"You got a plane?" Knox said, stunned. "Already?"

Bradley shrugged. "I've had it for a few years. Fly it myself. Now the other thing. I had to drive all the way to the feed store in Richfield this morning, but they had exactly what we needed, so all we gotta do is eat this delicious lunch Gloria's fixed and get on our way."

Now that his plan was about to become reality, Knox was feeling more than a bit stunned. If Bill Skeene ever found out, he'd lose his job for sure. And he wasn't sure it would work. At least, not with just one pass over the forest.

"We're going to have to keep doing this, you know," Knox said. "For as long as it takes."

"You explained all that," Bradley said. "Many times, in case you don't remember. Also, you shot down my idea of burning the whole place down, so this is what we're left with."

Knox shot a panicked glance at Gloria, but the woman seemed too busy loading up their plates to pay much attention to their conversation.

Bradley flapped a dismissive hand at him. "Don't worry about her. Gloria doesn't speak much English." He paused, grinning. "Or at least, she pretends not to. Not that I care. The woman is a jewel, and if she weren't married already, I'd marry her."

She bustled over and set down a plate in front of Knox. Steak. Scrambled eggs with cheese. Refried beans, and a flour tortilla slathered with butter. His stomach grumbled.

Without further conversation, the two men ate. Halfway through his meal, Knox felt a stab of guilt for enjoying food so soon after Colleen's death. What kind of man did that? A hungry man. A man who needed energy to see his crazy plan through. He was filled with trepidation. His plan wasn't a bad one, but it would have no immediate impact. There was no telling how long it might take to get the results he hoped for, and in the meantime, the monster, the Root Witch, would continue to threaten visitors. All because he lacked the guts to do anything more destructive. He was getting the animals to do his dirty work.

When they finished lunch, they walked to Bradley's truck. The rancher stopped at the long bed and lifted a tarp. "This was the only brand they carried," he said.

Knox glanced at the fifty-pound bags of deer and elk pellets, then looked away. "They'll work," he said.

On the short drive to the airport, Bradley turned uncharacteristically chatty. Knox hardly knew the man, but he suspected the bearded rancher was trying to distract him from his grief. His body felt oddly heavy and stiff. He half listened as Bradley went on about how he'd found Gloria working at the Mexican restaurant in Loa and convinced her to come work for him as a housekeeper and cook.

There wasn't much to the small airport outside town. A few hangars. Several rickety metal towers, one festooned with an orange windsock. A runway streaked black around the edges, not even a fence to separate it from the endless expanse of dirt fields and tumbleweeds. If it weren't for the mountain range, it would be easy to lose one's sense of direction in the wide-open space.

Bradley's plane was a single-engine four-seater Cessna. They loaded as many bags as the plane could safely carry. Knox sat in the back seat and cut off the top of the feed bags with scissors while Bradley inspected the plane and checked the fuel.

They put on headphones just before take-off. Knox didn't need any instructions. He'd grown up flying with his father.

The plane raced down the runway and climbed into the deep blue sky. Over the microphone, Bradley said, "You were pretty shitfaced last night, so I just want to get this straight in my head. We're going to drop those food pellets into the forest, and that will attract more deer and elk and get them to hang around. And because they love nothing more than eating, they'll chomp on the aspen shoots too, and the forest won't be able to replace the old dying trees. If we're lucky, there will be so many deer and elk, the Root Witch won't be able to kill them all."

"That's about it," Knox said. His heart sank, hearing his words repeated in a sober state. It sounded absurd.

"How long do you think all that is going to take?" Bradley said.

"Too long," Knox replied, staring at the steel bucket at his feet. Bradley had warned him it would be an awkward business throwing the feed out the window.

"Hey Knox," Bradley said. "There's something ahead. Looks like smoke."

Knox peered out the side window, squinting. He could see it too—gray columns rising into the air. An electric prickle raced down his spine. He gripped the back of the seat in front of him.

As they drew closer, Knox saw angry flames had replaced the golden canopy of the aspens. Swaths of forest were unscathed, while others glowed fiery red. Not the typical course of a wildland fire, not in calm weather. They didn't develop in random spots like that.

"Looks like someone beat us to it, buddy," Bradley said.

A chill spread across his neck. "We need to check how far this has spread. Make sure no one's in trouble."

"I can't believe I'm about to say this," Bradley said. "But should I call it in or hold off for a while?"

Knox hesitated. There was only one right answer, yet he wasn't willing to give it. The simple word stuck in his throat.

"I'll take that as hold off a minute," Bradley said. "Looks like someone did us a big fucking fat favor, Knox. You think it's just a fire bug, or someone with an agenda?"

Knox craned his neck to get a better look. Bradley was doing his best to avoid the billowing clouds of smoke as the Cessna sped toward the lake. The campground was empty. On the road, he could see two RVs and several cars headed down the main road, away from the blaze.

"Someone had to call it in already," Knox said. "There's a payphone at Doctor Creek Campground."

"Then I'm not going to bother. But where the hell are the fire crews? There's not a single engine down there."

"I'm sure they're coming," Knox said. "But you're right. Somebody started this, in different spots, and probably used an accelerant. It's burning way too fast."

A few moments later, the radio crackled to life, and Knox heard a man's voice. "Be aware of air attack crews coming into your area. There's a fast-burning fire in the aspen grove west of Fish Lake. Can you see it?"

"I'd have to be blind not to," Bradley replied.

The man in the air tower chuckled. "Lakeside Lodge is on pre-evacuation orders. Ground crews are on their way."

Minutes later, they watched an air tanker drop a load of red slurry near the area where the two TV reporters had been killed. The fire was most intense there.

That was no mistake. The only question was, who started it?

"I'm gonna give these guys some room," Bradley said.

The plane turned right over the southern tip of Fish Lake. On a small dirt road, Knox saw a truck speeding along.

"Do you have binoculars?" he said.

Bradley handed them over the seat. Heart pounding, Knox raised them to his eyes. He immediately recognized the red and white truck and the blond head inside. Mitch. A dark-haired woman was half-out of the passenger-side window, looking up at the plane. Mitch's producer girlfriend.

"You think those are our fire bugs?" Bradley asked.

In the last four days, Knox lost his wife and came to believe in a monster. He'd also devised a plan to kill it, but someone with stronger resolve had done what he'd rejected as too extreme. He'd met Sandy only once, briefly, but he'd heard her loud and clear in the satellite truck.

Bradley gave a long, low whistle. "Looks like those planes are just trying to keep the fire from spreading. Maybe your bosses decided to let it burn down."

When Knox looked out at the puffy, orange-tinged clouds, he knew the rancher had hit on the truth. Bill Skeene was calling the shots. The aspen forest, beset by overgrazing and other challenges, would eventually die without bold measures to protect it, measures Bill had no stomach to champion. Most forests burned, eventually. This fire would solve lots of problems, like the pesky legend of the Root Witch. If the blaze was kept from spreading, no structures would be lost, and the rest of the park would continue, untouched and unharmed.

Bill was probably in his office at that very moment, talking about natural cycles and forward-thinking fire management.,

Bradley followed the fast-moving truck. Then, Knox saw it slow and pull to the side of the road.

There was another road up, on the other side of the mountain, one not closed by fire crews.

It was time for a conversation.

"Can we go back?" Knox said. "There's some place I ought to be."

Chapter 41

Bradley wanted to tag along, but Knox wouldn't let him. He was grateful for all the man had done, but this next part was for him alone. The rancher followed him to his truck, rocking on the heels of his cowboy boots, scowling.

"You're coming back, right? We've got another bottle of whiskey with our names on it, and Gloria's making enchiladas."

Knox nodded, mostly out of relief because he had nowhere else to go, and he didn't like the idea of being alone. He'd have to face up to it eventually, but not yet. Bradley slapped the side of the truck before he drove off, then ambled toward the big house.

Most of Highway 25 was shut down, so he went as far as he could, then turned right onto West County Road 4528. After passing a few homes, he followed a dirt road leading into the hills. He spotted Mitch's truck parked in a clearing with a view of the forest.

Mitch and Sandy were leaning on the truck, looking across the valley at the burning forest.

"How'd you do it?" Knox said, nodding in the direction of the fire.

Mitch frowned. "Who said we did?"

"I'm not here to arrest you," Knox said. "Hell, if you did it, I don't even plan to report you." He sighed. "You saw that plane buzzing around? I was in it. Out on a little secret mission of my own, except my plan was going to take a lot longer and might not have worked. Yours seems to have worked just fine." His face was wet again. Knox had never been the crying type, and now he couldn't seem to stop.

Sandy was medium height, but Mitch towered over her. Without the heavy eye make-up she'd worn at the Xenon Club, she looked younger, more vulnerable. They both smelled strongly of smoke.

"I'm sorry about your wife," she said. "That might have been me too, when I was ten. But somehow, I survived. Maybe the Root Witch wasn't as strong as it is now." She grimaced. "Was. I hope it fucking fried."

He blinked, confused. And then he remembered the newspaper clipping he'd read, written in 1970.

"That was you? The kid who went missing during a camping trip? The one who wasn't expected to survive?"

"That was me. You can see why I might be a little pissed off about the big-bad-bear-did-it bullshit." Her head tilted as her eyes narrowed. "You didn't have anything to do with that, did you?"

He rushed to reassure her. "No, of course not. They wouldn't listen to me. The sheriff and the district manager, they thought telling the truth would make them look bad." When she'd relaxed, he added, "I'm glad. I'm glad you did it."

Mitch moved away toward the edge of the hill and stared at the haze of smoke. "Sandy thinks she heard it screaming," he said over his shoulder. "Do you think it's dead?"

"I hope so," Knox replied. "I still want to know how you started that fire." He was still a ranger, after all. There were still thousands of miles of woodland in his district.

Mitch turned around and shoved his hands into his pockets. Knox watched the couple exchange uneasy glances.

The young woman bit her lip, then nodded. Mitch went to the back of the truck and opened the glass door. Knox peered inside. It was dim, but his eyes quickly adjusted, and he saw the cans of kerosene and jugs of grain alcohol. It was only when he noticed the roll of heavy tape and strips of cloth that it all clicked into place.

"You made Molotov cocktails," he said, voice rising.

If they were ever caught, they'd go to prison. Face penalties. It would end their careers. They'd taken an enormous risk.

"You've got to get rid of this stuff," he said, panic blooming in his chest.

"Not here," Mitch said. "This is a popular spot. On a good day."

Knox thought for a moment. They needed to unload their illicit cargo, preferably on private property that would require a warrant to search. They also needed a place to shower and wash their smokey clothes. And, most importantly, they needed a place where some busybody wouldn't get suspicious and call the police. Driving all those miles to Salt Lake, carrying a load of incriminating evidence, was out of the question.

Bradley. He would help.

"I have a friend," he said. "He's a rancher. We can unload there, mix it in with his stuff. Wash out the truck. You can clean up there too."

Mitch's eyes widened. "That's a lot to ask, Knox. Won't he mind?"

"No. He was flying the plane. He's already onboard, so to speak." He managed a weak smile.

Sandy was staring at him, brown eyes glistening.

The three of them stood surveying the chaos below. The fire had filled in the untouched pockets of trees. It looked like the whole aspen forest would be lost. There was no saving it now. The planes and engines had kept the blaze from spreading. The weather was cooperating. Not even a breeze.

Mitch had an arm around Sandy's shoulders, her head leaning against him. Knox's throat spasmed. It was hard to be in the presence of a couple. He realized, with a start, that he was a widower now. A widower with responsibilities. He needed to call Colleen's brother and friends, find out when the medical examiner would release her body, and decide where to bury her. But first, he needed to help Mitch and Sandy.

"Will it grow back?" Sandy said. "The forest?"

A sudden heaviness descended, starting in his chest, radiating down into his limbs. Knox closed his eyes, imagining what the forest might look like in two years. The fire would stimulate the surviving roots to produce new sprouts. The growth would quickly spread, and within twenty years, the forest would have just as many aspens as it did before they lobbed the first Molotov cocktail. It would live on and thrive.

Knox knew the Root Witch was the product of a dying forest protecting itself. He had an agonizing choice to make—stay on as ranger and remain the forest's steward, its guardian. But if he did that, he'd spend the rest of his working life tethered to the thing that killed his wife. Or he could leave, find a new job far away. But how long before he was consumed with worry about the place he'd left behind and its innocent visitors, knowing he might have made a difference?

"Yes, it will grow back," he said, "Eventually."

Sandy winced, then looked up at Mitch. "We need to call the station," she said. "Have them send a crew to cover the fire."

The End

Author's Note

Thank you for reading *The Root Witch*! You may wonder if that aspen forest is real. It is. Today, it's known as Pando, which is Latin for "I spread." Much has written about the aspen clone forest and the efforts to save the giant single organism from dying. It's fascinating stuff. The legend of the thing that haunts it, however, is something my dark mind conjured after reading about Pando.

All those technical details about working in a local TV newsroom in 1986? All true. I got my start as a news producer in Salt Lake City. No cell phones meant no easy way to communicate with crews in the field. What happened in the story is a projection of my worst nightmares back then.

If you enjoyed the novel, I hope you consider leaving a review on Amazon and Goodreads. It doesn't have to be long. If you don't have time, please consider hitting those stars before you go. Reviews are especially important to indie authors like me. Reviews and ratings make it easier for other readers to find the book.

Thank you, and happy reading!

Debra

Some grudges never die.

Chapter 1

George Cunliffe teetered on the edge of the Lower Prestwich Bridge, his back to the yawning open-pit mine and everything that had made his life a misery.

What he did not feel was guilt. What he had done, he would do again.

He could not remember the drive to the mine, where he had left his truck with the evidence inside, or how he'd come to choose this spot to end his life.

Oblivious to the icy wind against his face, he stared down at the enormous tailings pond, the liquid a reddish orange on one side, running to a sickly yellowish green on the other.

The wind pushed the hood of his jacket from his head. Wooden floor beams of the old trestle bridge groaned beneath his feet.

Time to get going.

His hands were stiff but steady as he tested the strength of the vertical post closest to him and found it solid. After looping the old, frayed rope around the base of the iron shaft, he tied a knot, then slipped the noose around his neck. He'd intended to get right to it—leap into the air, arms spread wide, welcoming death—but he found he wanted to prolong his time on the bridge, just a little. Long enough to remember the one good, beautiful thing in his pathetic life that had brought him joy.

He picked up a small rock from the railbed and scratched words into the rusted track. When he was done, he tossed the rock into the tailings pond and admired his work.

I CURSE THIS PLACE.

Lowering himself onto the rail ties, he swung his legs over the side, one hand gripping a diagonal brace. He kicked off his boots and flicked the rope behind his neck, as if it were a scarf getting in his way. Then, before he could think about another thing, he pushed himself off.

A scream escaped his lips.

He hadn't meant to scream. The noise ended abruptly, and for one long moment, pain seared his neck as the rope tightened. His hands flew up to the noose, fingers clawing at the fibers, and then he was falling.

His body slammed into the pond's sludgy, sucking bank.

He lay there for how long?

Seconds? Minutes?

The rope had snapped, that much he understood. Even though death was not instantaneous, it was surely just a matter of minutes. His insides had to be smashed to bits. His mouth tasted like blood and metal. He stared up at the sky, the clouds turning a murky and sinister orange.

Or was the copper color of the water altering his vision?

Rain drops hit his face, sharp and distinct. By some miracle, he was still alive, standing. Floating above the tailings pond. He gazed down at his still body in wonder.

Transformed. That's what he was. His thoughts came in flashes. Images. Thinking in this strange new language.

His old life was over. His mind—the one that had been attached to his broken body—had carried over into this new, strange existence he'd yet to explore. It was like a warm yellow glow coming from under a door. He yearned to push it open and see what was there. Or *who* was there.

"Son?" he cried.

Instead, he heard the distant shouting of men and felt the wetness of rain falling upon his face. Then all was dark, except his mind.

More Books by Debra Castaneda

Dark Earth Rising
Themed novels that can be read in any order

The Spore Queen
A charming reporter, an ailing tech mogul, and two strangers hiding secrets are brought together by a mysterious fungus, one that will either save them or destroy them.

The Devil's Shallows
Eight miles of mystery. One night of terror. Residents trapped in a remote neighborhood confront the unimaginable.

The Copper Man
Haunted tunnels. Unexplained deaths. Eerie sightings. Decades after The Copper Man killed her brother, Leah Shaw returns to the remote mining town of Tribulation Gulch where a lethal mystery awaits.

A Dark and Rising Tide
When a massive storm surge hits the central coast of California, the ferocious surf destroys buildings, floods streets, and washes up something sinister from the depths of the Monterey Bay.

Circus at Devil's Landing

Creatures that howl in the night, a mysterious circus, and a clash between a ringmaster and a woman determined to rescue her captured lover.

Chavez Ravine Novels

Stand-alone novels set in Chavez Ravine, Los Angeles during turbulent times

The Monsters of Chavez Ravine

A 2021 International Latino Book Awards Gold Medal Winner! Before Dodger Stadium, dark forces terrorized Chavez Ravine.

The Night Lady

A rebel curandera, a plucky seamstress, and a young reporter are pulled into the investigation of a killer terrorizing Chavez Ravine.

The Haunting of Chavez Ravine

La Llorona is terrorizing people in the hills of Chavez Ravine, and a sassy curandera and her clever young niece must stop her.

The Christmas Cucuy

It's Christmas Eve, 1949, and Kiki's dreams are about to come true: she'll be singing at Palladium with her old bandmates. But when she threatens her rambunctious son with El Cucuy, her plans change.

www.ingramcontent.com/pod-product-compliance
Lightning Source LLC
Chambersburg PA
CBHW022110310726
48972CB00007B/1970